CREATING
STANLEY

J.J.R. LAY

Black Eyes Publishing UK

CREATING STANLEY

© J.J.R. Lay 2015, 2022

Published in 2022
Black Eyes Publishing UK
50 Boverton Drive
Brockworth, Gloucester
GL3 4DA (UK)

www.blackeyespublishinguk.co.uk

ISBN: 978-1-913195-20-5

A CIP catalogue record for this title is available from the British Library.

An earlier version of this book, with a different title, was previously self-published in 2015.

Original cover photo: Josephine Lay

Cover design: Jason Conway, The Daydream Academy.
www.thedaydreamacademy.com

I'd like to thank:
Black Eyes Publishing UK, for their unerring support and encouragement throughout the writing and re-writing of several versions of this book.

Also, all my beta readers who gave me invaluable feedback, especially Penny Brinnen, Derek Dohren, Chloë Jacquet and Anna Saunders.

The story takes place in 1998 and is loosely based in the City of Gloucester but some places and place names are fictional. For the purposes of the story, I've brought forward the date of the Gloucester Quays development and the building of certain blocks of apartments in that area, by a year or two.

For Peter

CREATING STANLEY

Yesterday, when I returned home after taking the child to school, the strangest thing happened. I went upstairs to the bathroom, and found a fat, white man, naked to the waist, gazing into my mirror. I was shocked. I stepped out, shut the door and ran down to the kitchen, wondering if I should call the police. But then I thought Guy might have invited a colleague to stay and forgotten to tell me. Surely, if that was the case, the man would come down to introduce himself. After a while, when this didn't happen, I slowly climbed the stairs again, calling out as I went. I couldn't hear a sound. I knocked on the bathroom door. No reply. When I turned the handle and opened it, there was no one there. I checked the spare bedroom. Nothing.

I spent all day thinking about the man. I didn't ask Guy about him. It was obvious Guy hadn't brought any one home, and I didn't want him to think I was seeing things.

One

Today, after I drop the child off at school, I keep thinking of the fat man in my bathroom. I enter the hall and listen. The house is silent except for the ticking of the clock in the sitting room. I climb the stairs. The bathroom door is slightly open. I can see light from the little window through a haze of steam, as though the shower's been running. I push the door, and there he is. The same fat, white man, a towel around his waist, shaving in front of the mirror.

I stand on the landing, legs shaking, staring at this apparition. I have to sit down. I go into my bedroom and sit on the edge of the bed. But I desperately need to pee; I have to go to the bathroom. When I finally do, there's no one there. As I pick up the soap to wash my hands, I notice that the bar is damp.

Downstairs, I make myself a cup of sweet tea and sit in the kitchen. Gradually the shock fades, and I come to the conclusion I might be hallucinating. All morning the man's image haunts me: his white skin, his expanding belly, the white towel around his waist. I run scenarios in my mind. What would have happened if he'd turned towards me? Would he have seen me? Would he have smiled? The desire to see him once more becomes overwhelming. I climb the stairs and sit on the side of the bath considering an alarming thought; is this my illness returning? I've never had hallucinations before, but perhaps I need a change of medication?

I pace around the house till I feel tired. In the kitchen, I sit at the table and pick up a pen. There's an old exercise book on the table, left behind by Guy's daughter, I pull it towards me. It has a couple of empty pages at the back. Chewing the tip of the pen, I visualise the fat man standing in his own bathroom in front of his mirror. It's a much shabbier bathroom and the mirror is old and marked in places. His ice blue eyes regard his reflection with sadness.

I scribble a description of him. Pause to let ideas and phrases flow, and then I write them down: a layout of his flat, the thoughts in his head, the reason he feels lost.

Stan regards his reflection in the mirror. The skin on his chest is pale and dotted with several moles. He looks down at the balloon of his stomach. *How did I let it get that bad?* Several emotions pass through his mind, but so quickly that Stan doesn't register them, he's merely aware of wasted years. He studies his face, briefly wondering if any woman would be able to love him. Running a hand over his chin he feels the rough growth of beard and tries to recall the last few days.

He remembers buying several packs of beer and a bottle of whiskey after his mother's funeral. He remembers filling the fridge with the cans, and looking out of the window at the small patch of muddy lawn outside his flat. For some reason, the sight of it had depressed him more than the funeral service. He knows he shut the curtains and sat on the sofa drinking beer in front of the TV, but the rest of the week is a blur.

In the kitchen, he makes a fried egg sandwich with the last of the stale bread and eats it with pleasure, even though there's no ketchup.

Stan stands in the shower for a long while, letting the hot water pour over his head. *I'll miss you, Mum, and your dependence on me. Nobody needs me now.* When he finishes showering, he wipes the steam from the bathroom mirror and contemplates the grey bristles with dismay. Wrapping a towel around his waist, he lathers his cheeks and starts to shave. As an experiment, he leaves a moustache on his top lip and a small goatee on his chin. When he wipes the foam from his face, he's pleasantly surprised; the silver bristles under his nose echo the silver hair at the sides of his face. *Kind of distinguished, I should get a haircut, go on a diet, and stop drinking beer.* The thought of beer makes him nauseous, a sensation that intensifies when he returns, still naked, to the sitting room and sees empty cans and beer stains on the carpet. He goes in to the kitchen for a black bin liner and stuffs all the rubbish into it.

Later that afternoon, Stan visits the local barber. The young man works magic on his hair, and Stan leaves the shop happy with the result. He goes shopping, buys himself black jeans and black T-shirts, in the hope they might make him look slimmer.

Two

This morning, as soon as I get home, I'm anxious to know if the fat man will re-appear. I climb the stairs, heart beating fast. Do I really want to see him? The bathroom door is ajar. I push it open. There he is, wiping condensation from the mirror. My mouth is dry. I slam the door shut. This is madness. I walk up and down the landing wondering what to do. I want to see him, and don't want to see him, in equal measure. When finally, I get the courage to open the door again, he's vanished. Only a faint damp patch on the bathroom floor shows where he stood.

I search the house for my father's old, portable typewriter. I know I kept it. I pull out shoes and shoe boxes from the bottoms of wardrobes leaving a mess I'll have to clear up before Guy returns from work. Eventually, I find the typewriter stuffed at the back of the airing cupboard behind the wash basket. I pull it out, and take it down to the kitchen table. It looks fine, not even dusty. I open it, put in a sheet of paper, and press a key. It works.

First, I type the notes I made in the exercise book, then I cut out the pages and throw them away. Leaving any papers around where Guy might find them would be silly, he wouldn't understand. He'd accuse me of wasting time. Sitting with my fingers on the keys of the typewriter, I visualise the flat, where the fat man lives. A first floor flat in a block on a run-down estate, much like the one near where I live.

❖

Stan walks along the high-street reviewing his situation. *I need to get a job, but with no qualifications and a four-year gap in employment, that's not going to be easy?*

Stan recalls the first time his mother suffered a stroke, and he'd moved back into the two-bed flat. It had seemed the best idea at the time; he was a bachelor and not in a full-time relationship. After her second stroke, he'd given up his job to care for her.

But now the carer's allowance has stopped, and his only option is to sign on at the Job Centre. He stands in the queue, looking at the grey-haired men in front of him, all dressed in sombre colours. He feels their hopelessness. Every so often the line shuffles forward, but when Stan finally gets to a desk and speaks to someone, they aren't very helpful. He fills in the interminable forms and experiences what it's like to be another supplicant trying to get money from the state. He leaves the building, walks back past the queue, which has grown longer, and has no idea how he's going to afford to live.

Back at his flat, Stan pushes open the front door against the mound of post that he hasn't picked up since the day of the funeral. He bends to collect it and carries it through to the kitchen table. He fills the kettle and while he's waiting for it to boil, he starts sifting through the pile. Most of the letters are bills, which he doesn't open, or circulars, which he throws in the bin but one, an A5 white envelope, comes from his mother's solicitors. Surprised that they should be writing to him so soon after his recent meeting with them, he opens it and starts to read. He can't believe what he sees. Stunned, he sits on the nearest chair and re-reads the contents. It appears that his mother took out a small Life

Insurance policy, and attached to the letter is a cheque for £5,000.

Stan starts to laugh. He does a dance into the living room and collapses on to the sofa. 'You're a miracle, Mum,' he says out loud to the corner of the room where he has the impression, she can hear him. 'However, did you manage to pay the premiums?' Stan can't wait. He puts the cheque in his wallet, leaves the messy flat, and goes to his bank. Having paid it into his account, he walks to the DIY shop, buys a large tin of white emulsion and a collection of brushes and rollers. *I might live in a run-down estate, but the inside of my flat doesn't have to reflect that.* Stan carries his purchases home on the bus, still reeling from his good fortune, and the rest of his day is spent decorating.

As he paints the living room, he thinks about his father. 'We always hated each other, Dad and me,' Stan says to his mother's corner. 'Best thing that happened was when the bastard moved out on my sixteenth birthday.' Stan remembers leaving school immediately and getting a job, a rather unusual job for a young man, he'd trained as a machinist in a clothing factory. 'But they were happy years, Mum, working alongside women.'

Within the week, the flat is transformed. Stan moves all his things into his mother's bedroom and turns the smaller room into an office. He buys a computer and a modem for the internet. Each day, he searches online and in the local papers for jobs and finally comes across a position that might just suit him: the local estate agent, 'Payntons', is looking for a viewing person to work four days a week and alternate weekends. Stan applies by email.

He gets a reply the next morning, offering him an interview that very afternoon. Stan's a bit stressed by the speed of events, and begins to type a refusal, but then he looks out at the back of his flat at the shabby estate and thinks, *I've nothing to lose, I might even escape this place.* So, he emails back an acceptance.

Dressing smartly: a jacket over new black t-shirt and jeans, Stan gets the bus into town, and at the Estate Agents' office, he introduces himself. 'Hi, I'm Stan Baker, I've come for an interview.' The woman looks at her list and ticks off his name, 'Ahh yes, Mr Baker, please take a seat. Maureen Carter, our manager will be with you soon.'

He's interviewed by a smart, professional woman in her forties and at the end of the interview, the manager looks him straight in the eye for a few moments, as though trying to see beyond his outward appearance. 'On the face of it Mr. Baker...'

'Please call me Stan,' says Stan.

'...on the face of it,' she repeats, ignoring his comment, 'you're not a likely candidate. Your CV is poor, to say the least. But, there's something about you I find appealing and that probably means our clients will too. Besides, it might be a good idea to have a man about the office.' She stands up and offers Stan her hand. 'The job is yours if you want it,' she says. 'There is one condition.'

'Anything,' agrees Stan, shaking her hand and holding it just a little longer than required.

Maureen Carter pauses for a brief moment but she smiles slightly. 'We will refer to you as 'Mr. Baker' or 'Stanley' in the office. In a superior establishment like Payntons, the name Stan will not do.'

'Perfectly understood, Mrs. Carter.' Stan gives a slight bow.

'Ms Carter, actually,' she corrects him. 'Training will begin next week. I'll meet you here on Monday morning at

9.00am sharp. Goodbye Mr. Baker.'

Stan walks out of the Estate Agents with a smile on his face; not only has he got a job, but he's to work amongst women again.

Three

I can hear the shower running as I open the front door and there's a faint smell of aftershave. For a horrifying moment, I think Guy must be back. Then I hear a man's voice singing. That's certainly not Guy, he can't sing in tune. The velvet voice makes my skin tingle. Slowly, I climb the stairs, push open the door a crack and look at the fat man through the steam. The new haircut makes him look younger. Cautiously, I take a couple of steps inside the bathroom, he stops singing but he doesn't seem to notice me. The goatee and moustache have been neatly trimmed and his skin is smoother, as though he's been using moisturiser. I move behind him, wondering whether he might see my face reflected in the mirror. But as he starts to turn towards me, my nerve fails. I dart out, slam the door and run down the stairs as fast as I can.

In the kitchen, I switch on the kettle to make tea and place my shaking hands in hot soapy water. Should I contact someone? I can't face all those questions from the well-meaning but uncomprehending people. And if I did, Guy would flip. He thinks I'm over all that. I finish the washing up, dry my hands and sit at the table with my tea. Apart from this daily hallucination, it seems I'm perfectly fine. I decide to fetch the typewriter from the airing cupboard. From the top of the stairs, I can see the bathroom door is open and there's no one there.

I focus on typing my story. I've no problem typing; I took lessons before I became ill, but I realise parts of the typewriter ribbon are fraying and several letters are faint. Maybe keeping the typewriter in the airing cupboard is drying out the ink. Where else can I store it, though, without it being noticed? I'll need to buy a new ribbon, but that will mean going to the shops, and there lies my problem. I'm not good at going into town, not by myself, anyway. All those people pushing in front of me makes me feel invisible. The wide streets and parks bring on panic attacks. I can feel my pulse rate rising at the very thought. Taking a deep breath, I focus on the task of hiding all these typed sheets of paper. In the sitting room, I search through the bureau for an empty file, label it 'Miscellaneous' and clip in the pages then I push it in amongst the household files on the kitchen shelf. Hopefully, Guy will never notice it.

Stan now has a routine: four mornings a week he goes to work at Payntons, and each evening, he comes home, heats up an oven-ready meal and eats it in front of the TV. Then at about 9.00pm, he goes into his office, turns on his computer and connects to the internet. He's found a new, online dating website. Stan's never considered himself a potential family man; a dad with several kids around his ankles, and he's never found anyone special enough for a marriage proposal. However, he does appreciate women, especially mature women, and when he sees how many of them are looking for love, he's amazed. He emails a few ladies, choosing ones around his age. Two reply: the first is Amy, who is a little younger than him and describes herself as 'a fun-loving widow'; the other is Linda, a divorcee. She's a bit older than Stan, but she looks young in her photo. Stan summons his courage and suggests to Linda that they might meet. She replies immediately, asking him to join her the next evening for a drink.

Stan walks quickly towards the Robert Raikes Hotel where he's arranged to meet Linda. The door is open, and he enters the hallway looking for the bar. The building is Georgian and refurbished in that style. There are several small rooms off the main hall, some with tables set for dining, some with easy chairs and settees. Sitting at the bar, he orders a single malt. He's early as he wants to familiarise himself with the surroundings. Despite the fact that he now visits prestigious properties as part of his job, he still finds the ambience of places like this a little daunting. Linda told him she'd be wearing a dark blue suit with a cream blouse and he hopes he'll recognise her as he's only seen a photo of her head and shoulders.

He starts to worry; *how many years is it since I dated anyone?* He takes a generous gulp of whisky. *Not since Ruth, and that was over four years ago.* He remembers Ruth's reaction when he told her he might move back in with his mother. Her actual words were, 'Well, if you do, you can kiss goodbye to our arrangement. I can't stand the old bat.' Of course, Stan defended his mother, and that ended the affair.

Stan sees a woman hovering uncertainly in the doorway, she's wearing a dark suit with a straight skirt, but he can't tell the colour in the dim light. She's petite with a good pair of legs in her high heels. *That must be her?* His nerves kick in, but he stands up and calls out, 'Linda?'

On hearing her name, Linda turns and for a split second, Stan sees an expression of concern, or is it disappointment, on her face as she notices his large body. Ignoring a tremor of insecurity, Stan moves to shake her hand and holds it for a second longer than is required. 'Hi, I'm Stan. So glad you could make it.' Smiling, he makes eye contact and she returns the smile. 'You look lovely,' he says genuinely. Her photo didn't do her justice, or maybe it's the muted light falling softly on her pale hair. Is it blonde or silver? He can't tell but her oval face is small, her eyes large and dark, and her smile is real not forced. 'What would you like to drink?' he asks.

'Oh, a white wine spritzer please, with soda and ice.' Linda smiles her thanks and looks around the bar.

Stan orders her drink and another single malt for himself. They move into one of the little rooms off the hallway and sit opposite each other in easy chairs. Stan tries to relax as he watches Linda compose herself. 'So, tell me all about yourself,' he says. 'Why does such an attractive lady need to go on a dating site?'

'Oh, you know,' she shrugs. 'The usual story.

'Which is?' he prompts.

She sips her drink, then says bitterly, 'My marriage has failed, and my ex-husband is starting another family with someone not much older than our daughter.' Her voice breaks and the hand holding the glass trembles slightly.

'I'm guessing you're still very angry with him, then?' Stan asks.

Linda sighs. 'I keep trying to put it behind me and get on with my life, hence the dating. But actually, the life I want is the life I had before. Linda puts her glass down, 'But hey, you don't want to hear all of this.' she laughs awkwardly.

Stan leans forward and touches the back of her hand, 'Actually, it's fine, I'd like to get to know you, and obviously this is a large part of you.' Linda doesn't pull away but sits looking at his large hand next to hers.

She looks up at him. 'Do you really want to know all this rubbish about my life, or is this just a new chat up line?'

'No honestly, I'm interested. Talk to me about your daughter. How old is she?' Stan allows himself to unwind. The initial contact is over, he's had a drink or two and is feeling more confident, besides, he's truly attracted to this woman. He sits and listens to her slightly husky voice. Linda has relaxed back into the leather cushions of her chair, and as she talks about her life, he watches her mannerisms: the brushing of her skirt with her hands, the crossing of her feet at the ankles, the looking up to the ceiling as she considers a question.

At the end of the evening, Stan walks her home. She explains that she shares a small semi with another woman who has also split up from her husband. 'So, I can't ask you in for a coffee, I'm afraid, but thank you for a lovely evening and for being such a good listener.'

'It's been a pleasure,' he says. He places a small kiss on the back of her hand before saying goodnight.

Stan is walking away when he hears the clicking of high heels on the pavement. He turns and Linda practically falls into his arms. 'Stan,' she breathes into his ear as she gives him a hug. 'You're an unusual man, can we…?'

'Can we do this again?' Stan smiles down at her. 'Of course,' he says, and he smells her perfume as he bends to lightly touch his lips to hers. 'I have your number; I'll ring you tomorrow.'

Four

How weird to look forward to my daily hallucination? Each morning, I walk into the bathroom to watch this fat man preen himself in front of the mirror; this man of my typed notes. Today, he has a white towel around his neck, and he's standing up straight, trying to pull in his stomach as much as he can. There's a small secret smile on his lips, as though the meeting with Linda has given him confidence.

I leave him humming to himself. I don't have much time. I type for about an hour, struggling with the faint print of the letters. Focusing on this process is taking me away from my domestic chores, and Guy is beginning to notice. Early this morning, he had to wait while I ironed him a shirt, which made him late and angry. He asks questions like, 'what the hell do you do all day?' and, 'are you turning into a lazy slut?'

I have to be careful; he could so easily get fed up with me and I could end up in halfway accommodation or worse. I'm safe here. I'm warm and fed and I don't have to worry. I can't manage to work, at least, not in a shop or an office, or anywhere public. So, the domestic chores and the sex are a small price to pay for this security.

I place some household bills and letters either side of the typed sheets, in case he should find the file. Then I clean up. I don't want Guy thinking I'm getting ill. I must stay on top of things. I'm aware his eyes follow me at times, watching for signs of my old complaint, it makes me nervous. I wish he'd forget my past, let me be.

Next morning, Stan's in a good mood. Linda is lovely, his date went well, and it appears he hasn't lost his touch with the opposite sex. Looking closely at his eyes in the mirror though, he sees how bloodshot they are. *Too many whiskies, I definitely ought to drink less.*

It's Saturday, and his weekend off. After breakfast, he rings Linda and arranges to see her again during the week. He's really pleased, but despite that he's tempted to ask other ladies out at the same time. Sitting at the computer, with the morning sun flooding his office, Stan's spirits lift further as he sees that the lady, called Amy, left him a message last night. 'Hi Stanley,' it reads. 'Sorry we couldn't chat tonight. Hope you're having an enjoyable evening. I've quite missed talking to you, please get in touch if you have the time. Love Amy.' He is intrigued that she's typed his name in full, but he replies to her email and asks if she'd like to meet.

Stan decides to spend the weekend sorting out his bedroom. The bed, he realises, has seen better days, it's only four-foot-wide, and the mattress is sagging badly. *I really can't ask any woman to sleep on that, let alone do anything else on it.* The room doesn't need re-decorating, but it would benefit from new curtains, new bedding and a rug on the floor. Stan takes a trip to Argos, where he flips through the large catalogue for beds, he's heard that Argos are fairly quick at delivering. He chooses a double bed with a black leather headboard and a firm mattress. At the counter the man confirms delivery on Tuesday and says there is an option to have the old bed, removed. Stan immediately acepts and is happy to pay a little extra for the service.

On the Monday morning, Stan returns to work pleased

with his efforts on his flat. When he arrives, the manager, Maureen, is waiting for him and asks him into the office for a chat. 'Stanley, I do hope you are settling down,' she says placing a hand on his arm and squeezing lightly, 'I want you to feel that any difficulties you may encounter can always be discussed with me.' She smiles at him in a way that makes him feel a bit awkward and he can't wait to get back to his desk.

That evening, he goes straight to his small office with a sandwich he's bought on his way home. He eats it in front of his computer, hoping that Amy has emailed, but she hasn't. *Oh well, it's only 6.30pm. A bit early.* Amy finally messages him just before 11.00pm. She's been out to the theatre and sounds excited. As a place to meet, she suggests an upmarket pub on the edge of the Cotswolds. This concerns Stan on two counts: firstly, he will have to get a bus and try to find it and secondly, his little stash of money is dwindling fast. Still, her humour is so infectious, and she looks so delicious in her photos, Stan certainly wants to meet her.

However, the next evening, when Amy turns up to the country pub in a red Alfa Romeo convertible, Stan is almost speechless. Dressed in a black trouser suit that accentuates her curves, with her red, brown hair, loose around her shoulders, she's like something out of *Cosmopolitan*. Sitting at the bar, Amy's smile lights up her face as she orders a glass of Champagne while proceeding to tell him that she's a wealthy woman, looking for fun. She's way out of Stan's league, and he isn't sure what to do. He starts to lose confidence and tries to think of an excuse to leave. But Amy takes their drinks to a quiet corner of the pub and reassures him that she's only rich, because her husband, who was very well insured, died just over two years ago. 'Now don't feel sorry for me, Stanley. I can call you Stanley? I've gone through the grief and now I want to enjoy myself.' She leans over and smooths away the frown lines on his brow with her fingers. 'Relax and have a drink on me. I liked the look of your profile, and what you said about loving women, I think it's beautiful. Now that I've met you, I can tell you're genuine, and I want you to help me have a good time and enjoy myself.' Despite his reservations, Stan finds himself delighting in her company, she's so good natured and amusing.

The following day, Stan takes Amy to an Italian restaurant and, as she says she 'adores' sparkling wine, he orders a bottle with their meal. Stan's sure she means she 'adores' Champagne, but luckily for him she's happy with the Prosecco. They talk and laugh throughout the meal and Amy doesn't move her hand away when Stan covers it with his and strokes the smooth skin of her wrist with his thumb. He finds himself confiding in her, talking about his mother and Ruth and the decisions that have led him to this point. Amy is such a good listener that the time passes and the waiter is hovering, obviously wanting to clear their table.

'Thank you, for listening,' he says as they finally leave the restaurant.

'Don't thank me, I was enjoying your story. Do you need to get away? Or do you fancy coming to my place for some real champagne?' she says unlocking the car.'

'Are you sure you should be driving?' asks Stan nervously.

'Don't worry darling, I only had a couple of glasses and that was with a meal. Besides I know this road like the back of the proverbial.' She squeezes Stan's right knee as she changes gear, and they head out of Cheltenham. Amy swings the red car around the bends of a very twisty lane. 'Isn't this fun on a lovely spring evening? Relax Stan, only five minutes away from my house now.' She turns the car into a wider road that runs between beautifully kept lawns of several large, detached houses. Most of them look Edwardian, but some owners have obviously sold part of their land for development, as every so often there is a more modern house sporting a shorter drive and a smaller front garden. It's into one of these 'bijou' residences that Amy turns the Alfa and pulls up in front of a neo-Georgian facade. She jumps out of the car and runs up the steps to open the front door. Stan follows more slowly, intimidated by her opulent lifestyle.

'Come on darling, let's open the real bubbly!' Amy says, taking him by the hand and leading him into a kitchen that's big enough to swallow most of his flat. She points to a monster of a fridge. 'Open up a bottle while I go and slip into something more comfortable,' she says, giving Stan a kiss full on the lips before disappearing upstairs. Stan opens the fridge which contains several bottles of Champagne of a brand he's never heard of but guesses is exceedingly expensive. He finds some flutes in a display cabinet, successfully opens a bottle without spilling any and pours out the frothing liquid.

He's nervous of what is to come and how he should proceed. *What on earth will she think of my large body? Surely, she's used to sophisticated hunks of men I can't possibly compete with?* He's just wondering if he might call a taxi and make his apologies, when Amy comes downstairs. She's dressed in a cream satin robe and her auburn hair is brushed out across her shoulders. At the sight of her, his mouth dies up, tongue literally sticking to the roof of his mouth, and he has to drink more Champagne before he can murmur, 'You look fantastic.'

Putting down his glass, he takes her hand and kisses it then he puts his arm around her waist and draws her towards him. She doesn't resist. *This must be a dream and I'm about to wake up.*

He kisses Amy on the lips with the lightest of touches. Then he stops and looks into her eyes. 'I'm not sure I can give you what you deserve. I'm older than you, and not a fine specimen of manhood, I won't be offended if you change your mind.'

'Don't be silly, Stanley, I want you to make love to me. I like the way you pay me attention, the way you want to please me and not just yourself. I know how you make me feel and I want more of it.' Amy puts her arms around his neck, presses her body against him and when her robe falls open to reveal her nakedness, he is lost.

Later, lying in Amy's king-sized bed, Stan runs his hand over her hips and caresses her thighs. 'You are very beautiful,' he says as he kisses her shoulder.

'I'm too heavy to be really beautiful,' she says wistfully. 'I binged on chocolate and rich foods after Gordon died, and I can't seem to lose the weight now.'

'Nonsense,' breathes Stan, his face against her neck smelling her perfume. 'I love your curves,' he says, tracing the arc of her breast. 'And the dip of your waist. And this fullness,' he murmurs as he runs his hand over the wide curve of her hips. Hearing her sharp intake of breath, he slips his hand between her thighs and whispers, 'This time, we take it slowly.'

Five

I'm ridiculously proud of myself. Yesterday, after dropping the child off at her school, I went into town to buy a new typewriter ribbon. I haven't been shopping on my own for years. By the end of it I was sweating, breathless and lightheaded but I managed it! Of course, I won't mention it to Guy. I don't know why but I get the impression he wouldn't like the idea; that for some reason he'd rather I didn't become too independent.

My typing speed is increasing and I'm proud of the way things are progressing. Who'd have thought I could type a love scene? I've never done anything like this before, it's boosting my confidence, but I have to limit myself to three hours a day. That way I can still get all the chores done before Guy comes home from work.

The fat, white man hasn't appeared in my bathroom for a couple days, now. It scares me how much I miss seeing him. I tell myself that surely, it's a good sign if the hallucinations have stopped. But I break from writing and creep upstairs just to see if he's there. Each day feels like a week. Perhaps I've made his life so exciting, he's not bothered with me, now? What kind of man am I creating? I think he's getting cheeky. I preferred it when he was sad and insecure.

Depressed and anxious, I go in to the kitchen, and type up my thoughts and some notes I made on the back of a shopping list. I must remember to destroy any scraps of paper with scribbled ideas on them.

❖

Stan's new bed is in place, his bedroom is finished and he's no longer worried about people visiting his flat. He invites Linda home for a meal. However, he's no cook, so he goes to a supermarket on his way home from work and chooses ready-made meals: Duck a L'Orange, a Vegetable medley, dauphinoise potatoes, and a bottle of wine.

Stan's glad to be away from work for a bit because his relationship with Maureen is becoming rather difficult. She keeps calling him into her office on the slightest of pretexts, and the rest of the staff are beginning to grump about it. Today, she introduced him to a Mrs Eileen Fanshaw, a client from Edinburgh, staying in the vicinity while she looks for a house for herself and her husband. Apparently, this woman has specifically asked for Stan to show her around various houses over the next two weeks. She's an impressive lady in her mid-fifties, who dresses in an extrovert style and wears lots of jewellery, especially rings. Fortunately, Stan has booked tomorrow off as holiday, and then it's his free weekend. *So, if it turns into a late night tonight, it won't matter.* He's feeling hopeful. However, Stan's head is in a bit of a whirl, because he's also seeing Amy again on Saturday. He can't believe how everything is going so well. Life is suddenly so exciting and although work is a necessary evil, he doesn't want it to interfere with his new experiences. *Fanny Fanshaw will have to make do with Maureen for the next few days.*

Stan reflects on the two women he's dating without any feelings of guilt or discord. With Amy he is the entertainer; he needs to be witty and attentive as she loves to be adored, and when he's in her company, he does adore her. With Linda it's different, Stan's become her confidant. She's gone through so much, he thinks, that she needs support and reassurance. *But she also needs to feel like a woman again.*

The doorbell rings just as he's placing the duck into the oven. Stan quickly puts on the timer for thirty minutes, then runs down the stairs to let Linda in. 'You look lovely,' he says as he bends to kiss her cheek. The lilac top she's wearing sets off her pale gold hair to perfection. 'Follow me.' He takes her hand as they climb the stairs, then leads her into the sitting room where he's set up a small table for two by the window. He's even found a red candle in a holder that his mother bought one Christmas.

The meal is a success and afterwards they sit either end of the settee sipping wine and chatting. But Stan realises Linda is still tense around him and he wonders what he can do about it. He gets up and puts on a CD. The golden voice of Andrea Bocelli floats into the space between them and Linda smiles and stretches out her legs. 'Oh, I love 'Romanza',' she says. 'How did you guess?'

Stan tops up her glass, 'I love the tenor voice, mine's a baritone and that's always made me sad.'

'Oh, do you sing? And, are you trying to get me drunk?'

'I used to sing in a church choir. And, no, I'm trying to get you to relax.' Stan says sitting nearer to her and putting his hand on her arm. Linda doesn't move away so he puts his arm around her shoulders. They sit listening to the music and when her glass is empty, he takes it from her, and bends to kiss her. She closes her eyes and leans against him, Stan lightly touches her cool lips with his warm ones.

'Those little kisses of yours are quite dangerous,' she whispers.

'Are they?' he says as he places a few more on her slightly opened lips.

'Yes, they are like butterfly kisses; so innocent, so

friendly, but so erotic that I want more.'

'That is the idea,' breathes Stan as he gently flicks his tongue between her lips.

'Please don't take me too far too soon,' she says as she turns to him.

'Don't worry, I promise not to make love to you tonight even if you beg me. I just want you to enjoy feeling sensuous.' He pulls her towards him, moves his hand down to her breast. But when he realises that she is not wearing a bra, Stan almost regrets his rashly made promise.

Six

There's no pattern to the fat, white man's appearances, although, he never presents himself when Guy and his daughter are here. Each weekday, when I return from the school run, I look for him. I turn the key in the lock, push open the front door and stand in the hall, listening. If the silence of the house is broken by the shower running or by his voice, singing, I quickly climb the stairs. But often, it's only the tick of the clock I hear, and then I know he's not coming. I try not to let his absence affect my typing, I get the typewriter out and set it up on the kitchen table anyway.

Recently, when I'm standing at the kitchen sink, I see an old woman at the end of our path. Some days she stops as she walks her little dog, and stares at the house as though, despite the net curtains, she can see me. Often, I think she might come to the door and knock; her dog watches the house too. I don't know who she is and she only ever appears when I'm alone; just like the fat, white man, I suppose.

Today, when I sit at the table, I find myself writing about her. I'm convinced that this elderly lady knows my fat man. Perhaps she lives near him, or has spoken to him on several occasions. When she walks along, her little dog trailing behind, she looks as if she's studying the pavement in case she might trip. She dresses in an old navy raincoat, belted at the waist, and wears a battered black hat stuffed onto her head so that strands of grey hair stick out from under it.

I've nick-named her 'The Watcher' because of her habit of peering into windows. She appears harmless but I sense that's a ploy. The Watcher observes everything on her daily walks.

On the day after the funeral, the Watcher observes the drawn curtains in Stan's flat. She becomes concerned when she sees them remain closed for several days. Each day, she stops outside the entrance to his block, ostensibly to let her little dog sniff around the trees. A few days later, she notices: empty beer cans overflowing from a wheelie bin, an open window, the curtains drawn back. Reassured, she walks on, resolving to keep an eye on Stan, and to speak to him if she meets him in the street.

One morning, she sees him taking delivery of a large, heavy cardboard case. She calls to him. 'How are things going?'

Stan gives her a beaming smile, 'Very well thanks.'

'Whatever is that?' she adds, pointing to the large box in his arms.

'A new computer,' he says, shifting the weight of it. 'Excuse me, I need to get this upstairs, it's rather heavy.'

The Watcher walks on smiling. She's never had children as her husband was killed in the war and no one else has ever taken his place. But she's developed an affection for her friend's little boy, who's grown into this large, generous man.

She sees Stan coming home with a woman; she notices how he's smartened himself up, and when she takes the bus into town for her weekly shop, she learns he's working in the local Estate Agents. The Watcher makes a resolution to congratulate him when they next meet. However, she has difficulty in catching Stan because when she walks her dog in the morning he's left for work, and when she walks her dog in the evening he's often gone out.

So, the next Sunday morning, the Watcher decides to alter her routine. Ignoring the pleading look in her dog's eyes as the time for their walk comes and goes, she delays till her clock chimes eleven. The little dog waits impatiently in the hall while the Watcher puts on her coat and hat, then they set off in the full sunlight. It's very warm and neither of them is accustomed to the heat, so the walk takes a little longer than usual.

As they turn the corner, a bright red, convertible sports car comes racing along the road and pulls up sharply in front of Stan's block of flats. The roof is down, and the Watcher can see the driver, a lady in her late forties, long red hair tied with a green scarf. The driver hoots twice on the horn which makes the little dog bark and the Watcher tugs on the lead to quieten him but it's too late, Stan comes out of the entrance and is walking down the path. He waves to the exotic driver, turns to face the Watcher, and bends down to fondle the little dog who responds with licks to Stan's hands. 'Hello little fellow,' he says as he looks up into the face of the Watcher. He doesn't think he has ever really looked at her before, but the piercing blue eyes remind him of his poor mother, and he's moved by this. 'Hi,' he says straightening up, 'You both look rather warm. Isn't it a bit late for your usual walk?'

The Watcher is momentarily flustered, 'Yes, it's late and warm,' she says. 'We need to be getting into the shade.'

'I'd offer you a drink if I wasn't about to go out.'

'That's kind,' says the Watcher moving away from him 'but we only live just around the corner, Flat 4. Burnside.

You're welcome to come and have a drink with us whenever you're passing.' With that the Watcher and her little dog shuffle off towards their home.

Seven

I stand stock still at the sink with my hands in the warm water. I dare not turn around. I know that she is in the room. The Watcher and her little dog are here. Here in my kitchen. I don't know how they got in, I'm sure I closed the front door.

Very slowly, I reach for a tea towel and dry my hands. Then, full of dread, I turn to face them. The old woman's not as scary as I feared, her face is lined but her eyes are kind, and when I get over the initial shock of seeing her, I'm certain she means me no harm. In fact, I get an intense impression she has something to tell me. I don't speak to her or ask her any of the questions that arise in my mind. I dare not talk to these apparitions in the empty house, or speak of them to anyone, out of fear that I'm going mad. Opening any kind of dialogue is unthinkable.

With my hands still trembling I sit down at the table and pull the typewriter towards me. I type her into the sheets of paper and as I type, she sits opposite me, her little dog on her lap. I wonder if her presence will interfere with my typing, but it's quite the reverse, her company is soothing and my fingers type faster than they've ever done before.

While I work, the Watcher gets up from her seat, goes over to the window and moves the edge of the net curtain to look at a passer-by. I'm not surprised that she's a 'curtain-twitcher', I imagine her peering into every lighted window, especially in the evening when people are slow to close their curtains. I'm sure she sees scenarios, decors, and secrets that people are unaware of showing her. I'll weave all this into my story, somehow.

Stan turns to Amy who is waiting for him in the car. He climbs into the passenger seat, closes the door, and they speed off down the road raising a dust cloud as they pass the old woman. 'Who was that?' Amy asks as they drive away from his estate.

'Oh, just some old biddy that walks her dog past my flat every day. I haven't seen her for a while but then I've been a bit busy,' he says smiling conspiratorially at her and squeezing her thigh. 'I think she used to know my mother. But enough on that. Tell me, how you are today my beauty. I must say you are looking incredibly tasty in that dress.' Amy laughs, and the sound of her laughter is whisked away in the wind and thrown back at the shabby blocks of flats and the sparse grass of his estate.

Stan becomes uncomfortably aware of the area in which he lives and has lived for most of his life. He tries to see it through the eyes of someone like Amy, who is used to luxury and designer architecture, and he wonders what she must really think of him, the thought sobers him. He reflects on inequality: the spectrum of human affluence; from the rundown flats in a backwater of Gloucester to the mansions in Cheltenham that Amy is accustomed to.

'A penny for them.' Amy nudges his arm with her elbow as they drive away from the city towards the M5. 'Where shall we go?'

Stan shakes off his reflective mood. 'If I'm honest I would like nothing better than to go back to yours,' he says as he strokes her bare leg with one finger just below the material of her dress.

Amy giggles, 'OK, Stanley, as long as you take me out for a meal this evening, I'm at your command.'

But, as she turns the little car around at the next roundabout and drives towards her luxury house, he knows she is not at his command. She'll only do what she wants to, and only when she wants to. That suits him fine for the moment, but what will happen when he finally has to tell her he can't support this fun lifestyle financially; when he tells her that he has to stop seeing her.

Eight

At last, he's back, this fat, white man whose life I type. There he is standing in his boxer shorts, weighing himself on my bathroom scales. He's obviously pleased with the result; I can tell he's lost weight and toned up. But I want to ask him how he is, because there's a melancholy expression on his face. Standing behind him, I almost catch his eye in the bathroom mirror. I can see my reflexion: my pale, anxious face; my long straight, brown hair, my lips slightly open, and my eyes, wide and dark. I long for him to see me but as he turns his face towards the door, I panic again and run to the safety of the kitchen.

However, I can't escape my apparitions, there at the kitchen table sits the Watcher, her little dog at her feet. She looks right at me as though she's waiting for me to ask her something. I'm tempted to turn tail and run out of the house, and not return until I bring the child back from school. Or even then to stay away till Guy returns home from work, but what explanation could I give him for doing that? The stress of keeping this weird existence to myself is beginning to make my behaviour erratic and Guy is noticing. I must be stronger and face my crazy spectres. I stand still in the centre of the room trying to pluck up the courage to speak. The Watcher knows a lot about my fat man, I'm convinced of that, but the words won't come out of my mouth. Instead, I type everything I imagine she would tell me into the story, and the sheets start to pile up on the table.

❖

When Linda arrives on Sunday, Stan immediately knows something is wrong. 'Come upstairs and tell me all about it,' he says putting his arm around her shoulders.

'I always seem to be moaning about something when I see you, I am so sorry.'

'Don't be silly. What's happened?'

'It's Bryony, my daughter...' Linda's voice breaks slightly but she controls herself and continues, 'she's told me she wants to go and stay with her father, and to be there for the birth of the baby. She wants to help look after it.'

'Well, I suppose it is, or will be, her half-brother or sister.'

'I know but I feel as though I am losing her as well. I just don't know what to do.'

Stan holds Linda tightly as she cries. 'Let it out,' he says gently as he strokes her hair. 'Let it all out.' Her sobs come in waves and he feels her body shaking against him.

'I am so sorry,' she mumbles into his collar.

'It's OK,' he assures her. 'You need this, just cry and don't fight it.' Standing there in the middle of his sitting room, enveloping her with his warmth, he feels the sobs gradually lessen, and she fumbles for a tissue and wipes her eyes. Linda draws in a huge shuddering breath as Stan releases her and she laughs. 'I've made your shirt all wet and there are streaks of mascara. I'm so sorry.' She dabs at them ineffectually with her tissue making it worse. 'Can I have a glass of water please?'

'Of course, and I'll get you some more tissues. Don't worry about the shirt it'll wash out.' Stan goes into the kitchen and fills a tumbler with water from the tap, he also pours a measure of single malt into a smaller glass. He takes them back to the sitting room.

Linda takes the water and drinks gratefully, and then eyes the whisky doubtfully. 'I don't like whisky, I'm afraid.'

'This isn't your usual sort of whisky, and it's medicinal, so hold your nose and drink. Although it's a sacrilege to say that when referring to a single malt.'

Linda drinks and gasps, then coughs. 'My God, that's strong,' but she tries it again and this time manages more.

Stan smiles. 'That's it, try one more sip, you can stop when you feel the fire reaching your bloodstream.'

She stands up to smooth down her dress and brushes back her pale gold hair. 'I need to go and freshen up a bit. I must look a mess.'

'You look lovely.' Stan says softly, placing one of his special kisses on her lips as she passes him.

When she returns, she's touched up her make-up and composed herself. 'Thank you for being there for me.' Stan hands her the rest of her whisky. 'I'm not sure I can drink anymore.'

'Of course, you can. I admit it is an acquired taste, but one which you'll have to get used to if you're around me for any length of time. Sip slowly and allow its fire to warm you.'

Pulling a slight face, she drinks and then smiles. 'I think we should get that wet shirt off you.' She puts down her drink and starts to unbutton it.

Stan holds her hands away. 'I must warn you if you unbutton this shirt, I won't be able to stop there. I won't make another promise because I want you in my bed, now.'

Linda wraps her arms around Stan's neck. 'Then we had better go and find your bed.'

Stan puts his hands on her waist and leads her to his bedroom. He unzips the back of her dress and it slips to the floor. Linda steps out of it. 'You are lovely,' he whispers as he kisses the soft swell of her breasts above the edge of her bra. 'You are soft,' he says as he unhooks it and slips it off her arms. 'And you smell divine.'

Realising that Linda is swaying and barely able to stand, Stan guides her on to the bed. Kissing her belly he slips his fingers under the edge of the lace knickers, and pulls the garment down over her feet. He strokes her smooth thighs until she is clinging on to him. *This*, he thinks, as he looks down at her naked body, while struggling out of his own clothes, *this was definitely worth waiting for*.

Nine

It seemed a very long weekend, Guy and his daughter went into town on Saturday. I didn't know how long they would be away, so couldn't risk getting the typewriter down. And yesterday Guy wanted me to sit with him all day, he wouldn't leave me alone, kissing and fondling till it was time for bed and we had sex.

This morning, when I get back from the school, the Watcher is sitting in my kitchen; she comes most mornings now. Sometimes, I've thought of putting out a bowl of water for her dog, he's always panting, poor thing. This time he looks so hot, I decide to try it. I fill a metal bowl to the brim and place it on the floor. The little dog runs over to it, and immediately begins to drink. I watch in amazement as drips of water splatter across the floor and I hear him drinking.

When I go upstairs to get my typewriter, I look in to the bathroom but it's empty. I'm sorry that my nerve failed me when I last saw him. Next time, when he turns towards me, I'll stay. I'll look into his eyes and see what happens. Next time, I resolve, I will not run away.

I set everything up on the table in front of the Watcher and as I begin to type I hear her voice in my head for the first time. She is softly spoken but not apologetic, there's a concern underlying her tone as she says, 'Stan is going to be trapped between two women at work.'

I'm so startled that my fingers freeze above the keys. I look up and stare straight into her eyes. She smiles at me, and I manage to return a brief smile at her and her dog, who has climbed up onto her knee. I watch as his little pink tongue licks at the drops of water on his fur around his muzzle. I still haven't replied to her. I still haven't asked any of the questions she is waiting for me to ask.

How is it that the dog is real? How can he drink water and lick drops from his fur when she is an apparition?

But her words remain in my mind as I continue to type.

When Stan gets into work on the Monday morning, he finds a note on his desk from Maureen informing him that Mrs Fanshaw will be coming in at 9.30am. He's to take her in the company car to three properties. One of the addresses is 'Newland's Farm', an isolated, rural location. Stan realises with despair that it may take him a good while to walk the boundary of the property if the client so requests. Hopefully, Maureen won't expect him back into the office until the afternoon. The note also mentions that Maureen wants a private word with him at the end of the day, and would be grateful if he would stay to discuss certain matters after the office closes. Stan's heart sinks, he's been avoiding Maureen for a while now. He has the impression that she wants him to ask her out but he feels sure that combining business with pleasure would not be a good idea.

Eileen Fanshaw arrives on the dot of 9.30, sweeps into the office, and walks straight up to Stan, 'Stanley, good morning. Are you ready to show me around today? I must say I am looking forward to it.' She sits her considerable girth on the chair opposite him and places her chubby, heavily ringed fingers on his desk.

'Good morning, Mrs Fanshaw, I have...'

'Oh, do call me Eileen, please!' she gushes. Stan feels his face redden, especially when he hears the stifled giggles from the girls working at the back of the office.

'Of course, Mrs... I mean Eileen. I just have to get the keys and the particulars, and then I'll bring the car round and pick you up at the front door. Would you like a coffee while you're waiting?'

'If you're making it, Stanley, I'd love one,' she coos.

'Well, I won't be able to do that and get the keys, but I'm sure Emily will be only too pleased to get you one, won't you Emily?' Stan turns a pair of beseeching eyes on his colleague seated at the desk behind him.

'Of course,' Emily says trying to smother her amusement.

Eileen Fanshaw looks disgruntled but agrees, though Stan feels her eyes follow him as he goes into the back office. Emily makes the coffee while he selects the keys he'll need. She's a mousey young woman of about twenty-two, but friendly enough. 'You'd better watch your step with that one, Stan, she fancies you.' Emily is the only person in the office to call him Stan and he likes her for it.

'Oh God, don't please. I'm not looking forward to today at all.' He takes the car keys off the hook and leaves by the back door.

The first few viewings proceed fairly well and except for putting a heavily ringed hand on Stan's arm a few times Eileen Fanshaw behaves herself. But when they get back into the car to drive to Newland's Farm her manner changes and she begins to flirt openly with him. 'You know, Stanley, you're a very attractive man,' she says placing a hand lightly on his knee. As Stan is changing gear, he has difficulty in moving his leg out of the way. 'It's

47

very grim for a woman, Stanley, when she is attracted to a man, especially if she's married. When my husband is away for weeks or months at a time, I do have needs. A man can always find somewhere to go to fulfil those needs, even if he has to pay. But a woman, especially one of my age, is unable to arrange that, even if she wants to. Where can a lady buy comfort? She's forced to throw herself on the mercy of the man she fancies at the risk of being ridiculed or worse.'

Her hand is warm and gentle on his knee, and Stan almost feels sorry for her. Giving her hand, what he hopes is a reassuring pat, he keeps his eyes steadily on the road in front, but her words make him reflect. *I guess Society still frowns on women of a certain age who admit that they have physical needs.* 'I'm sure it must be difficult for you Eileen,' Stan says, repeating the pat, while internally sighing with relief to find they're approaching the farm.

The farmhouse is Victorian, luxurious, and although unoccupied, furnished throughout. It so happens, that it's one of those rare properties on Payntons books, which is both 'For Sale', and 'To Let' depending on whichever contract they can arrange first. Eileen walks around the old building with a dreamy look on her face, all that brashness has gone and her manner becomes wistful. She tells Stan that she lived in just such a farmhouse as a child, and of the hopes she had of marrying into a farming family, as she loved the countryside. 'But I fell in love with an accountant who holidayed at the farm one summer,' she explains, 'and he whisked me off my feet, and took me to Greece. We got married there and the rest is history. I was far too young.' Eileen sighs as she gazes out of the window at the surrounding fields. 'The children I'd hoped for failed to materialise, and though I'm happy enough in the life we have, I always have the feeling that I've missed something.' She wipes away a tear and Stan feeling sympathy for her offers her a freshly laundered handkerchief. 'You really are a sweet man. I knew it the first time I saw you. I know this is beyond the call of duty and not very professional but would you just hug me for a minute?' Eileen's eyes look into his, and he sees they are pretty, hazel eyes, that are pleading with him to take pity. Stan, always a soft touch, takes pity and puts his arms around her generous shoulders. They stand in the middle of the large farmhouse kitchen, hugging. The old house is silent and still, and it's rather lovely.

It's past 3 o'clock when he gets back to the office, having dropped Eileen off at her hotel, and having declined the offer of a late lunch. So, it's a tired and hungry Stan that faces Maureen, who is obviously in a foul mood. 'Good afternoon, Stanley, kind of you to finally grace us with your company. How did you get on? Have you made a sale?'

'I think she may be interested in Newland's, it reminded her of where she grew up.'

'Oh, did it, well let's hope all the reminiscing gets us somewhere, because our monthly figures are down, and your sales are non-existent. Write up your notes on each visit, and then get onto the phone and try to get some more viewings for tomorrow, and don't forget, my office as soon as we close.' Maureen stumps off to answer her phone, which luckily for Stan has started its insistent jangle.

'Could you do with a coffee?' Emily asks him.

'I could murder for one.' Stan laughs.

'I'll get it. I need one too.' She returns with the coffee and hands Stan a packet of biscuits. 'Maureen's been like that ever since you left with the Fanshaw woman this morning. It's been hell.'

'I wonder why?' says Stan, tucking into the biscuits.

'It's her age.' Emily returns to her desk dropping her voice to a loud whisper. 'The menopause I reckon.'

By the end of the day Stan has managed to arrange several visits over the next couple of days, and one of them is with Eileen, who wants a second visit to Newland's Farm. When the office closes, he's able to show a nearly full diary to Maureen, he also brings her in a cup of coffee. She's calmed down enough to smile her thanks at the gesture. She takes the diary from him and peruses the appointments. 'That's better, Stanley.' Putting the diary down on her desk, she says. 'Err... I wanted the opportunity of being frank with you, Stanley. You have been here for a while now, and I would like the chance to get to know you better.'

Stan notices that she is wearing a new suit in a French navy material and a soft pink blouse. Deciding that flattery may help the situation he mentions her outfit. 'I like your suit very much,' he smiles, 'I personally think skirts are more attractive than trousers.'

'Well thank you, Stanley.' Maureen gets up and looks at herself appraisingly in a long mirror on the wall by her desk, obviously put there for this purpose.

Stan looks at her reflection too. She's an attractive woman, although a little too slim for his taste. Her brown hair is always worn up for the office, and he finds himself wondering what it would look like down, and how long it was. *Careful Stan, don't mix business with pleasure.*

However, that is just what Maureen seems to be suggesting. 'I wanted to ask you...' she hesitates for a moment, then blushing slightly continues, 'I've been given two complimentary tickets for the theatre next Thursday evening, from a satisfied customer of ours, but I've no one to accompany me. I'd really like it, Stanley, if you would come with me.'

Stan has a presentiment, a shiver of ill omen, but how can he refuse? 'Yes, that would be nice, thank you,' he says.

Ten

This morning, when I get home the house is silent, the shower isn't running and there's no light in the bathroom. However, as I stand in the hall listening to the ticking of the clock and the occasional drip of the kitchen tap, I'm sure he's here. I go to the airing cupboard, get out my typewriter and set it up on the kitchen table. There's no sign of the Watcher or her little dog, but I feel someone is here.

The file is getting heavy and full, and soon I'll have to start another, or Guy will notice something. Guy is a good man. He provides for me and the child, and all he asks in return is a clean home, a meal on the table when he gets back, and fairly frequent comfort from my body. But I don't feel close to him. Even when we have sex, I'm distanced. He takes his pleasure of me and then falls asleep. Sometimes he'll kiss me on the cheek or pat me on the behind before he dozes off, but otherwise once he's satisfied, he isn't interested in me.

I place my fingers on the typewriter keys but no words come. The sense of a presence is so strong. I go into the sitting room, but there's no one there, so I climb the stairs, heart pounding in my ears. Cautiously, I push the bedroom door and there he is, dressed all in black, sitting on the side of my bed staring into my dressing table mirror. Our eyes meet in the glass. I'm electrified by the icy blue of his irises and the fact that he's noticed me. He smiles wearily at my reflection, then gets up and walks past me to the stairs. He's gone. The front door's open and I can hear the shrieks of the children in the playground of the nearby school.

The next morning, Stan calls for Eileen in the company car, and drives her to Newland's Farm for her second viewing. She's less extravagantly turned out, wearing a simple dress and jacket in blue which suits her and Stan compliments her. They drive in silence for a while till Eileen suddenly asks him. 'What are you doing in this job, Stanley?'

Stan's taken aback by the directness of her question. 'Well, I suppose I'm earning money and I like meeting people.'

'You're too good for this kind of work, I can see you meeting and greeting in a large corporation or working in haute-couture, perhaps designing or selling women's fashions.'

Stan is not expecting this turn of the conversation. 'Oh, gosh… It is strange you should say that, though, because if I could have my time over again that's exactly the kind of thing I'd like to do.'

'I knew it! You see despite my overbearing manner I'm very perceptive. I can tell you love women: their femininity, the clothes, the perfume and make-up, everything that goes with it. You notice things and you delight in them. I think you should find an alternative source of income that will give you more satisfaction and utilise your talents.'

Stan laughs. 'That's easier said than done. I think I'm a bit old in the tooth to learn dress design.'

Eileen places her hand on his knee and squeezes. 'Maybe. I'll give it some thought, I'm sure I can think of an alternative occupation for you.'

Stan finds himself relaxing in her company and by the

time they are looking over the farmhouse for the second time, he's beginning to find her amusing in a quirky way. They climb the wide staircase and Stan waits on the landing while Eileen wanders in and out of the bedrooms. 'What do you think then?' he asks, returning the conversation to the job in hand. 'Would you consider making an offer?'

Eileen regards him as though she's trying to weigh something up in her mind. 'Do you know, Stanley, I think I might. But there's one thing that you could do for me, that would make it a certainty.'

'What's that?' asks Stan.

An amused but crafty expression crosses her face. She takes hold of his tie and pulls him towards her. 'Make love to me, Stanley.'

'What!' Stan is incredulous. *The woman has gone mad.*

'Make love to me here and now.'

Stan is horrified. He really doesn't know how to handle the situation. Is she serious or having a joke with him? He tries to loosen her fingers from his tie, but she pulls him into the main bedroom and towards the large bed. 'Sit down, Stanley, and listen to me.'

Stan sits down heavily, and Eileen stands in front of him. 'Gus and I have been married for nearly thirty years. Most of the time we get on fine, but the excitement has lessened, especially in the bedroom. Now, if I had the memory of you making love to me on this bed, in this room, then it might add spice to making love to him. It might rekindle my passion; remind me of how I used to feel in those early days in Greece.'

Stan shakes his head and tries to get up. 'Eileen you must see this is madness. I could lose my job. You could lose your marriage.'

'How? Who would know?' She puts her hands on his

shoulders and gently pushes him down, then sits beside him. Her eyes are wide and dark with the dilation of pupil. Those pretty hazel eyes that plead with him till, in spite of his better judgement, he feels the first stirrings of desire. His body is betraying him. He makes one last desperate effort. 'Maureen will suspect something,' he says trying to get up from the bed, 'and we'll be late getting back.'

'Nonsense, Stanley.' Eileen strokes his face; her hands are soft and gentle. 'How long would it take for us to walk the boundary of this property and go over the barn and outbuildings?'

'About half an hour I suppose.' He's feeling hot and his collar is too tight.

'Well then, let's say we don't do that, and if you allow me, the client, ten or fifteen minutes to make up my mind that gives us forty-five minutes to make love. Then you'll return to Maureen with a clinched deal. Who is going to mind?'

Much to Stan's amazement he feels his will weakening. Her close proximity, her perfume and the whole crazy situation is becoming erotic. When she bends to kiss him gently but firmly, he finds himself responding. 'I really shouldn't do this,' he says trying to detach her hands from his body.

'Oh, but you should, Stanley. Please do this for me just this once. You don't know how much it will mean to me; how much I want to feel again.' She is kissing him passionately; his eyes, his lips, his neck. She loosens his tie, unbuttons his shirt and slips her soft, ringed fingers onto his chest. Stan feels the contrasting hardness of the jewellery on her soft hands strangely sensual, and he finds himself thinking, *perhaps this is why people have piercings.*

The whole scenario is so bizarre, but when she bends her

head, puts her warm lips on his nipple, and gently bites, he's lost. He stops fighting the sensations he's experiencing. Lying back on the bed, he makes no protest when she climbs beside him and undoes the rest of his clothing.

She's a good lover. Never has Stanley experienced anything like it. In control from the start, Eileen sits astride him and rides like someone possessed, moaning in ecstasy. She pleasures him till he can hold back no longer and he comes beneath her, bellowing loudly. Finally, she collapses back on the bed laughing and he turns to kiss her, 'You are a mad, amazing woman, Eileen Fanshaw.'

'She laughs. 'Well thank you, Stanley, for the compliment. You've no idea how much I needed that.'

'I think I've an inkling,' he says softly as he strokes the curve of her ample breast, but he catches sight of the time on his watch and becomes serious. 'We really need to get going.' He gets up and reaches for his trousers and it's then he sees the mess they have made of the duvet. 'Shit! What are we going to do with that?'

'Calm down Stanley. We'll turn it over and I'll buy all the furniture and fittings with the house. No-one will ever know. Give me one last kiss and we'll be on our way.'

'When you've got dressed,' he says, as he hugs her fondly. 'Now hurry.'

When Stan gets back to the office Maureen is still there but everyone else has gone. She turns on him as soon as he gets through the door. 'Stanley you're late.' She sounds as though she is about to get angry, but controls herself, 'Never mind the important thing is, have we got a sale?'

Stan is relieved to be able to say, 'Yes. Mrs. Fanshaw is definitely going to purchase Newland's Farm, and I have her solicitor's details with me.' He hands a piece of paper to

Maureen.

'Oh, well done, Stanley.' I think, this calls for a celebration. I was thinking we could shut up shop a little early next Thursday and go for a bite to eat before the play.'

'Err… yes of course why not?' says Stan noticing that Maureen's staring at him. He just hopes there's nothing about him that might give a clue to what he's just been doing.

'That's settled then, we can go straight from here and have a meal first.' Maureen smiles happily at him. 'Just one more thing, Stanley, before you go. That suit is looking very crumpled. Perhaps it's time you bought a new one, and got that one to the cleaners?'

Oh, great! Stan grumbles to himself as he walks home. *Now I need to buy a new suit. Shit, more expense. And will Maureen be expecting me to pay for a meal?*

Eleven

After dropping the child off at school, I'm forced to pluck up courage and visit the corner shop for a few groceries. Guy's morning trip into town last Saturday meant we didn't do our usual shop, and now there's not enough food left to make meals. I hate shopping for anything but Guy has left me some money and expects me to do it. As soon as I've paid, I run back home as fast as I can with the heavy bag of shopping to carry.

I can hear watery lapping sounds as I enter the hall, and when I open the kitchen door the dog stops drinking, looks up at me and wags his tail. The Watcher is sitting at the table, she smiles and nods her thanks for the water that I leave out most morning, now. Of course, I remove all traces before Guy returns home. I put the bag of shopping onto the worktop and start to empty the contents. I try not to look at the Watcher, but I know she's observing me. When I finish, I fetch my typewriter and sit down at the table opposite her. As she leans across, I hear her voice in my head, 'I think he is in trouble, financial trouble I mean.'

I look up at her because she has worried me, and I want to ask, 'What makes you think that?' I don't speak the words, and yet she seems to understand what I'm thinking, as she adds, 'I saw him having his lunch at the Community Centre café.' I realise that I'm conversing with an apparition, despite trying not to. Things are moving so fast: the dog drinks, the Watcher speaks and she knows what's happening with Stan before I do. And now in my tale, I'll have to add a new problem for my character to face. Stan has been living the high life for too long and can't afford it on a part-time wage. A bit of me is happy, because this might mean he'll be in my bathroom every morning, like before, and he will need me.

Stan is getting increasingly tense. Of course, he loves his new lifestyle with two girlfriends, and two other women chasing him. Who wouldn't like it at his age? But the downside is, he's running low on funds and now Maureen expects him to buy another suit for work, when really, the firm should supply one on the salary they pay.

It's nearly the weekend again, and he needs to do a shop as there's nothing left in the fridge. Stan walks the length of the High Street to see if any of the men's clothing shops have a sale, but of course they don't. So, he decides to try the big department store in the city centre as they stock his size. It was hard enough finding a suit for his mother's funeral, which is the suit he currently wears for work. If he hadn't been seduced by Eileen, his suit wouldn't have been crumpled, and he wouldn't be in this predicament. *Still,* he thinks as he remembers the pleasure, it *was worth it, mad woman!*

Stan buys a steel grey suit, a couple of shirts and a new tie, and writes out a cheque. He hands it to the attendant, crossing his fingers there's enough in the account to prevent it bouncing. As he gets off the bus on the way home, he remembers he hasn't been to the supermarket. *Damn, I'll be eating out this evening with Amy, but I'm hungry now.* He sees the Community Centre across the road with the sign outside for its little café. *Should be pretty cheap, I'll drop these bags home and go there.*

The sandwich he buys is delicious and only costs £2 with the cup of coffee. Looking around at the other occupants, he realizes they're mostly pensioners having senior citizen meal deals, or children in buggies being looked after by their grandmothers, but it's a cheerful place. The lady in the café is lively and appears to know everyone. Stan can't help reflecting on the differences between this environment, and the one he'll inhabit this evening when he takes Amy to one of her favourite restaurants. They are worlds apart. But there's an appeal in the friendliness of this place that he likes.

When he meets Amy, she loves the new suit. 'Suits you, Stanley,' she laughs as she turns him around to view it from all angles. She tucks her arm in his as they walk along the street, looking at their reflections in the shop windows. 'Don't we look the pair?' says Amy, her fitted blue dress flaring out at the hem. 'Perhaps we should go dancing after our meal. What do you think?'

Stan's heart sinks, but she's so happy, and her happiness is so infectious that he merely bows and says, 'Whatever the lady desires.'

'Chez Reynard' is a new restaurant, minimalistic and chic. For once, Stan doesn't feel too out of place and the waiters are deferential to him as well as Amy. When their food arrives, it is superbly placed on square white plates. The flavours are beautifully balanced. Every forkful tantalises and Stan is as impressed by the culinary expertise as he would be by any great creative ability. Never has he imagined that dining could be such an exquisite experience in itself. 'This food is superb,' he says.

'I know. There's no Chef like Renard. We're lucky he's

cooking tonight. He hires his services out for society functions and is in great demand as you can imagine.'

But as Stan finishes his meal, his euphoria gives way to fear. The prices are sure to be as rarefied as the food and way above his budget. The time has come to be honest. *Even if honesty ends our relationship here and now.*

Amy has finished eating and is sipping her Champagne, 'Top me up darling.' Stan makes no move. 'Stanley, darling, can you fill my glass please?'

Stan shakes his head, 'Sorry Amy I was miles away.' Taking the freezing cold bottle out of the silver bucket, he pours, watching the bubbles rise in the tall slim glass. In his mind, he suddenly sees the Community Centre café, and stops pouring while he tries to make sense of the two worlds.

Amy looks concerned, 'Stanley are you alright?'

Stan replaces the dripping bottle and wipes his hands on his napkin. Reaching across the table he picks up her hands and looks at the gold and diamond rings she wears on her fingers. He twists the rings with his thumbs so that the diamonds flash their cool fire in the candlelight. 'Amy, I've something I have to tell you.' he says. He leans closer so as to speak quietly. 'I can't take you to these wonderful restaurants every time we go out, I just can't afford to do it anymore. I'm sorry, but I want you to understand...'

Amy throws back her head and laughs out loud. Then she stops herself, becomes serious, and squeezes his hand. 'Is that all darling?' she says, 'I thought you were about to propose or something stupid. Of course, I understand. I didn't expect you to pay these prices on your salary. This is my treat. Oh dear, I should have told you.' She beckons to the waiter. 'Can I have the bill please?'

'Certainly Madam.' The tall, supercilious young man

brings the handwritten bill in a leather folder and presents it to Amy with a slight bow. 'Was everything to Madam's satisfaction?' He pointedly speaks to Amy, ignores Stan.

'Yes, everything was fine, thank you.' Amy pays, leaves a generous tip and receives another bow with a flashing of white teeth. After leaving the restaurant, Amy, who is high on Champagne, suggests going on to a night club or somewhere to dance, but Stan's just not in the mood. He apologises and makes the excuse of a stomach ache. Amy calls a taxi, which drops him off at his flat before taking her on to her house. She will pay of course. He gets out of the cab, and then leans back in to kiss her good night.

'I'm so sorry Amy, but I just can't party tonight. Thanks for a wonderful meal. Call me if you want to go out again, and please believe me, I'll understand if you don't.' He kisses her hand, backs away from the vehicle and stands watching the red lights of the taxi as they disappear down the road.

Twelve

As I open the front door, I know immediately that he's back. I run upstairs. I smell the faint aroma of his aftershave and I fling open the bathroom door, but he isn't there. I check in my bedroom but that's empty too. I get out my typewriter and set it up in the kitchen. The Watcher isn't there either. It's strange, nothing is as it should be: no little dog drinking his water, the bowl is untouched. I stand at the sink and look out of the window but there's no sign of the Watcher walking her dog. I'm tempted to do the unthinkable. Standing at the bottom of the stairs, I call out. 'Where are you?' The sound of my voice echoes around the house and I am shaking with fear. Do I really want a reply? I return to the kitchen and start to type. The keys clack, clack in the silence. Then I hear the door creak as it slowly opens behind me.

He comes in and sits at the table in front of me. I hold my breath. He puts his hands over his face. I think he might cry so I say nothing, just feel empathy. I notice his hands, the pink of his neatly-cut nails, the smoothness of his skin. I long to hold them. I could so easily fall in love with this man.

The phone rings loud and sharp. It cuts the air. I go into the hall to answer it, in case it's Guy checking up on me or the child having had an accident at school. It's neither. Just a wrong number. But the damage is done. When I go back into the kitchen he's standing, looking out of the window, and as I sit down, he walks out of the room. I hear the front door close gently behind him.

❖

Stan wakes up the next morning with a sense of loss. Suddenly he feels everything keenly: the death of his mother, the moment of honesty the previous evening, even the breakup with Ruth all those years ago. Normally, his way of dealing with pain is to get on with life. Stan sees no point being maudlin, but today his mood won't lift. He sits in the kitchen contemplating his position, his life and existence in general, until he's late for work. The thought of doing back-to-back viewings today is more than he can stand. He decides to ring in sick. Mechanically he gets up and pulls the overflowing bin bag out of the bin, ties it and takes it downstairs to add it to the pile of bags left for the rubbish lorry. As he opens the downstairs door, he sees the little dog sniffing around the piled up black bags. 'Hey little feller there's nothing for you there,' he says. As he bends to stroke the tiny dog, the shadow of the Watcher falls across his hands.

'Hello Stanley,' she says. 'I didn't expect to see you. I know you have to work some weekends. Are you alright?' She bends down and puts the lead back on the little dog's collar.

'Yes. Just a massive case of reality kicking in. I can't face work today, so I'm taking sick leave.'

'Oh, you be careful with 'reality kicking in,' young man.' Stan starts to laugh at the 'young man' bit. 'I mean you can get bogged down with that you know,' she says. 'Anyway, I'd better be getting along. Remember you can always call round for a coffee anytime or something stronger,' she adds with a wink. 'We're always there aren't we, Mutty?' She pats the dog on the head.

'Why don't you come upstairs for a drink with me, now? It's getting warm already and for once there's nothing I have to do.'

The old woman looks at Stan. 'If you're sure it won't be putting you out,' she says. 'My poor old bones could do with a sit down. I often think it would be good if there was a bench here on this little patch of grass, just so we could have a rest on our way round the estate.'

Back up in his flat, Stan fills the kettle and switches it on. The Watcher and her little dog sit at his kitchen table. 'I'll not be a moment,' Stan tells them. 'I just have to phone my manager.' He goes into the sitting room and phones Maureen on her home number, she answers straight away as though she was expecting his call. He tells her he's too ill to come in.

'Well, if you are, I guess there's nothing we can do about it, but it's very inconvenient. You're booked in for viewings all morning and to take Mrs Fanshaw back to measure up and see what furniture she wishes to keep.'

Stan had forgotten about Eileen. 'Oh dear, well tell her I'll take her Monday, or perhaps, if you could spare the time today…'

'I'm not going in on a weekend especially for her, or anyone else for that matter. Besides I don't think she is as enamoured with me as she is with you, and we want to keep her sweet; this sale has to go through to keep our figures healthy. Luckily, I brought the diary home with me so I'll ring round and cancel for you, but you will have to rearrange everything tomorrow. Get better Stanley, I need these viewings done.'

Stan returns to the kitchen and makes two coffees and gets a bowl of water for the dog. He sits opposite the old lady and suddenly has the urge to confide in her. 'To tell you the truth, I'm missing Mum more than a bit. I could tell her anything and she'd always have something sensible to say about it.'

'Yes, Vera was a wise woman. Do you remember playing with my dog on the green out there while your mother and I chatted?'

Stan thinks for a moment. 'It was a little black poodle, wasn't it? A totally mad thing, I used to throw sticks for it, but it never brought them back.'

'Yes, that's right. I was going through a bad patch at that time and your mother was very helpful, I owe her a lot. So, I want the chance to help you if I can, Stanley.'

'Thanks, but I'm not sure you can. I've started a new lifestyle that I can't afford to keep, it's as simple as that. I can just hear Mum saying, 'You've got ideas above your station, Stanley, that's heading for trouble.'

'True in a way, but sometimes you need to move on, and I think you have hidden potential. For instance, have you ever thought about running your own business?'

Stan laughs. 'Doing what?'

'I don't know, but look around, there must be something you can do. Perhaps your red-headed lady in the sports car could help you.'

'Amy?' Stan thinks for a moment. 'I suppose it's worth talking to her about it.'

Thirteen

Today, I'm very agitated. The weekend has been stressful. Guy just followed me all around the house criticising everything I did. Now that he's left for work, I want to set my typewriter out as usual, but the Gas man is coming to service our boiler. The problem is I don't know when. I don't want to get involved with anything. I have my fingers crossed that neither the fat, white man nor the Watcher will appear today. I pace around the house checking every corner, but no one's there, and part of me is sorry. I'm scared these secret interactions are becoming addictive, and I wonder if I should talk to someone about them. I decide to do the chores now, while I am waiting, and with luck there will be time to get my typewriter out later, when the boiler man has been.

While I'm waiting, I sit at the table thinking of what I might type next. I'm not sure I have any idea where it's all going. Nothing is as I anticipated. Things seem to move on in unexpected ways that have nothing to do with me.

When Stan gets to the office on Monday morning Maureen is already there. 'Morning Stanley, I trust you're better. Here's a list of people to contact. The ones at the top are the people I had to cancel, and as you might imagine none of them were pleased. I've said that you should be able to rebook for next Sunday morning, so I am hoping you'll agree to work then.'

Stan groans inwardly but agrees to work the Sunday. He picks up the phone and starts dialling. When he calls Eileen's number there's no reply, so he leaves a message. He's a little concerned; he just hopes she's not looking at other properties with another agent, that would not go down well with Maureen. He makes sure he finishes Maureen's list before he breaks for lunch, then he goes to the nearest cash machine to check his balance. It's as he thought, right on the limit, and he can't get any cash out. *Jesus, pay day is nearly two weeks away! Thank God I have no rent to pay, but what am I going to do for food?* Stan checks his wallet and counts out £30 and some loose change. He decides lunch had better be coffee and biscuits back at the office.

In the afternoon, he calls Eileen's number again and this time to his relief she does pick up. 'Stanley darling,' she coos at him. 'How are you? I missed you.'

'I'm sorry about that, Eileen, I can take you to the farm on Sunday.'

'Oh, Stanley I can't wait that long, can't you do something one day this week? What about Thursday afternoon?'

Stan looks at the diary and for some reason he sees that the appointments stop at 3.00pm. 'Yes, OK that should be possible, I can pick you up around 3.30.'

'Brilliant Stanley, that's a date then. Remember I shall need a little time for measuring up and other things.' Eileen laughs. Stan hopes she doesn't mean what he thinks she does. He writes her name and Newlands Farm in the 4.00pm slot in the diary, then puts it back on Maureen's desk. Taking his list of viewings, he collects the keys, and escapes for the afternoon.

One of the appointments, is at a flat not far from his own, and when he's finished, he realises how hungry he is. He's about to drive past the Community café, so he pulls over, parks, and goes in. Stan orders a jacket potato with salad, which only sets him back £2.50. He takes a glass of tap water from a jug left out for that purpose, and sits in a corner feeling a little over dressed as everyone else seems to be wearing jeans, even the grannies. When his food arrives, he eats it hungrily while watching people come and go. It seems a lot happens here. As he's finishing his meal, he notices the diminutive figure of a middle-aged, Eurasian lady. Her black hair is cut in a shoulder length bob, her face is pretty but determined and she's wearing a trouser suit which adds to her professional manner. She greets several people, and Stan watches her with interest, wondering what her role is: manager, social worker, counsellor? Whatever it is, she's certainly attractive, and as she turns to climb the stairs, she looks in his direction. Their eyes meet, just for a second, but Stan gains an instinctive impression that his destiny will be in some way linked with hers. Then the moment passes, and he looks at his watch realising he will be late for his next appointment.

Later that evening Stan rings Linda. *Here's a lady, who won't want to cost him a fortune, and who will comfort him without question.*

'Hi Linda, how are things?'

'Stan, nice to hear from you,' she sounds light and happy.

'Sorry I haven't been in touch for a while,' says Stan feeling a bit guilty.

'That's OK. Things have been looking up here. Bryony and I had a long chat and I told her how I felt about her going to her dad's. Anyway, the result is that she'll just go over there at the weekends at the moment, and so I will have her here during the week.'

'That's brilliant! I'm happy for you. Shall we celebrate tomorrow with a meal here at my flat?'

'Can we make it at the weekend Stan? I want to make the most of the evenings with Bryony while I can.'

'Yes of course,' says Stan, trying to hide his disappointment. 'But I'm working next weekend, so it will have to be Sunday after six.'

'That's fine. Shall I make a pudding to bring?'

'That would be great! See you then.' He sends a kiss down the phone, but when he puts the phone down, he immediately feels the depression returning. It's stupid, although he is pleased things are working out for Linda, he's scared it may mean she'll no longer need him. He goes to the fridge and finds a couple of beers left over from his after-funeral binge. As he opens the can he recalls how he felt then, and he realises depression isn't so easy to escape.

Fourteen

The fat man returns each day, although he's nowhere near as fat as he was. I'm so excited. But when I glance at his reflection, I realise we are back to the way things were. He doesn't seem to see me or my face in the mirror. If only he could sit at the table while I type, like the Watcher does. But I know I wouldn't dare speak to him. So, I leave him shaving and return to the kitchen, where the Watcher is seated in her usual chair. She looks at me sadly and her words sound in my head, 'It would be so much simpler if you'd speak to us.'

I shake my head and refuse to look at her, then start to type as quickly as I can, tapping out the words that pour through my head. If only I could type faster, I lose some of the words as they pile up behind the dam of my fingers, it's so frustrating. When is the Watcher going to realise that this is the only way I can speak to them? I hear her sigh as she gets up from her chair, only then do I look up to see her walk out of the door, her little dog trots behind her his claws making a clicking sound on the tiles as he goes.

I go back upstairs but the bathroom is empty.

Maureen is waiting for Stan, and as soon as he walks through the door, she barks out. 'My office Stanley, please.' She has the diary open in her hands and her face is thunderous. Elsie gives him a little smile of sympathy as he puts his keys down on the desk and follows Maureen's receding back. When he closes the door, she starts on him before he has the chance to sit down. 'You have booked an appointment on Thursday afternoon when I deliberately put a pencil line through the four o'clock appointment slot.'

Stan can't understand her fury. 'Mrs Fanshaw wanted to see Newland's before next Sunday,' he explains, 'and since there were no other slots big enough to give her the time she needs I thought ...'

'The trouble is Stanley you didn't think. On Thursday we're going to the theatre, and I crossed it out so that there was no chance of your being late back. Had you forgotten?' She throws the diary onto the desk.

Stan curses under his breath. 'Yes, sorry, I did forget momentarily, but then I thought I would be able to be back in time.' he lies.

'In time for the theatre may be but not in time for us to have a meal beforehand.' Maureen sits down and puts a hand over her eyes.

'I'm sorry Maureen,' he says. 'But I decided that making sure Mrs Fanshaw went through with the purchase was as important as the meal, and I do think I can do it. If I get her there by 4.00pm and we leave before 5.00, even allowing for the traffic, I should be back here by 6.00pm.'

Maureen takes a deep breath. 'Stanley it's not your job to make such decisions without running them past me first. Still, this time I grant you, we can probably fit it all in and the Newland's deal is kingpin to our figures. OK, but do not waste time. Get her on track from the start, she's a bloody difficult woman, if you keep focused you should do it. I want you back here by six and not a minute later. Understood?'

'Understood.' Stan breathes easier as he exits her office. He feels like a football kicked between these two women, and he can't wait for Eileen and her husband to sign on the dotted line and get the contract exchanged. He goes back to his desk where Elsie has made him a coffee. 'You're an angel,' he says with conviction.

Much later, after an evening meal that consists of a cereal and a yogurt, Stan goes onto his computer to check his emails. There's one from Amy. It reads: Hi Stanley, just wanted to say that I miss your company. Please don't let pride spoil a beautiful relationship. I can't help being rich and you can't help being less well-off, but with effort on both sides I'm sure we can resolve things. Lots and lots of love. Amy x x

Stan smiles to himself as he reads it. She is a sweet lady. Is it just his pride that's the problem? Perhaps it is, but can he resolve that? He recalls the attitude of the waiter in 'Chez Renard' when Amy paid the bill. Can he put up with that sort of social put down over and over again? Picking up the phone he calls her number. After all, he's at a loose end till Thursday.

Fifteen

I watch his hands as he shaves; sculpts his side-burns and moustache. I've an urgent wish for him to touch me, to know how those hands would feel on my skin. I imagine them smooth, warm and sensual. I feel faint and aroused, and move away, shocked by the strength of my emotions.

I can't even remember what Guy's hands are like. I don't think I've ever noticed them. They travel across my body without sensitivity, they never woo me. How did I meet Guy? How did I get involved with him? Well, I was lonely and finding it hard to cope in the outside world. I couldn't make ends meet, and he had this baby girl to look after. Yes, the child is his not mine. But I've loved her in my own way, especially when she was little and needed me. Now? Things are different. I think she finds me strange.

Back in the kitchen I type out my passion, flood it into the story. I type frenetically till I hear the front door close. Then I stop. The silence in the house presses down on me. His absence is like loss. I never notice Guy's absence. I listen to the ticking of the clock in the sitting room and gradually the words form. I type on.

The next evening, Amy comes over to meet Stan, she doesn't hoot as usual, but gets out of the car and rings his bell. When Stan opens the door, he's not expecting her yet and shock is written all over his face. She laughs, 'I want to see your flat, Stanley, aren't you going to invite me in?' Dressed in white slacks and a white T-shirt with a gold motif on the front, she carries a gold leather shoulder bag and has matching gold pumps on her feet. Her hair is braided and held in place with a gold clasp. She couldn't appear more out of place in this dingy estate. Stan follows her up the stairs with a mixture of emotions: pleasure at seeing her, excitement that she has come to his home, and a real fear of what she might think of his rather cramped flat. He opens the door for her and as she enters, she gives him a kiss. 'Don't look so scared, Stanley, I'm not about to eat you, yet.'

He makes coffee, choosing mugs that don't have any flippant comments on the side, and takes them into the sitting room. He sits on the edge of the settee and watches her look around. 'Not what you're used to, my humble abode.' He makes a mock bow of his head.

Amy is not amused. 'Stop it, Stanley! Stop putting yourself down. You really have to realise that what you are as a person has very little to do with how much money you have.'

'It helps other people's perception of you, though.' Stan mumbles frowning into his coffee and wondering where all this is going.

'Please stop feeling sorry for yourself.' Amy puts down her coffee and comes to kneel at his feet.

Stan puts his hand on her shoulder. 'I'm sorry, it's just that I want to be able to take you out and treat you to things. I need to find a way of earning more money than my stupid, little job with 'Payntons' gives me.'

'Well, that's why I've come to your flat today because I want to help but I want you to remember most of my motivation is purely selfish.' She stretches up and gives him a kiss.

Stan strokes her hair. 'I have to tell you I can't bear to go around with you paying for everything. I do have some pride and I can't take people like that waiter at 'Chez Renard' looking down their noses at me when you pay the bill.'

'Which is why I have a proposal to make to you.'

'Are you going to proposition me, shall we go into the bedroom?'

'Quiet... Be serious for a moment, this is difficult.' Amy gets up and sits at the other end of the sofa. There's a frown of concentration on her face and the light heartedness has gone. 'I've been giving the situation a lot of thought. I want to go on having fun with you, at least two or three times a week, both in bed and out of it. So, what if... And please don't take this the wrong way, what if I pay you for the time you spend with me?'

'What?' Stan is horrified. He gets up, moves away from her and stands by the window, trying to contain his rising anger. 'I don't relish being bought, or being paid for services rendered.'

Amy gets up and comes over to him. 'Please, it's not like that. What if I pay you for three evenings a week? No listen. If I gave you say £50 an hour...'

Stan brakes in, furious with her. 'I can't believe I'm hearing this.'

'No, wait Stanley.' Amy catches hold of his arm. 'If I pay you to escort me wherever I want to go: theatre, restaurants, night clubs, and you pay the costs out of what I pay you so that you are never embarrassed like before. What do you say?'

Stan looks at her, at her pretty face which is so serious and concerned. He's struggling to know what to think. The idea is preposterous, absurd.

'Please, Stanley, think rationally,' Amy pleads. 'Don't let your pride blind you to what might be a sensible solution.'

Pacing back and forth, wearing the already worn carpet, Stan endeavours to control his temper. He doesn't want to shout at her. He knows she's genuinely trying to help but her solution is impossible. Amy catches hold of his arm, stopping him. He stands stiffly, unable to reach out to her though he wants to. He wants to ravish her, bury himself in her. He knows he doesn't want to lose her. He tries to see the situation through her eyes, and although it's still abhorrent to him, he calms down and says, 'Alright, I'll think about it.' Amy smiles with relief.

'But... and it is a big BUT,' Stan continues, holding her away from him, 'I won't be paid for our love making or when we go out for the day as friends or lovers'.

'I understand, that's fine, but whenever I want to go somewhere expensive?'

'We'll see. I said I'll 'think' about it but now, right now I just want to have you. Will you accept my humble bed, or do we need to drive to yours?'

Amy puts her arms round his generous girth and squeezes. 'Take me to your humble bed Mr Baker, I've missed having you inside me.'

Sixteen

Yesterday evening seemed to last for ever. I could hardly wait for the morning in the hope that my hero might come. I kept looking at the clock while we were watching the TV, so much so that Guy remarked on it. 'Did I want an early night and some sadistic sex?' he asked, leering up at me from the sofa he was lolling on. 'Should we go up now?' He started to get up. I quickly said I was fine and fortunately for me the football was about to start.

Today, I return home feeling hopeful but there's nothing, not a sign of my fat man. Did he sense what I was thinking when I watched his hands that last time? Would those half-formed emotions prevent him returning? The Watcher is absent too. I take out my typewriter as usual but words don't come. I'm just sitting in the kitchen with my fingers poised over the keys. What's happening? Why didn't I speak to both of them when I had the chance? I could have said something to my fat man when we looked at each other in the mirror. I should have asked the questions the Watcher is waiting for me to ask.

I sit and feel abandoned, then it comes to me; tomorrow I'll go out. Not just to take the child to school no, I'll go out, and walk around and try to see the Watcher and her little dog. A spike of fear runs through my body at the thought of it, but I know the time she usually appears on my garden path, and if I wait just at the end of it? The plan calms me and I feel more in control. I relax and my fingers tap the keys as words start to flow.

Thursday dawns bright and sunny, and as Stan puts his suit jacket on, he can already feel the heat rising. He's not looking forward to today. Firstly, he's feeling tired from the evening before with Amy, who was insatiable. Secondly, he has to manage a difficult day at work culminating with the viewing at Newland's, and finally, there's the trip to the theatre with Maureen which he's increasingly aware is a big mistake. As he enters the office Maureen is standing by his desk with the diary open in her hands, 'Morning Stanley, warm, isn't it?' She's dressed smartly and her hair is different, shorter and slightly curled but for once Stan doesn't mention it. 'I'm sorry to add to your already busy schedule today, Maureen continues, 'but I've added a second viewing at No. 23 Grace Street. Mr and Mrs Belmont would appreciate a quick visit, I've told them you won't have much time.' She breaks off, looking at him expectantly and when he doesn't respond she shrugs her shoulders and goes off to her office.

Stan slumps down at his desk, looks at the diary and rubs his eyes. Back-to-back bookings in this heat with no time for lunch. Oh well, he'd better get started.

The day gets hotter and by the time he picks Eileen up at her hotel he's wilting. She comes out carrying a woven shopping bag, looking as fresh as a daisy and with a great smile on her face at seeing him there. 'Oh, you poor thing you look so hot.' Eileen rummages around in her bag and takes out a flask. 'Here have some iced tea and a slice of banana bread. Now, park in the shade of that tree over there and eat this before we go any further.'

'But we need to get going I haven't got much time.' Stan tries to take control of the situation but the thought of iced tea weakens his will and he pulls over under a large oak tree.

'This won't take more than a few minutes,' Eileen says, handing him a tall glass out of her bag, into which she pours the amber tea from the flask. 'Drink that and then eat this,' she unwraps a little foil package to reveal two slices of buttered fruit bread. 'I bet you haven't had time for any lunch.'

'Stan doesn't reply immediately for when he begins to drink, he can't stop. He's so thirsty and the tea is smooth and tangy with a hint of lemon. 'Gosh that's good. You're a wonder Eileen, thank you,' he says as he takes the bread and eats hungrily. 'No, I didn't have time for lunch.'

'I thought so, that boss of yours works you too hard, I think I should have words with her.'

'No please don't,' Stan splutters, 'that wouldn't help at all.' He shudders at the thought of what Maureen would say if she were told what to do by this woman.

Stan hands the glass back and starts the engine, 'I feel like a new man,' he laughs. 'Thanks. You're a life saver, but we must go.'

'Stanley,' Eileen says when they've been driving for a while. 'I've been thinking about your situation. I'm sure you don't earn much at this job, and I'm guessing you don't get bonuses when you get a sale, do you?'

Stan laughs. 'No Eileen I don't, on both counts. I'm not an Estate Agent, any bonus goes to them at the end of each quarter.'

'And yet you're doing a lot of the work. You form the relationship with the clients, you get to know what they like, you suggest alternative viewings, and you go on working with them until a sale is reached. I think it's a very poor show.' She puts her heavily ringed hand on his knee and pats it.

'It's kind of you to be so concerned, Eileen, but you shouldn't lose any sleep over it. I'll manage. I might have the chance of a little extra cash anyway.'

'Really doing what?

'Well, I have a lady friend who needs someone to take her to events and shows and things.' Stan wonders why he is telling Eileen this but continues, 'I've been doing this as a friend, but I can't afford to keep doing it. So, she has asked me if I will be an Escort for her. She'll pay me a salary, out of which I can pay for the tickets etc. I haven't actually said I will yet, but I'm thinking about it.'

'But that's a brilliant idea! Of course, now it all fits…'

'What does?' asks Stan feeling slightly worried.

'Why, 'escorting' of course! You're made for it. Attentive, kind, reliable, charming, interested in people…' Eileen's counting his attributes on her bejewelled fingers, she continues on the other hand; '…courteous, a good conversationalist, a good listener, loves women, and you readily make eye contact with your beautiful blue eyes.' She laughs with delight clapping her hands.

'Oh, come on Eileen don't go overboard, this isn't sounding like me at all!' Stan is feeling distinctly uncomfortable. What has he started? Why do all these women suddenly want to run his life for him?

'Will you provide any extras on the side?'

'I beg your pardon?'

'Well, any extra services if required,' Eileen asks with a glint in her eyes. 'You know, massages or intimate input, so to speak.'

'Eileen certainly not!' Stan swerves to avoid a cyclist he almost didn't see.

'Don't be such a prude Stanley. The real question is,

could you respond to such requests, or rather, would you?'

With a sense of relief Stan sees the sign to Newland's Farm, turns off the road onto the long drive and draws up in front of the house. He looks at his watch, 4 o'clock, they've made it in record time. 'Let's go,' he says.

Eileen remains seated. 'Not till you answer my question.'

'Oh, Eileen come on, I don't know what you're on about.' He takes out the keys and opens the front door. Inside, the large hall is deliciously cool.

Eileen follows him in at last, comes up to him, and putting her arms around his neck, kisses him. He holds her away. 'Eileen be good, we haven't time for anything like that. Now, what did you want to measure up?'

'You,' she says giggling. 'OK, the bedroom curtains perhaps.' She says walking towards the stairs.

Once in the main bedroom, she won't take no for an answer. She kicks off her shoes and stands with her hands on her ample hips, 'Stanley, we can waste a lot of time arguing about it or we can do it, and get away on time. What's it to be?'

'I thought once was all you needed to spice things up with the memory of being ravished, or actually, ravishing me as it happened?'

'You can't have too many memories, and besides as you so quaintly put it, I wasn't ravished.'

Stan sighs but with amusement as well as resignation. 'I got into a lot of hot water last time for having a crumpled suit; Maureen got me to fork out on another,'

'Well take it off before we begin,' she says taking off her stockings. She unbuttons her shirt slowly, then unzips her skirt and lets if fall. She stands there in nothing but a pair of white lace French knickers and matching bra.

For her age and size, she has a good body. *Firm, white,*

with smooth, smooth skin, He likes the brazenness of her, her confidence in herself, her knowledge of him and his response to her desire. He takes off his suit and shirt, folding them carefully this time, and under her gaze he removes his boxers and lastly his socks. He wriggles his toes in the thick wool pile of the carpet. It feels good. 'Let's do it here on the floor, throw me a couple of pillows.'

Eileen obeys chucking them at his head but missing. 'Stop playing about, if you want ravishing, you'd better get over here. Now!'

'Yes sir!' she mocks, but her cheekiness dissolves as he kisses her, running his hands over her breasts.

'Lie on your back.' She does as he tells her. 'Put this under your hips,' he says as he pushes a thick pillow under her. Then he slowly slips her knickers over her ankles, kissing her as he does so.

Stan caresses her till the movement of her body tells him she's ready. Then, without warning, he thrusts into her. She squeals out in surprise and pleasure. He leans over her, 'Now I'm going to take my revenge,' he says biting her neck, shoulders, breasts, while rhythmically moving within her. He feels the waves at her centre, the tightening of her belly, her attempts to move under him. But he's in control, she'll have to wait till he decides it's the right moment. He slows down and she moans. He thrusts deeper.

'Oh God, Stanley! Please… Please,' she begs as she arches her spine.

Then he can't hold back any longer, he's groaning at the sharp pleasure of her. She's so bloody sexy this large, generous woman, so earthy, so animal.

It's nearly 5.30 and Stan is driving as fast as he dares. He knows Maureen will have begun to pace around the office because he's late. 'Eileen,' he says keeping his eyes on the road, 'You are some mad woman. Mad and amazing, do you know that? But you'll be the death of me.'

'You're pretty amazing yourself. Honestly, your talents are wasted in this occupation.' She fumbles in her handbag and draws out a handful of £20 banknotes and when Stan pulls up at her apartment, she tries to hand them to him. 'Please don't be offended. This is to pay for the suit I made all crumpled, I'm sure it was an expense you didn't need.'

'Eileen put it away please!' Stan is hurt and bewildered by the gesture. 'There's no need.'

'But I feel responsible. I backed you into a corner which cost you money. I've enjoyed myself more than I could have ever imagined, but I don't want to think that by doing that, I've made things difficult for you financially.'

'Eileen, I haven't got the time to discuss this now, Maureen is waiting for me. I have to go. He leans over and kisses her goodbye before she gets out of the car.

She puts an arm round his waist and squeezes him. 'Alright, we'll talk another time, but call me, please.'

'OK, next week. I will.'

Maureen is not at all pleased he's late, but Stan can see she's making a supreme effort not to let it show. 'I was beginning to worry you wouldn't make it,' she smiles at him.

'Sorry Maureen.' He puts his bunch of keys back on their correct hooks in the cupboard. 'I just need to freshen up a little,' he says making for the toilet.

Stripping to the waist he washes his hands, face and underarms, it's not easy drying himself on paper towels but he manages it. *God, I could do with a shower, and I'm so tired. I just hope I don't nod off during the play.* Stan dresses, checks himself in the mirror and smiles ruefully at his reflection. When he returns, he sees that Maureen has made them a picnic of coffee and supermarket sandwiches. Stan's mouth is dry and the whole situation feels so awkward, he can hardly swallow the plastic bread and cheese. Between sips of coffee he manages to blurt out, 'Your new hairstyle suits you.'

Maureen flashes a brilliant smile at him, 'Thank you, Stanley. Your new suit looks good, too. I meant to say that a couple of days ago.'

Stan's never really seen her smile, not with her whole face and he finds himself saying, 'You should smile more often,' and then wishes he hadn't but she doesn't seem to mind.

'You're right, Stanley, I'm a very focused and ambitious woman, and I need to relax a bit more. Life should be enjoyed. I'll make it a resolution, beginning with this evening.' She takes the tickets and a program out of her bag.

'What are we seeing?'

'Oscar Wilde's 'The Importance of being Earnest'. Have you seen it before?'

'No.' Stan looks through the program, his heart sinking. 'A period drama, is it?' He can't think of anything worse.

'It's so full of wit you could probably set it in any era. I think you'll enjoy it.'

'Then we better go and see it. Do I owe you anything for the sandwiches?' Stan puts his hand in his pocket for his last few pound coins, and finds instead a wad of notes. He looks at them incredulously. They are all £20 notes. *Eileen, she must have…* He puts them hurriedly back in his pocket.

'No, my treat,' says Maureen as she gets her jacket.

The evening goes well, and to Stan's surprise, he really

enjoys the play. He says so to Maureen as they leave the theatre. She takes his arm, and says, 'That's good. Perhaps we can do it again?'

Stan hesitates, he doesn't think it wise but he doesn't want to hurt her feelings. 'Yes, that might be nice.'

'Would you like to come back for a night cap?' she asks still holding on to his arm.

Stan gently moves away, patting her hand as he removes it. 'I'm sorry, Maureen, but I wouldn't be much company tonight.'

Maureen's manner becomes crisp. 'I don't often ask men in for a drink you know.'

'I'm sure you don't, and I'm honoured, but I'm bushed. Some other time maybe?' He raises his hand in farewell. But, as he leaves her, he's sure he can hear anger in the clicking of her high heels as she walks away.

Seventeen

From the minute I open my eyes, I'm longing to see my fat man. I'm awake early but, for once, so is Guy. It's hot in our bedroom, I get out of bed to open the window, and stand for a moment in the cool breeze. He gets out of bed as well. This is a problem as I want to get up and start breakfast but he comes up behind me and puts his hands on my breasts. I can feel his hardness urgent against my back and I know I can't escape. His hands aren't hot but they feel sweaty, or is it my skin? They drag at my flesh as they move. I feel like a lump of dough that he is kneading as he pulls me back to our bed. He doesn't speak and neither do I.

I climb onto the mattress and attempt to lie down but he stops me. Guy wants me on my knees. He pushes my night dress up till it falls around my neck and face, and I've no chance to take it off. He spreads my knees apart, bends to moisten me with his tongue and then he enters. I'm stuck on the bed, my hands by the pillows, my backside in the air, and my face pressed down on the sheet. He holds me in place by my breasts which hurts. I don't mind him having me, it's natural, but I wish he'd give me time so I could share it with him. I count his thrusts 1,2,3,4, then I give up and wait. If I'm quiescent it'll be over sooner. Only this morning it isn't. Guy turns me over and climbs on top of me. I try not to look at him. He doesn't like it. Once, when I looked into his eyes while he was in me, he got really angry. He said my eyes were pleading with him. I said, 'pleading for what?' He said he didn't know but he couldn't stand it. Instead, I look at the clouds moving past our window, it's like we are moving - sailing.

When Guy's finished, I go to the bathroom and wash. I can't wait for him to go to work. I stay in the bathroom as long as I can so as to avoid him. I wonder what my fat man would think if he could see me now. Will he come today? I do need to see him.

After taking the child to school, I run back as fast as I can but as I enter the house, I know he isn't there. I retrieve the typewriter and go into the kitchen. The Watcher is waiting for me and I smile sadly at her. She smiles sadly back, as though she understands.

Stan wakes early, he didn't eat properly yesterday and now he's really hungry. As he puts two slices of bread in the toaster, he suddenly realises it's his day off, and he's got nothing to do. Stan begins to sing, letting the sound echo back from the bare, yellow walls of his kitchen and not caring if the neighbours hear him. *I won't have to see Maureen till Monday.* He recalls the sound of her footsteps when they parted. Was it just his imagination that had made them sound angry? Probably not. He'd refused her, slighted her. *She won't forgive me for that.* He munches his toast standing by the open window. The sky is clear and the early morning sun is warming the bleak buildings around the square of grass. The estate almost looks beautiful, so he decides to go for a walk.

The road is quiet as he sets out, only one solitary car passes by him. *Someone returning from night shift?* he wonders, and for a moment he imagines the life of the tired driver. Stan considers his own situation: his problems with

Maureen, and the low pay for the hours he puts in. Perhaps he should look for another job, but doing what? Anything he does will be badly paid. Amy's proposition is tempting, but he still feels uncomfortable about it. There's no doubt that she can afford the money, and he certainly needs it but will it spoil their relationship? And now Eileen has stuffed money into his pocket. *Mad woman*. He remembers the feel of her. Stan is so taken up with his thoughts that he doesn't see the Watcher's little dog running towards him till he nearly trips over it.

'Morning, Stanley, you're out early,' says the Watcher stopping to put the lead back on her dog. She's a little out of breath as though she's been hurrying.

'Hi. Yes, I woke up early and wanted to be outside on this lovely morning.'

'I know just how you feel. How are things with you?' She turns and starts to walk back the way she came and Stan follows her.

'Well, to be honest things are rather complicated at the moment.'

'Do you want to talk about it?' she asks, stopping in front of a set of flats that's a carbon copy of Stan's block: red brick, three stories.

Stan laughs, 'How long have you got?'

'All the time you want. How about a cuppa? I live here on the ground floor and I owe you a drink, remember?'

Stan is about to decline but stops himself. 'OK, thanks,' he says, after all he could do with someone to talk to.

The Watcher's flat is very neat but old fashioned, with faded wallpaper and patterned carpets that are spotlessly clean but threadbare. He sits at her kitchen table while she puts the kettle on and gives her dog a bowl of water. Two of the walls are covered with photographs. On one wall the pictures are monochrome and mixed in with cuttings from local newspapers. In the centre of the other wall is a cork board with several pieces of paper pinned in rows, these are interspersed with more recent, coloured snaps. Stan gets up from the table and takes a closer look. Most of the photos are of the estate and, he guesses, of people who live, or have lived, on it. Others are of the City Centre and Gloucester Docks showing the various stages of decay and re-development. 'You have been busy over the years,' Stan says.

The Watcher turns to look at him. 'Yes, that's always been a bit of a hobby of mine until quite recently. My camera was stolen last year, so now, I just watch and keep it all in here,' she taps the side of her forehead, moving the grey strands of hair that stick out from under her hat. She places two mugs of steaming tea on the table. 'Do you take sugar?'

'Err... No thanks,' says Stan vaguely. 'When was it stolen?'

'Last summer. Mutty and I sat down in the kids play ground, and Mutty ran after their ball, wouldn't give it up. So, I went to retrieve it for them. I left the camera on the bench. I was only away a moment but when I got back it was gone. It was broad daylight, nowhere to hide but no one saw anything.' The Watcher shook her head, removed her hat and ran her fingers through the mop of unruly, grey hair. 'I thought maybe one of the kids had pinched it but they said not and I believed them. Weird though, I'd just used up a film taking shots of a blue van that was parked near the Community Centre. The driver came back, saw me and was very angry. I thought he was going to snatch it then and there but he drove off in a hurry.'

Stan looks at her with concern. 'Did you report it to the

police? The theft I mean.'

'Nah. It was an old camera, not worth much. But there were a few shots of several unmarked vans that were parked up on the estate that summer.'

Stan goes on looking at the photos while she talks and sees an old photo of someone he recognises. Unsticking it from the wall he brings it back to his seat. 'Is this who I think it is?'

'Yes, that's your mother, Vera, taken just after the war.'

'Who's the man? She has her arm through his as though they're a couple.'

'They were, that's Christopher. Did she never mention him to you?'

'No. I didn't know she'd ever been out with anyone except my father.' Stan sips his tea but can't take his eyes from the young, pretty woman whose radiance shines out from the faded snap. 'She looks so happy. What happened to him?'

'He was posted to the Russian, German border soon after this picture was taken. He was lost, presumed dead.'

'Did she ever see him again?' Stan sees for the first time what a vibrant young woman his mother must have been. A very different woman to the cowed creature his tyrannical father had fashioned over the years.

'No, sadly.' says the Watcher sitting down at the table opposite Stan, 'I did though. Several years later he turned up asking for your mother but by then she was married and had you. When I told him, he said to leave it, to say nothing as he was sailing for America very soon. Rightly or wrongly I never mentioned his visit. Well, she'd done all the grieving and I didn't want to open old scars.' The Watcher gazes into her mug, 'I wish I had said something now, at least before she died. Just so she could have known he did come back, that he was alive, and did think of her.'

'Why did she marry my father of all people?'

'Well, she was pregnant with you and needed someone to provide a home.'

Stan is thunderstruck! 'You mean I'm not my father's... Reg's son?'

'No, you were not Reginald's child but he never knew it. He'd been hanging around your mother for months, she worked as his secretary and he was besotted with her, although she wasn't interested. For a start he was nearly old enough to be her dad, but, when the telegram came saying Chris was missing, presumed dead, she didn't know what to do. Reg kept trying to get her to go out with him and in a kind of numb panic she did. When she told him she was pregnant, he never questioned that it wasn't his and they got married.'

Stan gets up and paces around the kitchen. He is shocked and yet relieved. 'I knew I wasn't anything to do with that bastard, and oh, how he hated me. I'm surprised he never twigged. I didn't even look like him, and certainly I couldn't be what he wanted in a son.'

'That's why your middle name is Christopher. Reg wanted it to be Reginald after him but your mother held out for that name, so that's what you were christened.'

'But why didn't she tell me?' Stan sits down again and puts his head in his hands. 'When everything was so bad between him and me, or when he left us, why didn't she tell me then? It would have made all the difference. I thought I was destined to become like him. I vowed I'd never have kids of my own, so as not to create a similar hell for any other child.'

'I don't know her reasons, Stanley, but you must realise she and I came from a different time, when sex before marriage or having a child out of wedlock, were dreadful sins. Maybe she didn't want to risk losing your respect.' The Watcher gets up and refills the kettle. 'Have another cup, Stanley, and we'll have something a little stronger with it,' she says reaching up to a cupboard for a bottle of single malt. 'I know it's early but you could do with a shot after that news.'

'How did she meet my real father? What was he like?'

The Watcher sets two glasses on the table and pours out the tawny spirit, more into his glass than hers. 'We were at school together. When we left, we both went to work at Benson's clothing factory, making uniforms for the troops. On my 19th birthday we went to a dance. There was bunting everywhere and people were celebrating the end of the war. Christopher Mcloughlin was a young officer on leave, he and another soldier, Phillip Grey, were at the dance. Anyway, they asked us to dance and the four of us went out together, several times in the next few weeks. I fell in love with Phillip and we got engaged, and the four of us celebrated. We all drank a little too much, and Vera and Chris disappeared to a room upstairs.'

The Watcher sips at her whisky. 'Both men were in the regular army and so weren't demobbed, but were sent off on active duty. Phillip and I got married just before they left. Their platoon was ambushed. Phil was killed, and Chris, as I said, was missing.

'Jesus,' breathes Stan. 'What did you do?'

'We clung to each other. When Vera found she was pregnant, I agreed she should get married to Reginald. Of course, at the time, neither of us knew what he was really like, he seemed OK, very attentive. I got on with my life. I didn't want anyone else. I started walking, walking miles and watching, watching people as a hobby, and I always liked taking photos.'

Stan drains the rest of his whiskey and stands up. 'I'm sorry but if you'll excuse me, I think I need to go. It's all been a bit of a shock.' At the door, Stan turns to look back at the Watcher. 'Thanks for telling me, I do appreciate it. Don't for a minute think it wasn't wise. I'd like to come and talk to you again sometime.'

'Anytime Stanley.' The Watcher smiles sadly at him. 'I have more to tell you about Vera, but that's enough for today.'

Eighteen

Immediately I open the front door, I know he's back. I go up to the bedroom and there he is, sitting on the bed like before gazing into my dressing table mirror. There's a sadness in his eyes and I have an overpowering compulsion to put my arms around him. But, like a lightning flash in my brain, I realise that I can't because he isn't really there. Just for a few, clear moments I know this fat, white man is a figment of my imagination. I've created him because I need someone to love. I turn to look at him expecting him to disappear but he doesn't. I stand in front of him and wonder whether, if I put out my hand, I could touch him? But I'm suddenly scared for my sanity and quickly leave the room.

I get out my typewriter, and with sharp feelings of despair I start to type. I've already written about his mother and this confuses me, why is it important? But I don't try and analyse, I just type the words that come to me from the ether, or from some place deep inside me, that I could never find even if I wanted to. When I finally look up the Watcher is sitting opposite me and her little dog is on her lap gazing at me with his big brown eyes. I stop typing and hold my breath. I get up and move towards her, put out my trembling hand and touch the dog. Under my fingertips his fur is soft and the warmth of him comes through his thick coat. Then he turns his head and I feel the warm, wet touch of his little tongue on my wrist.

On Saturday morning, Stan goes shopping and buys steaks and salad for his evening meal with Linda, he hums to himself as he shops. He's got over the shock of finding out about his parentage. He's so happy to find that he doesn't carry Reginald's rogue genes, and he's also pleased that his mother experienced happiness, however brief, and that he was sired in love and passion. This is what he is, a passionate man who's been held back by fear; fear of his own feelings and a nasty streak that he now knows he can't have inherited. He's free to see himself differently. When Linda arrives at his flat in the afternoon, the sun is shining in a clear sky. She's wearing blue slacks and T-shirt and her pale hair gleams in the strong light. Stan hugs her and gives her a long lingering kiss, 'You look good enough to eat.'

She laughs throwing back her head against his shoulder. 'What's brought this on?' You look happy.'

'I am happy and I've lots to tell you, but would you mind if we went for a walk while I talk?'

'No, of course not.'

As they walk, Stan notices everything around him: the same shabby blocks of flats, the concrete walk ways between them and the areas of dead grass, but for once this familiar landscape doesn't depress him. Linda's presence gives a joy to the cries of children playing on the swings. She helps him notice the attempts of residents to smarten up the area: flowerbeds outside ground-floor flats, bright curtains at some of the windows. He smells mown grass and sees the sharp shaded area under a chestnut tree. As Linda walks beside him along the broken concrete path, he senses a quiet companionship. Taking hold of her hand, he realises how happy he is. Stan tells her about the Watcher and what she's told him.

Linda squeezes his hand, 'I'm so happy for you Stan. Honestly, I can't think of anyone less likely to be bitter and twisted than you.'

'Well, I think I was, inside. And when I remember all those wasted years when I didn't dare commit to anyone or anything. I feel very angry.'

'Get sad, Stan, not angry. Nothing's wasted. Those years have made you what you are today: a son who cared for his mother, and a man who helps people whenever he can. Not to mention a passionate lover.' Linda laughs, putting her arm through his. They're walking towards the Watcher's block of flats and Stan sees the lace curtain in her kitchen window move slightly to one side and then drop back. He smiles to himself. 'Would you mind making a brief call on an old lady and her dog?' he asks Linda.

Stan introduces Linda to the Watcher and they sit in her kitchen while she puts on the kettle. 'I'm glad you came, she says, 'I've looked out another photo for you.' She passes him a larger and much more recent, colour photograph of his mother taken about ten years ago. Vera's wearing a pale blue dress and coat and looks smarter than he's ever seen her look. She has her hand on the arm of a middle-aged black man, smart in suit, shirt and tie. They're standing outside a West End theatre.

'When was this taken?' he asks surprised.

'Oh, it was taken by a passer-by on Arthur's camera when they went to London for the day. Is it alright to tell you everything in front of this young lady?'

Linda laughs at the 'young lady'. 'It's up to you Stan, I can leave you for a bit if you like.'

'No there's no problem. Carry on.'

'When you moved away to your bed-sit in the late

eighties, Vera started going out and about. She joined several evening classes and it was at one of these that she met Arthur. Arthur was a lovely man, but there was a problem, he was married, and his wife was in a wheelchair after a stroke. I guess it wasn't much of a marriage after that and he and your mother were only in their early fifties so love flourished. They had several happy years together, although on a part-time basis, but I think that suited Vera. She didn't want to get married again as she enjoyed her independence but she did have a good time.'

Once again, his mother amazes him, 'Why didn't she mention him to me?'

'I don't know, Stanley, maybe it was because he was married, maybe because he was black. He and his wife came from the Caribbean, Jamaica I believe. Anyway, it gradually came to an end when his wife became increasingly dependent on him and then when your mother had her stroke, well... Arthur just couldn't have looked after two disabled women. They kept in touch by letter for several years, till Vera's second stroke. When you moved back in it stopped. Sad really, but she was happier in those few years than I ever saw her.'

'Can I keep this?'

'Of course, and you can have the other one as well.' the Watcher says, giving him the photo of his mother and his natural father, Christopher.

'Thanks again.' Stan doesn't know what else to say. He takes hold of Linda's hand, 'We'd better be getting on.'

'Nice meeting you,' Linda says.

The Watcher smiles at her, 'Lovely to meet you.' She touches Linda on the arm, 'I think you might be good for Stanley.'

Back at his flat Stan opens a bottle of wine, ice cold Pinot

Grigio, so cold it makes the glasses mist and Linda sips at hers while looking at his music collection. Stan comes up behind her and kisses the back of her neck. 'There's not a lot there I'm afraid. What would you like to do?'

'I don't mind, I'm easy.' Linda leans back against him.

'Are you?'

'Am I what?'

'Easy,' Stan laughs as she elbows him in the ribs. He puts down his drink, takes her glass and puts it on the table, then turns her towards him, saying, 'I want you very badly.'

'Then we'd better do something about that.' Linda stands on tip toe and kisses him on the lips.

He runs his hands down her back and over the curve of her bottom, 'You have a lovely bottom, do you know that?' he whispers into her hair. 'In fact, you have a lovely body altogether,' he says cupping her breasts.'

'I think we had better lie down before my legs give way,' she says, holding onto him, 'I'm melting.'

'Are you? And where are you melting?'

He unzips her slacks, pushing them down her bare legs and she steps out of them. Holding her to him with one arm, he slips the fingers of his other hand under the silk of her knickers and into the warm wetness of her. He feels her breath on his neck as she makes a small mewing sound.

'Please Stan,' she whispers. 'Please.'

He helps her out of the rest of her clothes and leads her onto the wide bed. He struggles out of his own clothes and climbs onto the bed beside her. 'You are beautiful,' he breathes as he kneels over her.

Nineteen

I've been in mental turmoil for the whole weekend. No chance of seeing my fat man or the Watcher. I've a desperate need to know whether these people are real or figments of my imagination. If they're the latter, how can I touch the dog and how can he lick my arm? If I can touch the dog, could I touch my fat man? Even more scary, could he touch me?

All through the weekend I try to remain focused on the daily routine but I keep getting distracted by my thoughts, and Guy notices. I burn the toast in the morning, drop a bottle of milk as I put the shopping away, and later I singe a pair of his favourite jeans by leaving the iron on them when I go to answer the phone. He's furious. He says I'm a liability: I can't earn any money as I'm too scared, and then I waste money by destroying things around the house. Finally, he slams out and goes to the pub. Much later he comes home drunk and throws up in the toilet. I feel like saying 'at least I don't empty money down my throat.' But there's no point.

I wanted to get my typewriter out last evening, once the child had gone to bed, and while he was out, but I didn't dare because I wasn't sure when he would return.

Now it's Monday and the Watcher is here sitting quietly opposite me as she does. But she's making me nervous. What if I touched her or worse, what if I spoke to her and she replied out loud? That would really freak me out, but I'm tempted to try. What shall I do? I'm beginning to obsess and the last thing I want or need is to be sectioned again. I don't want to go back to that mental ward. I'm scared that Guy will send me back if he finds out what I'm doing.

'Writing a book is not the same as being mentally ill.' The words come to my ears clearly. The voice is warm in tone, soft, and comforting. The Watcher spoke to me out loud. I can't look at her. She's not real. I close down my typewriter and put it away. I daren't go out so I walk through the hall and into the sitting room and turn on the TV full blast. She's never come in here before so I think I'm safe. I'm shaking, and it's best if I stay in this room till it's time to collect the child.

When Stan gets to the office on Monday morning the atmosphere is heavy and tense. Emily comes out of the kitchen with two coffees and hands him one with a grimace. 'Keep your head down, Stan, Maureen's on the war path with a vengeance today.'

'Thanks for the warning,' he says taking his coffee and sitting down at his desk. He hasn't been looking forward to seeing Maureen anyway.

'Emily leans over her desk towards Stan and adds quietly, 'I don't know what it is you've done but there has been a complaint against you.'

'Oh great!' *Really this job is not worth the hassle.* He can hear Maureen's voice rising and falling in her office, she's obviously on the phone to a client. He gets out the sheet of people he needs to update on their sales but before he can start Maureen throws open her office door. It hits back against the wall with a bang that makes everyone jump.

'My office Stanley! Now!' She disappears back inside

and Stan follows, closing the door behind him.

'Stanley, I've had a complaint against you.'

'I'm sorry...'

'Please don't say anything. I'm incandescent with fury as there can be no excuse for what you've done. The complaint comes on behalf of the venders of Newland's Farm. It appears that the vendors had instructed another Lettings Agency, and until contracts are exchanged on the sale of Newland's, this other Letting Agent can still take prospective tenants to view.'

Maureen picks up a letter, her hand shaking visibly as she reads it.

'Dear Miss Carter,

I feel it incumbent upon me to make you aware of certain findings at Newland's Farmhouse. On our most recent viewing at this property on Friday last, we were appalled to find that there were marks on the duvet and on the carpet of the master bedroom, but worst of all there was a used condom floating in the toilet pan in the en-suite bathroom. I need hardly say that none of my staff know anything about this situation nor do the owners whom I have contacted. Therefore, I am forced to assume that the perpetrator must be amongst your staff... etc. etc.'

She threw the letter into Stan's lap and paced up and down behind his chair. 'We all know there's only one member of staff who has done viewings in that place in the last week, and only one client, that frightful Fanshaw woman.'

'I really don't...' Stan tries to speak,

'Don't even attempt to lie to me, Stanley, that makes it worse. I'm dismissing you immediately. You will get your things, return any keys you may have on you, and leave this establishment quickly and quietly. I might add what an utter, and bitter disappointment you have been to me personally. Now, get out of my sight.'

Stan exits from her office closing the door behind him and closing his eyes for a few moments. He doesn't want to face anyone or see any expressions of disgust or sadness in the eyes of the women around him. He can feel that his face is red and he's sweating. Going to his desk drawer, he takes out a few personal effects, pushes his chair under the desk and walks out of Payntons without looking back.

Stan feels numb. He's shocked and furious with himself. That bloody condom, he'd wrapped it in toilet paper and flushed it down the loo, but hadn't checked it had gone, as he was in such a hurry to get back to Maureen. He walks fast along the pavement oblivious to where he's going. What the hell is he going to do now? Go back on the dole? *You can't when you've been sacked, and there'll be no reference for another job. You've blown it you prat.* Stan walks on cursing himself and Eileen for leading him astray. *Not,* he admits, *that I took a great deal of persuasion.*

He looks up and sees how close he is to the Community Centre, so he crosses over the road and walks to the entrance. Feeling suddenly hungry, he realises he's had nothing to eat since the night before. He goes to the café serving hatch and orders a full English breakfast and takes one of Eileen's £20 notes to pay for it. *Perhaps I won't hand the money back, all things considered.*

'There you are ducks.' The cheery assistant hands over a plate brimming with food, 'Enjoy. You look as though you need cheering up.'

'I do,' says Stan. 'I certainly do.'

'Ah, well that should help,' she beams him a lovely smile.

He sits at a corner table and tucks in. He's amazed at his

appetite, and at how delicious the food is. He begins to feel better. *Well, it's not as though I loved the job,* he admits to himself. When he's nearly finished eating, he has an overwhelming urge to confide in someone. His first thought is Linda but he's not sure how she'd view his behaviour. *Amy then?* He can see her laughing at the whole ridiculous situation. *I'll message her tonight. Should I ring Eileen? Warn her? Does this mean she might lose the sale?* He decides to call her as soon as he gets back to his flat.

Stan is wiping up the last of his egg yolk with a piece of toast when the door to the stairwell opens and out comes the petite, Eurasian lady dressed in a smart dress and jacket. She stops to hand her empty coffee cup in at the hatch and the cheerful assistant shouts, 'Thanks Martina.' But he notices that Martina does not respond, there's no smile cracking that olive face as she walks self-importantly out of the centre. He watches her walk over to a large, black sedan parked on the other side of the road. The engine fires up as she opens the passenger door but he can't see who's driving as the windows are darkened. In spite of all his problems there's something about this woman that fascinates him.

Twenty

After a night of broken sleep and bad dreams, I wake up with a resolve to speak to the Watcher today, if she comes. I'm determined to screw up my courage and ask her to explain. But on my return from school, I can tell the fat man is in the shower. Instantly, there's a swarm of butterflies in my stomach. But I don't go straight to the bathroom. First, I get out my typewriter and set it up on the kitchen table as usual. Only when I hear the water stop running do I consider facing him. I give him a chance to wrap a towel around himself, then I push open the door a crack. I desperately try to make sense of my perceptions: I can see him, smell him, I breathe the steam from the shower, and if I touch his towel after he's dried himself, it will be damp. That much is reality it seems. But he only looks at me in mirrors and I've no idea what he sees. I wave my hand above my head as he gazes in to the steamy glass but today, he's preoccupied and doesn't look at me or my reflection.

I return to my typewriter and tap away telling his story. When I finally look up, I see the Watcher is observing me. I get her dog a bowl of water and again he drinks thirstily. That much is real. I take a deep breath, dig my fingernails into the palms of my hands, open my mouth and say, 'Are you real?' There, I've done it. Now what will happen? I hear her voice clearly in my ears. 'Of course, I am.' She smiles at me. I look down at what I've typed, confused. Then I realise, I didn't see her lips move as she spoke.

❖

Stan wakes with a lurch into reality; the reality that he has absolutely no way of making a living. He supposes he could sell the flat, *but how much would it make, eighty thousand or so? And how long would that last if I have to pay rent?* He gets up and has a shower standing under the jets of hot water for much longer than usual. When he's finally dressed, he decides to call Eileen and warn her about the situation, if she doesn't already know.

'Stanley, how lovely to hear from you,' Eileen coos. 'Are you alone, can you talk?'

'Yes Eileen, I'm at my flat.'

'Oh, no work today?'

'No. Err… Eileen, have you heard from Payntons?'

'Funny you should say I was just going to open a letter from them, the porter has just brought the mail. He's such a lovely man, reminds me of you a little bit.'

'Eileen, listen to me.' Stan hears paper being torn. 'Listen to me before you read it.'

'OK, Stanley, I'm listening. What's the mystery?'

'No mystery, but I have to tell you, I got the sack yesterday from Maureen.'

'But why? That's awful. I knew that woman…'

'Eileen for God's sake, listen to me. There was a complaint from another Agent who had a viewing at Newland's Farm.

'But I'm buying it, they said so. Why would anyone else go there?'

'I don't know but the problem is, the condom I used didn't get flushed away properly. They found it and the marks on the duvet. Maureen knows we were the only people to have gone there and…'

'Has guessed what we were up to. I see, and of course she is terribly jealous.'

'I'm not sure that's got anything to do with it.'

'Of course, it has. Now Stanley, you must be worried, you poor man, why don't you come to my hotel for coffee and we can discuss things.'

'Do you think that's wise?'

'What does it matter now, the cat is out of the carrier and it can't get any worse for you anyway.'

'True. OK, I'll be there about eleven.'

Eileen is waiting for him in the foyer and Stan is surprised how nice it is to see her. She kisses him on the cheek and leads him into the lounge where coffee and homemade biscuits are set out on a table between two very comfy settees.

'What did it say in the letter?' Stan asks as she pours him a cup of coffee.

Eileen sits opposite him sipping her coffee. She is dressed in a pale green kaftan, her hair is loose and she's wearing no make-up. Stan thinks how much younger she looks, softer and more vulnerable somehow.

'Well, it just asked me to confirm that I'm serious about the purchase of Newland's Farm. Then it stated that there's an issue concerning the state of the property after a viewing undertaken by a member of staff. It also asks me if I have any concerns or complaints about the treatment I've received from any member of Payntons' staff.' She laughs out loud. 'The cheek of that woman, does she think I am going to shout 'rape'?'

'I suppose she's giving you that option, though do rapists use condoms?' Stan starts to smile.

'Let's be serious for a moment, Stanley, what are you going to do?'

'I've no idea, Eileen. I won't get a reference and that will make getting another job almost impossible.'

'What about this lady who's offering to pay you to be her escort?'

'Amy? Yes, the offer is still open, though I haven't accepted yet. Oh, and by the way, how did you put these bank notes in my pocket without me knowing, you naughty woman?' He takes out several £20 notes from his wallet and holds them out to her. 'I had to use one yesterday I'm afraid.'

'Stanley, please put them away. I'm feeling bad enough about getting you into all this trouble through a whim of mine, and you'll need every penny you can get.'

Stan hesitates holding his open wallet in one hand and the notes in the other. On the one hand he wants to be a gentleman but on the other hand his need to have money is desperate.

'Please put it away and don't make me feel more of a worm than I do at this moment,' she leans forward and puts a hand on his knee. 'Keep it for my piece of mind.'

'Alright, if you insist.' Reluctantly he puts the notes back in his wallet and replaces it in his pocket.

'Now listen to me Stanley, I know you have your pride and I respect you for that but in this situation, you need to take anything that is offered. Call Amy and tell her you accept her proposition, that will give you a small income and give you time to work out what else you can do.'

Stan doesn't reply. He feels torn between necessity and pride, deep inside he knows she's right, it is the only solution.

'Stanley, you have to understand that you're not getting this money for nothing, this lady wants a companion and she wants to go to expensive places with that companion and she has chosen you because she likes you, you make her feel good about herself. She has money and you don't, that's the crunch. For her the simple answer is to give you money so that you can afford to take her out and give her a good time. Where's the harm in this? It solves both of your problems. There's no loss of dignity in giving good service for money.'

Stan scratches his head. 'It sounds sensible enough put like that but...'

Eileen squeezes his knee again, 'But you still feel bad about it. Don't worry you'll get used to it. Think of it as a job but a job you are good at, one that you can enjoy and one where you can use all your talents.'

Stan pours himself another coffee and takes a biscuit. 'Alright, I'll ring her.' He looks up at Eileen and smiles, 'You're an amazing woman Eileen, what would I do without you?'

'Well, you wouldn't be in this mess for a start. I'm pretty amazing at destroying other people's lives for my own pleasure,' she smiles at Stan. 'Which brings me to another suggestion. Will you escort me around for the next few weeks while I'm waiting for this purchase to go through? My husband is coming down next weekend to see the farm but after that he'll be away on business and I'll be at a loose end. Please let me pay you to take me out and about. I'll pay the same rate as Amy.'

Stan is shocked into saying, 'But you can't afford to do that. I can show you around with pleasure as I'll have plenty of spare time and you can pay for expenses if you want but...'

'You're not getting this are you, Stanley? You need to make money, and by the way, please don't make assumptions about what I can afford.'

'Sorry.'

'Go and call Amy and discuss this with her and then if it's fine by you, I'd like to meet her.'

'Why?' Stan has an uneasy feeling in his stomach. It's one thing to deal with one woman at a time but to put them together?

'Oh, I have a little proposition to put to her, if I like the look of her, that is. Don't worry it'll be to your advantage.' Eileen gets up and sits beside Stan, she puts her hand on his shoulder and kisses him. 'Now I'm afraid I have things I need to do so I'll say 'au revoir' for the moment darling. No, don't get up, finish the coffee and biscuits and then go and find Amy.'

Stan watches her walk out of the lounge and across the foyer to the stairs. She moves gracefully, the material of the loose kaftan flows around her and he wonders if she was a dancer in her youth. He sits thinking about what she's said and finishes the biscuits.

Stan's aware of a change in himself. It began with the images of his mother in the photos the Watcher gave him. Pictures of a private reality which his mother hadn't shared with him but in which she became alive and passionate. *Women need close relationships to bloom. How many middle-aged women live unexciting lives and are desperate for someone to add colour to their existence? Could I do this for them? Is this a talent of mine? If so, why shouldn't I use it and be paid for it?* He shakes his head, feeling confused and gets up to go. As he walks towards the foyer of the hotel, he sees the diminutive figure of Martina, the woman from the Community Centre. She's standing at the reception desk and is talking to a young man who is twice the height of her, and yet Stan forms the impression that she's the stronger of the two and she's definitely in control.

Twenty-One

I've nearly got over the shock of hearing the Watcher speak. I make another resolution to say something to her if she comes this morning. But the kitchen remains empty and the house is silent. I get my typewriter out and begin writing. I like being alone. It's only in the silence that I feel calm and can listen to the pattern of my thoughts. When people are around me, it's like white noise in my head. I struggle to fit in with their ways of thinking. Of course, it would get lonely if my life was quiet and empty all the time. But when the fat man is near me, I don't get that dissonant feeling. He just makes me feel warm and happy. Is it because he doesn't speak?

When I'm typing, I'm never at a loss for words, they just tumble from my fingers, and yet if I try to tell people what I'm thinking the words get clogged up behind my tongue and I forget some of them.

I've put the timer on. Three hours is such a short time, and I forget to stop typing. I must be careful as Guy is definitely suspicious. He keeps saying I'm distracted and that I 'go off on one' as he calls it. I type that I want the hero of my story to come to me tomorrow. Perhaps, he'll know and come because I've called him. I don't know what's happening to him, there's a change and it worries me.

Stan stands at his sink, looking out of the kitchen window

at the concrete area below. Several washing lines stretch out between the backs of the blocks of flats. Someone's black trousers have been out there on the line for days now, and one of the pegs has come off so that they're suspended by one leg only. In the wind the pegged leg balloons out like a windsock. Clouds scud across the windswept sky above and Stan has a sudden memory of another windy day, when he was a child. His mother had taken him to an air show, she'd shown him the windsock at the side of the airfield and explained that it showed the pilots the direction of the wind. A silly, small memory but one that links him to a better time.

Stan's rung Amy and she'll be arriving any minute. He's continually having to think about things these days, and he realises he knows very little about the internal desires and motivations of women. He loves them and their wiles and mind games but he feels vulnerable, it's as though they're organising his life. *Can I really earn an income and pay tax on such an occupation?* Stan's reverie is broken by the ringing of the doorbell, and he goes down to let her in.

'Darling Stanley,' Amy's arms reach for his neck as soon as he opens the door. 'You poor thing,' she kisses him passionately.

'Whoa, Amy,' he says holding her away from him with his hands on her waist, 'Hold on girl. You'll have the neighbours talking if you carry on this way.'

'They're probably talking already. I bet they've never seen anyone get a life before.' Amy giggles and catches hold of his hand as they climb the stairs. She's wearing designer jeans and a close-fitting top that accentuates every curve. Once in the flat she's in his arms and the passion takes them both. Finally, she's forced to break away in order to catch her breath. 'Stanley, I have missed you,' she says, huskily.

'I've missed you too. Let me put the kettle on and make some coffee, then it'll be a question of bed or kitchen table to talk.' He moves towards the sink but Amy grabs his arm and pulls him back.

'I'm not thirsty. Let's choose bed now. I don't think I can talk about anything seriously until I've had you.' And before he has time to think she is in his arms again. Her hair is around his neck, her perfume envelopes him, he didn't intend this but her obvious longing for him is arousing and she feels so good. They undress and climb into his bed. The feel of her skin against his chest is intoxicating, he suddenly remembers he hasn't changed the sheets since Linda was here. But it's too late now, and that fact makes it more erotic, as though the two women are here together, the memory of one, and reality of the other. He reaches for the drawer but Amy stops him, 'I want you 'au naturel' Stanley.' She is all over him, rubbing herself against his belly, biting his nipples, her legs around his body, till he has to have her.

He sits her on top of him and she cries out as she rides him. Stan watches her face and sees her expression of abandonment. It's beautiful. Amy is aware of nothing except the sensations of sex and its dance. He controls his reactions till he senses she's satisfied, and until her movements make it impossible for him to hold back any longer.

They lie together, she's curled in his arms. He listens to her quiet breathing as she sleeps and he can't understand why such a beautiful woman wants him. Wants him enough to pay for him. How can he take money for something that brings him so much pleasure? To be paid for this would cheapen it. To him it's precious, this sensuous joining of bodies. He shakes Amy gently; they do need to talk; he needs to talk. She opens her eyes and lifts her face to be kissed, which he does, but then he says, 'We should talk, Amy, if you can wake up enough.' She stretches deliciously, her body taught against his and he feels a flicking of desire. Stan rolls away from her before he is tempted to start all over again. He goes into the kitchen and makes coffee, Amy comes in her hair all tousled, she is naked under an old shirt of his, which she pulls around her as she sits at the table. Taking the coffee from him, she sniffs its aroma, her face is soft and sleepy. *She looks like a child.*

Stan sits opposite her in his dressing gown, and is again aware of the shabbiness of his environment: his old dressing gown, the bare yellow walls of the kitchen painted in gloss by his mother so that they could be washed down annually, and the Formica topped table scrubbed till the pattern has faded. But Amy seems unaware or unbothered by it as she asks for the sugar, which he's forgotten to get.

'Amy…' Finding no way of approaching the difficult subject of her paying him, he leaves the sound of her name hanging.

She smiles at his discomfort. 'Are you trying to say that you want to accept my offer and become my escort?'

'In a word, yes.' Stan is experiencing great difficulty in talking about it, but he stumbles on, 'If I hadn't lost my job, I wouldn't consider it but because of Eileen and her waywardness, I'm forced to make money anyway I can.'

'This Eileen what did she get you to do exactly?'

'She persuaded me to have sex with her in this farmhouse she's buying. Twice. We were found out.'

'Was it worth it, Stanley?' Amy giggles.

'It was good, yes, surprisingly so.' Stan's face turns red

as he explains. 'She's an amazing lady. She's feeling responsible for my predicament, I told her about your proposition and she wants me to do the same thing for her, while her husband's abroad.'

'Oh, Stanley you're so quaint. You're feeling awkward because you're telling me about having another woman, but I think it's very sexy.'

'How?'

'Well, I'm not the only one to find you alluring; it confirms my good taste. I like the fact that other women want you. Is there anyone else?' Amy asks looking him straight in the eyes and smiling cheekily.

'Err…'

'There is!' She claps her hands. 'Wow, Stanley, you dark horse, come on tell. Who is she?'

Stan finds it difficult to speak of Linda and his relationship with her. He realises that it's different to, more private than, his connection with Amy and Eileen. However, he gives a brief outline of their relationship.

'So, she's a little more special, is she? I'm jealous,' Amy pouts. 'Does she know about us?'

'No, you see…' Stan is struggling and finding this conversation challenging.

'She's more conventional, I'm guessing, and wouldn't understand?' Amy says.

'Something like that.'

'Don't you think you owe it to her to be honest?'

'Well, if she asks, which she hasn't yet, then yes, I will tell her but…'

'But she won't like it and it could be the end?' Amy puts her hand across the table and holds his. 'Poor old Stanley, life is so complicated with us women, isn't it?'

Stan grins, 'It is but I wouldn't have it any other way.

Eileen wants to meet you by the way.'

'Does she indeed? That's interesting. Is she free this evening?' Amy finishes her coffee, kisses Stan and goes back into the bedroom, 'Can I use your shower?'

'Yes of course, it's a bit basic though and I only have men's shower gel. I'll get you a towel.'

Amy is standing naked in his shower, her hair is curled up on top of her head and as he enters with a clean towel, she says, 'Your shower's fine darling, perfectly serviceable, hook the towel on the door, can you?' She starts soaping herself all over with his shower gel. He watches with an increasing desire to join her. 'Thank you, Stanley,' she dismisses him. 'Now you go and call Eileen and see if she is available to meet us.'

Stan rings Eileen and arranges for them to meet for dinner at Pizza Express in town at eight o'clock and as he replaces the receiver Amy walks in naked except for a towel around her head. 'Well, what did she say?'

'She'll meet us at eight at Pizza Express.' He walks up to Amy and strokes her still damp breasts, bends to kiss her nipples and pulls her to him as he feels himself harden again. 'That gives us time to go back to bed.'

Amy extricates herself from his embrace. 'No Stanley, sorry. I have to go home and get ready.'

'Get ready for what?'

'Meeting Eileen. I'm not going dressed in jeans and with messy hair.' She gives him a kiss and starts dressing.

Stan watches her. *What strange creatures women are. Here are two of them about to spend a couple of hours making themselves look good just for him.* 'Do you want me to smarten myself up too?'

'Of course!' She looks at him critically, 'I suppose it will have to be your suit again, we need to get you kitted out with some decent casual clothes.'

'I've got my black jeans and my leather jacket,' Stan is feeling a bit put out.

'Oh yes those will do for tonight. Now I must dash, I am sure Eileen will look her best and so must I. Bye darling.'

Watching her get into her little red car and drive away, Stan thinks ruefully that perhaps all this dressing up isn't for his benefit after all, but is a kind of duel between the two women. He decides he had better have a shower too.

Twenty-Two

Half an hour before I'm due to collect the child from school, I hear the shower running. I've put the typewriter away, and I'd given up on seeing either apparition. I go upstairs and there he is standing in the steam filled bathroom wiping the condensation off the mirror with a flannel. He looks so good. I'm sure he's lost more weight and gained a slight tan, which contrasts with his silver hair. He begins to shave carefully, accentuating the sharp lines of his goatee, moustache and tapering side burns. I stand slightly behind him breathing in his smell and looking into the mirror at his eyes. He glances at my reflection, holds my gaze for a second, and then winks! He smiles a warm and caring smile that turns my knees to jelly. I close my eyes, just for a moment, but when I open them, he's gone back to his shaving. I look at my watch. I'm late! I have to go. Reluctantly I turn away but as I go through the door, I'm sure I hear him blow me a kiss.

When Stan arrives at the restaurant the two women are already there seated at a table in the window, each with a glass of wine before them. Their heads are close together over the table as they talk earnestly. He sees them from the other side of the street and he assumes they're talking about him; comparing notes on his technique perhaps and this makes him feel nervous. One at a time is one thing, but to have two women comparing him, that's something else. He takes a deep breath, blowing the air out between his lips, he pulls his stomach in as much as possible, holds his shoulders back and walks across the road. As he enters Eileen sees him and stands up waving, 'Stanley, darling over here!'

Amy looks around and grins at him as he joins them. He kisses both women on the cheek, sits down at the table and picks up the menu. 'Have you chosen yet ladies?'

Amy laughs, 'No we've been too busy getting to know each other.' She picks up another menu.

Eileen leans towards him putting her hand on his arm, 'Stanley, you really fell on your feet when you met this lady, she's a diamond. We've been discussing your prospects and we are in complete agreement.'

'That's good, I think,' says Stan. 'Hopefully I get a say though.' Stan feels his anxiety building.

'Of course, you do darling.' Eileen picks up her menu, 'Let's order first and then we can talk. What are you drinking? We ordered glasses of Prosecco but shall we have a bottle?'

'Yes, that'll be good,' says Stan as the waiter arrives.

The waiter takes their order and brings Stan another glass and a chilled bottle of Prosecco. When he's gone, Stan sips gratefully; his throat feels parched. 'Right ladies, put me out of my misery and tell me what you've been plotting.'

'You make us sound heartless, Stanley,' Amy pouts prettily and gives him a frown, 'Whereas we have nothing but your best interests at heart. We know it'll be very hard for you to get any kind of employment without a reference and therefore we've come up with an alternative.'

'And I feel so responsible darling,' Eileen holds her

frosted glass with fingers even more heavily ringed than usual, 'If it hadn't been for my appetites, you wouldn't be in this predicament. So...' she looks across at Amy and nods for her to continue.

'So...' Amy takes a deep breath. 'We think you should set up in business with us as your first two clients.'

Stan is immediately concerned. 'What kind of business?'

'A select, private 'Escort' business,' Eileen gives Stan an encouraging smile.

'Doing what exactly?' asks Stan turning a pale.

'Why escorting ladies of course.' Amy puts out her hand to touch him but their food arrives so they stop talking as the waiter places the dishes before them. Stan pours himself another glass, he suddenly needs a lot to drink.

They eat in silence for a few minutes. Stan realises he's very hungry and the tiger prawns he's chosen are delicious, he starts to relax and enjoy himself. However, he's still wary of these two women, and he asks in a low voice, the question that's uppermost in his mind. 'What does this 'escorting' involve exactly?'

'Why escorting ladies wherever they wish to go,' Amy says reassuringly.

'Is that all?' Stan is nervous, 'I don't want any 'extras' as Eileen puts it.'

'No of course not darling, I was only joking,' Eileen coos. 'Although I still think...'

'Absolutely not,' Stan butts in. 'If I'm to do this it has to be on strict understandable guidelines of my making.'

'Absolutely!' Amy smiles at him. 'So, tell us please, will you accept us as your first clients?'

Stan takes another swallow of his wine and feels the bubbles fizz on his tongue. He considers his options or rather the lack of them and realises that if he should refuse these two friends, who are trying to help, then he'll have no-one and nothing.

'I'm tempted to say yes, but I must stress that I'll only accept payment for escorting you. Anything else is too personal, it would insult me and you, and it would spoil it somehow.'

'Darling!' Amy gets up and gives him a long kiss right there in the middle of the restaurant, 'I know you're doing the right thing; the only thing you can do.'

'Well done, Stanley,' Eileen beams at him. 'Now we have to discuss terms.'

'I suggested £50 per hour,' Amy says. 'I worked out that if Stanley took me out three evenings a week that would be about ten hours and if half of that money pays for the expenses, that would probably leave him around £250 per week.'

'Excellent! If I asked you to escort me at least once a week for around four hours on the same terms that would give you a further £100 at least, as I probably won't go to such prestigious places as Amy. So, together it should net you an income between two and three hundred pounds a week.'

'Will that be enough Stanley?' Amy asks with concern in her voice.

Stan almost chokes on his wine. 'More than enough! It's too generous. How about £40 an hour?'

'I really don't think that will be enough, Stanley and you don't want to sell your services too cheaply.' Amy puts her arm through his, 'You see you'll need to get clothes to suit the occasions, for instance a tuxedo and a selection of casual wear at the very minimum.'

And Stanley,' Eileen leans forward very serious for a moment, 'you'll have to register your business and pay tax on your earnings, though of course the expenses will be exempt. So, your take home pay will be less than £1000 per month to start with. You'll need to advertise for more clients.'

Stan reflects on this. Without needing to pay rent it's a good wage for doing what's enjoyable to him. 'Is there much of a call for this kind of thing, though?' he asks nervously.

'More than you might think, Stanley. I've been reading articles about the modern woman and her desire to go out into society, whether she has a man or not. Many professional and older women are prepared to pay for expert courtesy and companionship.'

'Well, I'll take your word for it.' Stan still feels uncertain.

Amy looks critically at him for a few moments. 'We will have to smarten you up a little, though. Will you consent to put yourself in our hands?'

Stan decides to take the plunge, after all what's he got to lose? 'OK. Yes, ladies, I'll do it.' He puts one hand on Amy's arm and the other on Eileen's ring covered fingers, 'I'm very grateful to you both.'

Amy claps her hands, 'You won't regret it.'

'You've made the right decision,' Eileen squeezes his hand.

'This calls for a bottle of the real stuff.' Amy calls the waiter over. 'A bottle of your best Champagne please.' When the bottle arrives in a bucket of ice and the fresh glasses are filled, Amy starts to propose another toast but then stops glass in mid-air. 'What are we going to call your business?'

'Baker Escort Services?' Asks Eileen, 'It doesn't sound terribly memorable though.'

'Sounds more like a mobile confectioner,' giggles Amy.

Stan's still thinking through all the implications of advertising his services, however restricted those services may be. He doesn't feel he wants to take out young women. 'Ladies, I think I would like to restrict my clients by age. I don't know if that's possible but I wouldn't know how to relate to anyone under, say, fifty.'

'I think that is perfectly sensible,' agrees Eileen. 'So, what have we got: escorting ladies who have to be over fifty and require select services of a non-sexual nature.'

'Over Fifty Escort what?' muses Stan.

'I have it!' Amy stands up from her chair and leans over to Stan, 'We'll call it 'The Over Fifty's Escort Agency?' Only perhaps use the number 50 in the title? What do you think?'

'That's brilliant!' Stan and Eileen both say at the same time.

'You'll have to advertise,' says Eileen.

Stan agrees, 'I'll place a series of adverts in the Western Daily Press, from next week.'

Amy holds her glass high. 'Here's to the success of 'The Over 50's Escort Agency'!'

Twenty-Three

This evening, on his return from work, Guy brings in a copy of the Western Daily Press. While he's watching a football match on the TV, I flip through the pages for something to do, and I look at the Classified Ads to see if there's anything we could buy the child for her birthday. My eye is suddenly caught by a boxed advert for 'The Over 50's Escort Agency'. I stare at the page in disbelief. Can someone else have thought up that title? Can they have actually opened an escort agency with it? Then I read the name, Stanley Baker. The name I created for the fat, white man, for the apparition, for my protagonist.

I barely conceal my panic. Quickly, I close the paper as if I'm tidying up, but Guy notices something's wrong. I cover by saying I've got a sudden stomach ache and I rush for the loo. Sitting in the bathroom, where the fat, white man first appeared, I try to make sense of it all. How can this have happened? I thought everything was a figment of my imagination. If it isn't, who put the advert in the paper? Did I do it? Did the Watcher? Did Stan?

It might be a coincidence. But can there be someone else called 'Stanley Baker' advertising this service? My hands shake each time I think about it. I call down the stairs to Guy and say I'm going to bed. I say I'm ill but I'm not sure he believes me. Panic is on the edge of my mind. I know I need to calm down before Guy comes to bed. I look at the clock. Guy always listens to the analysis after a match, so I have about half an hour to sort myself out. Tomorrow is

Saturday and it's a Bank Holiday weekend. There'll be no time to myself for three whole days, except when Guy's asleep. I won't see the Watcher or my fat man. I can't ask them the questions teeming through my head. Breathing deeply and rhythmically, I try to calm myself. I've almost succeeded when I realise how much time has passed. Guy is coming up the stairs to bed. I hear him in the bathroom and I begin to tremble again. It's Friday and if he isn't tired or drunk then he'll want sex before we sleep. I'm not sure I can take it tonight.

I pretend I've fallen asleep. I keep my eyes tight shut and remain absolutely still as he climbs into bed. But this doesn't stop him. His hands reach for my belly and he pulls me towards him. I murmur 'I'm not well.' So, he says, 'OK. I'll be gentle and I won't take long. Turn over.' I roll onto my back. I'm trembling, I can feel it, I just hope he doesn't. I hold my breath until he enters me and then I close my eyes and try to think of something beautiful. Tonight, I can't.

Stan is in Stroud to meet a prospective client, the first one since his advert came out in the Western Daily Press. He's sitting at a table in a café, with an untouched cappuccino in front of him, waiting. The woman lives in Stroud and wants to meet him before deciding whether to hire him as an escort. Outwardly, Stan has altered a lot since Amy and Eileen took him in hand over a month ago. He's dressed in smart casual clothes, his beard is sharply delineated and he looks smooth and groomed with his silver hair, tanned face and steel blue eyes. But inwardly, he's much the same Stan he always was. He doesn't quite understand how all these experiences keep happening to him. He's spent the best part of a month escorting his two ladies, and from these outings he's gained a kind of cultural education. With Eileen, he visits art galleries and museums; with Amy he goes to the theatre, concerts and plush restaurants. He is paid for these interesting trips; paid for the enjoyment of escorting two lovely women, one he admires, and one he adores. Every week he makes love to each lady. Once a week with Eileen at his flat and at least twice weekly with Amy in her large bed at her house. But he refuses payment for these times.

He is more confident and he's been able to look for other clients. However, one thing worries him, or one person, and that's Linda. She's been away and he hasn't told her about his business or about the adverts. Now that they're in the paper each week she's likely to see one. *How on earth will she react? I need to try and call her again tonight.* Watching the open door, Stan sips his coffee and reads the notes he's scribbled on an old envelope. The lady's name is Sasha. She's said she'll wear a blue denim skirt and jacket and high black boots. Looking up, he sees a woman walking up the steep hill of the High Street towards him. She's carrying a denim jacket and judging from the speed she's climbing, she's certainly fit. As she enters the café, Stan gets up to greet her. 'Hi, are you Sasha?'

'Yes. Stanley?' she asks in a soft voice. She smiles at him, though he can see she's a little surprised at his size.

'Have a seat. What would you like to drink?'

'A cappuccino please, a medium one if that's alright.' She sits down.

'Of course. Chocolate sprinkles?'

She laughs. 'Yes please.'

When Stan returns with her coffee, he sits opposite her and they regard each other for a moment in silence. She has a classic face framed with dark hair, cut into a bob. There is an impishness about her that's very attractive. 'Right,' says Stan, trying to take control of the situation, 'tell me how I can be of service? Feel free to ask any questions you like.'

'To be honest, I've rather a lot of questions. I'm intrigued, especially now that I've met you, to know how you got into this line of business?'

'That's rather a long story, but to cut it short; I've two good lady friends, and when I lost my job, they suggested they pay me for escorting them to events and functions. From that I set up this business and here I am.' Stan takes a long drink of his coffee which is now cold. 'Does that answer your question?'

Sasha smiles, 'I think so. Although, if you don't mind me saying, you do seem an unlikely candidate for this kind of work.'

Stan leans forward and touches her hand and squeezes gently. 'I think you're referring to my girth and age,' he says, sitting back in his chair.

Sasha's cheeks redden with embarrassment, 'I didn't mean to insult…'

'Don't worry, I think I'm an unlikely candidate too. However, my friends assure me that I make a considerate and attentive escort.' Stan smiles at her and looks straight into her eyes holding her gaze for just a moment. 'Tell me how you'd like me to help and then let's see if I'll do.'

Sasha looks down and stirs her coffee. When she looks up again her face is serious. 'Can you assure me that whatever I tell you will remain in strictest confidence?'

'Of course,' Stan leans towards her. 'But there's no need to tell me anything personal, I don't need to know why you need the services of an escort.'

'True.' Sasha looks at him intensely, 'But somehow, I'd

like to. Perhaps you have the makings of a counsellor, as well.' She takes a deep breath. 'My little sister is getting married, rather late in life. Not so little at the age of forty-two, but the problem is she thinks I am in a long-term relationship and wants me to bring him along.'

'And you're not?'

'Oh, I am, but he's married. I'm his mistress and have been for nearly eight years. My family have no idea. We're not a close family, and they all live in Surrey, so you see it has been easy to keep them at bay.'

'And you want me to act as your partner?'

'Yes. Is that too difficult?' She looks at him with pleading eyes.

Stan thinks about it for a moment, he's not sure how good an actor he can be. 'Well, it is possible I suppose, but it will take a bit of arranging. You'll have to brief me, and for us to seem comfortable in each other's company, I think we'd have to, at least, go out for a meal before the wedding. Can you afford that?'

'Money is no problem,' she smiles. 'Yes, we could go for a meal and I can tell you all you need to know.'

'Have you mentioned anything about your relationship, for example what he does for a living? Have you ever sent them a photo? Has anyone in your family ever met him?'

'No,' Sasha shakes her head, 'no one has ever seen him. I did say he travels a lot for his work as a reporter, it made it easier if on the odd occasion someone came to visit me'

'Is he a reporter?'

'No, he's a dentist, who has a disabled daughter.' she says sadly. 'Which is why he can't get a divorce.'

'I see.' Stan finishes his cold coffee while he thinks about the situation. *It's just my luck that my very first client has such a complicated remit. Why couldn't she have just wanted a theatre trip?* 'Well. I'm not sure which would be more difficult to play, the reporter or the dentist,' Stan says, 'as I've no knowledge of either.'

'It will have to be the reporter, although I haven't mentioned him for a couple of years or so. We could say he has changed occupation.'

'What? Become a dentist?'

'No,' she laughs. 'But seriously what do you think?'

'Hmm, I don't think this will be easy. Could he have become a writer?'

'Yes, that would be perfect! Could you do that?'

'Let me get a refill and I'll think about it.' Stan starts to get up but she stops him.

'No let me please.' She stands and gets her purse out of her bag. 'Would you like something to eat too?'

'Are you sure? A croissant would be good, thanks.'

Stan sits and ponders his ability to carry off such a ruse. If he's honest with himself, it's a rather exciting project, much more challenging than just taking someone out for a meal or an event. *Why would the reporter have retired?* Stan runs several scenarios in his head and thinks he may have hit on one that might work.

Sasha returns with two coffees and two croissants and puts them on the table. 'There you are,' she says as she puts her purse back in her bag and takes off her jacket before sitting down.

Stan can't help noticing her trim waist and curvy hips. 'Thank you,' he says realising he's very hungry and starting on his croissant immediately.

'Are you having second thoughts about it all?'

'No, still on first thoughts,' he laughs trying not to spit croissant crumbs across the table as he talks. 'I might have thought of a way around the reporter bit though. What about saying that I retired after covering a really traumatic event, for example a famine or a war, and it's something I don't like to talk about anymore. That should do it!'

Sasha claps her hands. 'Oh, that's brilliant and totally believable. You're good at this, Stanley. So, will you do it for me?'

'Well, as I said it will take some planning but yes, I think I can do it, if you want me to?' Stan looks at her, at her flushed face and her smiling eyes. *What a woman! Does this guy know how lucky he is?*

'Oh, thank you Stanley,' Sasha squeezes his arm. 'When shall we meet again?'

'When's the wedding?'

'Oh yes, I forgot to tell you, it's Saturday 17th October at 2.00pm in Kingston upon Thames. Can you do it? Are you booked?'

'That should be alright. Is it a prestigious wedding?' Stan asks, a little concerned, wondering if he can manage a society wedding. 'What should I wear?'

'Oh, just a suit and tie, it's only a small affair and the reception is being held at a local restaurant.' Sasha takes out her diary and looks at the following week. 'I could make Wednesday or Friday. Any good?'

'No, I'm afraid not. Is Tuesday OK? By the way we need to discuss terms. Stan clears his throat. It's awkward to talk about money but he steels himself to do it. 'I charge £50 per hour.'

'Stanley, whatever it is you charge, give me an invoice at the end and I assure you I will happily pay it. Yes, Tuesday is fine, shall we meet at The New Inn, in Gloucester?'

'That's good for me. Seven thirty, OK?'

'Perfect.' Sasha finishes her coffee and gets up to go. 'Thank you, Stanley, you've taken a load off my mind.' She puts out her hand. Stan takes it and holds it just a little longer than necessary. 'Till Tuesday then.'

Stan catches the bus back to Gloucester. He looks out of the window at the passing streets and then fields as they move through surrounding countryside. Stan decides that he must get a car as soon as possible. *I really can't escort ladies all over the place on the bus.* Perhaps after this wedding he'll be able to afford the deposit on one. He thinks of other questions he needs to ask Sasha. *Does he need to provide a car? Will he be driving?* He resolves to run the whole scenario past Amy and ask her opinion.

Twenty-Four

Guy's taken the child to school this morning as he is off on a business trip for the day. It's been a very difficult weekend. I've managed to be normal, I think. There was only one incident when I forgot to iron his blue shirt, he got cross and accused me of 'mooning about' but otherwise I got through it.

As I sit in front of the typewriter at the kitchen table waiting for the words to come, I hear the clicking of the little dog's claws on the hall floor The door opens and the Watcher comes in. I'm so pleased to see her; I smile and get up to fetch the dog some water. I desperately want to ask her about the advert in the paper. But my fear is so strong I can almost taste it in my mouth. Both of us know I have to ask. She waits patiently with a smile on her lips and pity in her eyes.

'The advert,' I stammer, 'how... how did it get in the paper?' There, I've spoken to her. I've spoken to one of my apparitions.

The Watcher takes part of a folded newspaper out of her pocket. It's a page from the Western Daily Press, dated the 27th August, and when she opens it, I see the classified columns. She gestures to me to read, which I do. Then I read it again. There's no advert regarding any Escort Agency. None at all. I look at her in confusion. 'What's happening?' I whisper. She smiles sadly. 'You're imagining things.' 'Does that mean I'm going mad?' I'm so scared of her answer I almost don't want to hear it.

'It means you're writing.' She smiles at me as she gets up. They leave quietly. I don't notice how they go.

Stan has called Linda. She's coming to his flat this afternoon. She sounded a bit distant on the phone but he doesn't know if he's just imagining it. *Could she have already seen one of his adverts?* Suddenly he realises how important Linda's opinion is. He wants her approbation; he needs her backing in this business venture. But he's very aware that she might not be able to do that. He puts a bottle of white wine in the fridge, then sits down and tries to read the newspaper. None of the words register. He's too anxious. Tossing the paper aside, he paces the floor until he hears his doorbell. Linda looks lovelier than usual. She's acquired a tan which is heightened by the cerise shirt she's wearing. She glows with health. Holding hands, they climb the stairs in silence. 'Are you alright?' he asks her, fear making his heart beat.

'Yes, I was wondering the same about you? You're very tense, and you haven't even tried to kiss me.'

'I'm sorry.' Stan pulls her to him, 'Try this…' and he kisses her full on the mouth his hands caressing her shoulders. He breaks off and looks at her. 'Did I ever tell you how beautiful you are?' he says, kissing her more slowly with short chaste kisses.

She breaks away and breaths deeply, her face is flushed under the tan. 'That's more like the old Stan.'

'Come and have some wine, Chablis, your favourite.'

They sit and drink in silence. Stan's at a loss to know how to behave, his secret weighs so heavily upon him. Attempting conversation, he asks, 'How was your break?

Lots of sun by the look of it.'

'It was lovely as I have already told you on the phone last night.' Linda looks at him with her head on one side, 'Come on Stan what is it? What are you trying not to tell me? Do you want to break off our relationship? Have you met someone else?'

'No! No, it's not that Linda.' Stan stands up and walks to the window. He looks out at the scrubby grass for a moment, and notices the leaves on the chestnut tree are just beginning to turn. *How quickly this year is passing, and how complicated my life is getting.*

He returns to sit on the far end of the sofa. 'Have you seen this Friday's Western Daily Press?'

'No, of course I haven't, I only got back on Saturday,' she looks confused. 'What's this all about Stan?'

Stan picks up the discarded newspaper and shows her the advert. Linda reads it and then reads it again. 'What does it mean? Is this your business, Stan?'

'Yes. I've started an Escort Agency for mature ladies who need companions to take them places.' Stan waits for her to say something but when she doesn't, he stumbles on. 'You see I lost my job at Payntons and Maureen won't give me a reference, so I can't get another position anywhere so...'

'Why won't she give you a reference?' Linda gets up and stands in front of him with the paper still in her hand.

'It's a long story.'

'We've plenty of time. What haven't you been telling me, Stanley Baker?' Linda's face is taught and her eyes angry or hurt, Stan isn't sure which.

'Please sit down again I've lots to tell you. I should have been up front before but I wasn't sure if you'd approve of what I was doing. I didn't want to stop seeing you.' Stan is distraught. Linda looks withdrawn. 'Please, if I tell you everything can you promise not to say anything, till I finish?'

Linda sits down again and pours herself more wine. 'OK, but be honest and tell me the truth.'

Stan takes a deep breath and starts with Amy.

When he's finished Linda remains quiet. She sits staring at her wine glass twisting the stem of it round and round in her fingers. At last, she raises her head and looks straight into his eyes, 'I guessed that I probably wasn't the only woman you were seeing Stan, but I thought with time you would grow fond enough of me to let anyone else go. You were so kind over Bryony and all my problems. I know I couldn't give as much time to you, to us, as you'd have liked me to. But what hurts the most is that you couldn't tell me your troubles, that you didn't feel you could even try to confide in me.'

'I'm so sorry Linda.' Stan sees how stupid he's been. 'I should have told you.'

Linda stands up and puts her glass down. She picks up her bag and slips it onto her shoulder, 'I'm sorry too Stan.'

'Don't go Linda,' he begs, trying to put his arm around her. But she moves away towards the door. 'What do you want me to do?'

'I don't want you to do anything, Stan, it's all been done. You have an agency to run and women to escort, and whatever else you do for them. Your life is full and so be it. I'll see myself out.'

The tight feeling in Stan's throat becomes so painful he can hardly croak out, 'Don't go Linda. Not like this.' But she's gone. He hears the door close in the lobby downstairs. From the window he sees her walk away. The muscles in his legs itch to run after her but he can't move. He needs to call out to her, so he opens the window and leans out, but no sound comes out of his mouth. He slumps down onto the settee and leans his head against the cushions.

After an hour of despair, Stan sits up and, unable to bear the confines of his flat any longer, goes for a walk. Outside, he turns towards the Watcher's flat and without knowing why he knocks on her door. There's no reply. So, Stan walks on aimlessly, head down, watching his feet appear one by one under his stomach. He feels so wretched and such a heel. He wanders around the estate looking at the drabness of the urban landscape he lives in. *Why shouldn't I try and escape this shabbiness before I'm too old?* His tumbling emotions colour his view. With a stab of regret, he remembers how sunny the day had been when he'd walked these streets with Linda and introduced her to the Watcher. Now, the shouts of children playing sound raucous and spiteful. The perspective she'd shown him has fled. All he wants is to get away from this pit, and live somewhere else. Determination begins to grow. *I'll damn well make enough money to escape. I'll do whatever it takes.* Pulling in his overhanging belly, and clenching his fists he power-walks on. *Somehow, I'll lose weight, get fit and walk out of this estate forever.* His anger buoys him up for a few moments but then as it diminishes, *I should have trusted Linda to understand. I should have given her the chance.*

Returning, he passes the Watcher's flat and looks again at her windows. The curtains twitch in her kitchen and Stan pauses at the top of her path unsure of what he wants to do. The Watcher opens the lobby door and steps out, the little dog races out from behind her and straight up to him. Absentmindedly he bends and fondles its ears.

'Stanley, are you all right?' The Watcher asks as she approaches him and puts a hand on his arm. 'You're shaking man. Come on, come inside and I'll get you a drink, a stiff one.'

Sitting at her kitchen table surrounded by her photos and sipping single malt, Stan tells her the whole story. He pours out all the words and emotions till there's nothing left to say. He just stares at the walls. Stares at people from the past who've been through it all and have escaped at last, but not in the way he wants to. The Watcher tops up his glass. 'Give her time Stanley, give her time to take it all in and find what she feels about it. I don't believe she has gone from your life forever. But what's done is done.' She gets up and fills the kettle setting it on the gas to boil. 'For now, you have other commitments you need to concentrate on. You've two lovely friends who are trying to support you and a new client who needs your help.'

Stan nods his head. 'Thank you,' he says giving her a weak smile. 'I know you're right.' He sighs as he finishes his whisky. 'I need to start thinking as a writer for this wedding, a writer who's running away from his past. What on earth could I be writing about? '

'Try 'life', Stanley. Tell them you're writing about life.' The Watcher goes to top up his glass again.

But Stan puts his hand over the glass and stops her, 'Thanks but no. I need to go back to the flat and get sorted for tomorrow. Thanks again for helping. I need to buy you a replacement bottle, I'm coming here so often.' Stan stoops to stroke the dog and leaves.

Outside the day is dying and lights are appearing in windows around the estate. Stan feels better for having talked to someone, there's nothing to be done right now. He needs to carry on. As he walks past the blocks of flats, he gains glimpses into rooms where curtains have not been pulled. He observes the different décors, the pictures on the walls. In some windows there's a flickering of TV screens in the darkening rooms, and he reflects that each of these dwellings is a cell. A cell containing human life in all its rawness: happy, sad, bored or excited, but mostly a combination of it all.

For a moment he understands the Watcher's passion for observing people.

Twenty-Five

I take the child to school and rush home as fast as possible. I'm convinced my hero will be there. Running up the stairs with shaky knees and heart thudding, I'm almost praying. He is there. I see his reflection in the steamy mirror, towel around his waist. His face, neck and forearms are tanned, his chest and back pale in contrast. I can't stop staring at him. At last, I know; I know I'm falling in love. The boldness that helped me speak to the Watcher, returns. I put out my hand, oh, so slowly, and touch his arm. His skin is cool, slightly damp, yet smooth. He starts at my touch and turns his head towards me. I don't know if he sees me because he returns to his shaving. My hands are shaking. I touched him. I touched this apparition; this man I created. I touched him and he didn't disappear. How can that be?

For the moment, I don't care. I'm happy to stand and watch. I'm happy to smell him; to hear him breathe. I see a drop of blood appear on his chin as the razor nicks. He swears. He is mine, this fat, white man; this hero of my story. I hug that fact to my heart as I leave.

I return to the kitchen, set up the typewriter and begin to write. My fingers race across the keys as the words come. I am happy, so happy.

Stan is up early. Standing at his open bedroom window he looks out at the sparse area of grass and the leaves on the chestnut tree that are speckled and turning brown. The morning is misty and there's an Autumnal chill in the air. Stan shivers and goes to the bathroom. There's a sadness at his centre. He thinks of Linda and wonders how she is and if he should try and phone her. He decides against it. The Watcher said leave her, but he feels he needs to do something. *I'll send her flowers and a note.* He turns on the shower.

He's been in the shower just long enough to get really wet when the phone rings. 'Bother,' he says out loud. Then thinking it might be Amy, he steps out, grabs a towel and drips his way to the sitting room. He answers the phone. 'Hi Amy?' But the voice that answers him is one he doesn't at first recognise.

'Hi Stanley. No, sorry it's me... Maureen.'

Stan is rocked by this, and is slow to reply.

'Are you still there?'

He can hear the tension in her voice as he manages to say, 'Yes.' He waits to hear what the devil she wants.

'I thought you might be tempted to put the phone down on me.'

'I should.'

'I know Stanley. I know how you must feel. I'm truly sorry the way things turned out... But I had no choice.'

'What do you want Maureen?'

'Err... I saw your advert in the paper and I just wanted to say well done you for the initiative. And also, how much I enjoyed our theatre trip. I don't go out much. I was wondering if... Would you escort me occasionally?'

Stan is speechless. Torn between feeling angry with her, and being amazed at her cheek, 'I don't think that would be very wise.'

'I'd pay you the going rate, all professional and so on. I

140

think it's a great idea especially for women like me and there's no other agencies doing this around here as far as I can tell.' Her voice brakes slightly and Stan wonders if she's close to tears. Aware of the large damp patch he is making on the carpet and of how cold he's feeling, he says, 'I need to get going, Maureen.'

'Well, will you at least meet me to discuss this further? Please Stanley.'

It shocks him to hear her plead with him. Against his better judgement he hears himself saying, 'Oh, alright, when?'

'Tomorrow?'

'Aren't you at work?'

'No, I'm off this week. Shall we say tomorrow morning at eleven, at the new cafe in Southgate Street?'

Stan sighs audibly. 'Alright, but I still...' he doesn't finish because Maureen has already rung off. He pads back to the bathroom and gets back into the shower, but the water is cold. He finishes his ablutions quickly and in a foul mood.

When he's dressed, he gets himself a bowl of cereal and stands in front of the sitting room window. Stan feels restless and stressed. *How could that woman have the cheek to ring me?* he fumes. *And how can she think that I'd want anything more to do with her?* His face feels hot as he remembers that awful day. The cereal is like cardboard in his mouth, so he goes back to the kitchen and throws the rest away. He makes a coffee and decides to call Amy. She answers straight away and gushes at him in her usual vibrant manner, so that by the time he's told her about Maureen he immediately feels better. 'Oh, Stanley, how awful for you, what a cheek that woman has. Do you want to come over for lunch? I'm going out at two but we can chat and have a glass of bubbly and I'll kiss everything better.' She giggles. Stan wonders if she's already had a glass or two.

He decides to take a taxi to Amy's, but goes to the florist first, orders some flowers for Linda. On the card he writes one word. 'Sorry.' And draws a little sad face. When the taxi drops him at Amy's house he pays and asks for a receipt. *God I'm getting more business-like by the day.* He tips the driver generously and walks up to the neo-Georgian porch. But before he has time to ring Amy opens the door and throws her arms around his neck. 'Stanley come in.' She's wearing a straight black skirt, black tights, and high heeled shoes and a wine-coloured jumper with a deep V neck.

'You look delicious.' Stan says as he closes the door behind him still caught in her embrace. He runs his hands over her hips. Smelling her perfume at the base of her neck, he bends lower to kiss the swell of her breasts that peek at him from the edge of her top.

Amy presses her body against him, but then pushes him away. 'No Stanley, I really haven't the time to get all made up again. She gives him one last kiss and leads him into the kitchen where she has prepared a light lunch of smoked salmon salad. Two glasses of Champagne stand, chilled and sparkling in the light from the window.

'This looks good!' Stan says brightly attempting to disguise his disappointment and his need for her body, which at this moment is rather strong.

They eat while Amy chatters on about her friends and a new dance class she is going to start. 'You could come along with me, Stanley, then we can go to dances together. Its Salsa dancing with a little Latin American thrown in. I'm sure you could manage it. It would be another talent to have as an escort.'

Stan drinks more Champagne, the last thing he can imagine himself doing is Latin American dancing. 'Thanks Amy,' he says decisively, 'but no thanks.'

'Oh, but it would firm you up and trim you down,' she says smiling and then seeing his discomfiture changes the subject. 'Right, Stanley, spill the beans, tell me what's been happening?'

Stan tells her everything; about Sasha and the wedding and about Maureen and meeting her for coffee. But he says nothing about Linda. 'So, I'm worried about both situations for different reasons. Can I manage to blag my way through, pretending to be a writer and Sasha's partner? And should I even consider seeing Maureen again?'

Amy sits sipping her wine, and the little furrows between her brows show her concentration. 'This wedding is a really brilliant opportunity to make a sizeable amount of money. You can't afford to let it go. I admit the role-playing element is a bit awkward. Perhaps you should turn yourself into a tall, silent thinker of a man. You know the type? They used to smoke pipes in educational establishments, before the pipe went out of fashion. When people asked them questions, they would puff several times, regard their pipe critically, scrape out the old tobacco and then refill it from a pouch taken from their pocket. All this displacement activity gave them gravitas, everyone hung on their pronouncements, with a kind of reverence.' Amy giggles. 'That's the kind of guy to be, without the pipe of course. Give a measured silence while you consider each comment you make. That'll give the impression that your thoughts are profound. It'll give you time to think, which will lessen the chance of a blunder. There, what do you think?'

Stan isn't sure he can quite manage that effect but says. 'Yes, I see what you mean. It'll help to slow everything down and it'll give Sasha a chance to butt in if she sees any problems, but I might have to practice a bit.'

'You can start now Stanley, consider my next question; how did you feel when you realised it was Maureen ringing you?' Amy puts her elbows on the table, places her hands together and rests her chin on the backs of them, her head on one side.

'Well...' Stan frowns.

'Don't start to talk straight away, think about what you're going to say,' she says her lips curving into a delicious smile.

Stan stops and looks at her mouth, *how kissable those lips are*. He forgets for a moment what he felt about Maureen, as he couldn't care less about her. Amy's eyes widen and she raises one eyebrow questioningly so he tries to be truthful. 'Initially, I felt irritated, and then angry at the cheek of the woman. There is something about her that I really don't like, and I don't think I could work with her again.'

'Well done, Stanley, I was hanging on your every word,' she smiles encouragingly. 'But I think you should look at Maureen from a different angle. Imagine this successful woman in a man's world. She is focused, ambitious and driven, she prides herself on being as good as any man but all that comes at a price. When that office door closes at the end of the day, she goes home to nothing, to no one. She has few friends and those she may have, are in relationships, probably have families. One day she employs an older man that she quite takes a fancy to and she cajoles him into going out with her, although she is aware, he's reluctant. When he turns down the offer of coffee after the event, she finds the situation very hurtful. Finally, she discovers from another agency that he has been having sex with a client during business hours in a vendor's property. What can she do but sack him if she wants to retain her credibility as a manager? That's what she has to do while still being hurt by his behaviour. Do you see her predicament?'

Stan shakes his head but pauses before replying and actually during that moment he reviews the picture Amy's just drawn. 'OK, I admit you have a point. That could be her position. My behaviour with Eileen was unacceptable on several levels. But doesn't she have any pride? Why would she come back and ask me to escort her?'

'I don't know, but perhaps you should go and discuss it.' Amy suddenly looks at the clock. 'Sorry Stanley darling, I have to go. Can I drop you back in town?'

Stan remains silent for a long-time watching Amy's face as she waits impatiently for his reply. She gets up and clears the table then stands by him and shakes his shoulder till he bursts out laughing. 'Yes Amy that would be good, thank you.'

She realises what he is doing and laughs too. Standing up, he holds her close, looking down into her eyes. 'For a woman who is only out for fun, you've a remarkably wise head on your shoulders.' He kisses her slowly and feels her relax against him. Then, reluctantly, he lets her go. 'It's a pity you're going out, we could have had an interesting afternoon.'

Twenty-Six

When the Watcher told me that I'm writing, I realised with relief I'm not going mad; I'm writing a book. Now, I'm determined to make the best use of my three hours at the typewriter each day, it's the highpoint of my life and helps me through the rest. The Watcher comes more frequently. She's here now looking at me, and though we haven't spoken since that day, I find her presence calming. Every so often, I look up, catch her eye, and she smiles at me encouragingly. I smile back before continuing to let the words tap out under my fingertips.

I don't recognise the words that come, I've no idea what I might write nor any understanding of whether it makes sense. I just let the words stream through me and enjoy them, the sound of them, the feel of them, and the way they group into smooth phrases. I love their diction. Sometimes, I imagine a famous actor speaking them, standing solitary in a spotlight on a dark stage. If this is a fantasy then it is fantastic, and heady, and I love it.

Stan meets Sasha as arranged at The New Inn. They sit at a polished table in an alcove. The old timbers in the ceiling have taken this building's weight for centuries. The scent of lavender polish infuses the air as the waiter brings them their drinks and the menus. Sasha's dressed in grey, except for a red scarf which adds a warming touch. Once more

Stan finds himself wondering about this man of hers. *How can he bear to keep her waiting in the wings of his life?* He knows it's none of his business. Stan explains that the meal will be absorbed by his fees. She doesn't have to worry about ready cash, if there are unexpected expenses, he'll add them to his invoice.

She smiles nervously. 'You seem to have thought of everything.'

'Well, I've had help thinking all this out.' Instinctively, he touches her fingers that are picking away at the table cloth, he holds them for a few seconds and says, 'Just relax and enjoy yourself.' Releasing his hold, he smiles reassuringly, 'I'm here to make the evening as agreeable for you as it can be.'

'Thanks, Stanley,' she says as she takes the menu from him. 'Have you thought any more about escorting me to the wedding?'

'Yes, I've given it quite a lot of thought,' Stan says. Then seeing how tense she is, he smiles at her. 'Don't look so worried. It'll be a pleasure to escort you, but there are several issues to discuss. Can I fire questions at you during this meal? Some of them might be a bit personal, but if I'm to appear as a partner of some years standing, I'll have to know a lot about you.' Stan stops talking as the waiter arrives to take their order. 'Is that alright?' He asks when they are alone again.

'Yes of course what do you want to know?'

'I'll ask them as they come to me, if that's all right, and I'll be jotting some of it down, although I'll destroy these notes after the event. OK?'

'Fire away.'

'How old are you?' Stan gets out a slim note book from his pocket and a pen.

'Forty-nine. I'll be fifty on November 5th.'

'Well, that is easy to remember so you always have fireworks on your birthday?'

'Yes, it's a bit boring, actually, I never manage a normal birthday party, it always ends with fireworks and friends complain if it doesn't.'

'Strictly speaking, I shouldn't be escorting you till after your next birthday but we won't worry about that. Have you any other siblings?'

'No just Laura. Her husband-to-be is called Adrian by the way, Adrian Durrell. He's forty-five and an interior designer.'

'Great,' Stan writes it down, 'and your mother and father's names?'

'Moira and Tony and they are sixty-nine and seventy-three. My father's a retired accountant and my mother was a nurse.'

The questions go on throughout the meal. Favourite colour; purple. Favourite flower; rose. Favourite drink; Archer's and lemonade; and so on till Stan has a whole list to learn. He puts the book back in his pocket and sits back with a sigh. 'Gosh, that was a marathon, sorry there were so many, but I want to do this properly, can you think of anything else I should know?'

Sasha tries to stifle a yawn. 'No, I think that's everything. But what about you? What should we both know about you?'

'Well, I think we should keep to my first name unless you have already mentioned a name?'

'No, I don't think I have... no, I'm sure not.'

The waiter returns to collect their plates. 'Can I get you anything else sir, madam?' Sasha shakes her head.

'Can we have coffee and take it into the lounge, if that's

possible?' Stan asked the waiter. 'Also, the bill please.'

'Certainly sir, I'll have the coffee brought into you if you would like to make yourselves comfortable.' Stan ushers Sasha into the old-fashioned lounge and they sit on sofas in the far corner, away from any guests. 'Right, I've thought long and hard about this. We'll turn my surname into Barker, as that's easy to remember. I'm fifty-three and a retired reporter turned writer. I'm going to be a rather ponderous sort who is monosyllabic; I'll weigh my words and use them sparingly. That way it gives me time to consider what to say, and for you to dash in if you see something going wrong. What do you think?'

Sasha laughs appreciatively. 'Bravo maestro, I think it's an excellent plan. Well done, Stanley, and she bends forward and gives him a peck on the cheek. She sits back her face flushed. 'You are clever, I can't begin to tell you what this means to me.'

'Well, don't thank me too much before the actual day, that's the important bit.'

They part after finalising how they'll to travel to Kingston and whether they'll stay overnight. In the end they decide Stan will hire a car and do the driving and they'll stay over at a hotel. Stan leaves feeling the evening's gone well and that he's remained professional but considerate. *Perhaps I might be good at this work, after all,* He walks back to the bus stop attempting to calculate how much he is likely to get paid. If they leave at ten in the morning and stay overnight, it'll be in the region of £1500 inclusive of expenses, and she'll owe him for this evening which is another £150! He can hardly believe it. Deep inside he feels mean for charging so much. The old feeling of discomfort at what he is doing, returns. He knows his mother wouldn't approve and neither would Linda. That's a big problem for him but on the other hand, he does have to survive, and if Sasha is happy to pay, why should he turn her down?

On the bus Stan tries to look out of the window but all he sees is his own reflection, that of a neat but middle aged, fat, white man. It's a reality he tends to forget for periods of time and facing his reflection sobers him. Only when they get into the city centre does he start to see through the glass to the bright lights and people on the pavements.

Twenty-Seven

Today neither of my apparitions appear. But I'm pleased as I need to continue creating this account of Stan's life. As I add more female characters to this chronicle, I wonder if what I'm writing is credible? Or is it an unlikely story? However, the words form and the stories of my characters unfold without any planning on my part. My fat man, my protagonist, is a man apart, an intriguing character that proves men don't need to be strikingly handsome to be lovable. Perhaps men just need to be genuine and honest. I continue to ponder on men in general and their often-overwhelming need for an ego. Is Stan believable? I can't imagine how it feels to be a man, but I know what I find attractive; I know this man is someone I can love.

Then I'm forced to stop cogitating, because the words are growing impatient to be written and I've very little time to get them all down.

Next morning, Stan reluctantly decides to go and meet Maureen. However, he takes his time and when he gets to the café, he can see she's already there sitting at a table near the window. He stops on the other side of the road and watches her. A coffee cup is in front of her, her bag is on another chair, and she has a newspaper on her lap but she isn't reading it. She glances at her watch and looks up at the ceiling and then back to the paper. Observing her in this way, Stan thinks she doesn't look like the steel woman he imagines her to be and he remembers Amy's words. He takes a deep breath, tries to swallow the bitterness in his heart and crosses the street to the café. At that moment Maureen looks up and sees him, the look of relief and obvious pleasure on her face disarms him. In spite of his better judgement, he raises his arm and waves.

She stands up as he enters, takes her bag from the other chair as though she's been saving it for him, and smiles. 'Hi Stanley, thanks for making it, what would you like?'

'Oh, I'll get it?' He reaches into his jacket pocket for his wallet.

But Maureen puts a hand on his arm. 'No this is on me.'

'I'll have a cappuccino then please.' Stan sits feeling at a disadvantage, as though things are out of his hands. He shakes his head. Amy had encouraged him to come, but now Maureen has him cornered, and obliged to her for buying him coffee, when he'd wanted it the other way around. He knows he's being petty but somehow it matters. Fortunately, there's a queue at the counter and he has the opportunity to rationalise his feelings of antagonism. By the time she returns with the coffee he's able to smile his thanks.

Maureen sits opposite him and after putting her purse in her bag, folding the paper and placing it on the table, she turns to him and looks him straight in the eye. 'I know this must be difficult for you, Stanley, and believe me it's not easy for me either, but can we put the past behind us, for a moment?'

Stan nods but says nothing.

'I was pleased and relieved to see your advert in the paper, it made me feel easier in my mind. I realised how difficult it was going to be for you to get another position.

This is something I think you're ideally suited to. So, I thought I could help us both by putting some work your way.' Maureen puts out a hand to stop Stan from breaking in. 'Please let me finish. I don't get out much, Stanley, and most of my friends are busy with family ties. If you could see a way to escort me to the theatre a couple of times a month, that would help us both. What do you say?'

Stan is about to reply when he stops himself. He decides to practice the pause before speaking so, he waits for a moment while Maureen sits forward expectantly. Finally, he says slowly, 'Maureen you're right, this isn't easy for me but I need to be professional about my agency and I won't always be able to pick and choose who I escort and where. There is one issue though and that's your age, are you over fifty?'

Maureen's face falls, 'I'm forty-nine in just over two weeks' time. In fact, I was wondering if you would escort me out for a meal to celebrate that. Can you make an exception in my case? Please Stanley.'

Stan sits back in his chair and considers the situation. He can hardly believe that Maureen is pleading with him like this, it seems so out of character, but perhaps he only knows her business persona. He's already made a concession where Sasha's concerned, but in this case, it would be for over a year, not merely a few weeks. If he does allow this, then where will it end? *I'll be escorting ladies of thirty-eight soon and God forbid even younger?* He looks at Maureen, who is obviously hanging on his decision. *This silent pause thing does seem to have a lot going for it.* 'Alright. The age is a problem because I chose 'over 50' for my agency for good reasons. I'll agree to escort you out for your birthday but I'll decide what to do after that. How does that suit you?'

'Oh, Stanley that's lovely of you.' Maureen gets up from her chair, moves over to him and gives him a kiss on his cheek, 'I won't forget this and I'll take any opportunity I can to put business your way.' She sits back down and drinks some coffee. She's looking so happy that the years seem to have fallen from her face, and for a moment he sees what she must have been like in her twenties, before determination and ambition soured her and hardened the lines around her mouth.

He smiles at her enthusiasm, 'I think I once said you should smile more often.'

'You did and you're right and if you escort me, I will make an effort to smile frequently.'

'It's not something you need to try to do,' Stan laughs, 'just relax and enjoy yourself. It'll happen automatically. Now where do you want me to take you and when?'

'The Everyman on the 14th September, please.'

'I shall book two tickets for that evening. Do you wish to eat out as well?'

'Yes, that would be great. An Italian restaurant, if possible' Maureen sits on the edge of her chair, almost like an expectant child, eyes shining.

'I'll find one and book a table.' Stan finishes his coffee and decides to keep it strictly professional. 'Now, I have to go. Is that everything?'

Maureen puts out her hand to stop him getting up, 'There's just one other thing, Stanley. I said I'd put more business your way. I have this friend or rather a business acquaintance who is interested in your agency. To set your mind at rest she is almost fifty and she's a life coach who needs a male escort every so often for business events. She asked me to mention her, and wants your details.' Maureen rummages around in her bag and takes out a card, which she holds out to Stan, 'Her name is Martina King. I've shown her your advert so, she'll probably be in touch in the next few days.' Stan looks at the card. There's something about the name which is jogging his memory, he has a sudden mental image of a very smart Eurasian lady, and he asks Maureen, 'Does she work at the Community Centre by any chance?'

'She rents a room there a couple of times a week I believe. Do you know her?'

'No, but I've seen her a couple of times; a very smart lady.'

'Yes, that's her, she's smart in everything. She's got lots of contacts and if she likes you, she could get you a lot of business.'

'Thanks Maureen.' Stan puts the card away in his wallet. 'I'll look forward to hearing from her. 'I must be going.'

Maureen stands as he gets up from his chair. 'Thanks Stanley, I'll see you on the 14th, that's brilliant.'

She moves towards him but he puts out his hand, takes hers and shakes it, not, holding it a second longer than is required. 'I'll pick you up from the office at 6.30 on the day.' He walks away leaving her standing there.

Twenty-Eight

Today, when I return from the school, I go straight upstairs to get the typewriter out of the airing cupboard. I hear the front door open and my heart beats fast as I leave the typewriter where it is and go to the banisters to look down into the hall. To my dismay it's Guy. He's come home for some reason. I'm so scared at the thought of what might have happened, I don't speak. He looks up at my scared face and says, 'You look like you've seen a ghost, whatever's the matter with you, woman?'

'Sorry, I just wondered who it was. I wasn't expecting you.' He tells me to come down and get him a cup of tea. I go down. Then he says, he could do with a diversion as he wants to forget something. I say, 'Why what's happened?' 'None of your business,' he growls. So, I just get his tea. I keep wondering if he is going to stay or not. Imagine what would happen if the Watcher came with her dog while he's here? Then I realise with some relief he won't be able to see her. Guy reads the paper while he drinks his tea and I hover at the sink not knowing what to do. This has quite put me out. I'm desperate to get back to my typing. My hands shake and I rattle the cups as I try to wash up. He looks up and asks me if I can't go and leave him in peace. I ask, 'Aren't you going back to work?' and he puts his paper down and says 'No, probably not.' My mouth goes dry but I manage to ask, 'Why not?' He gets up and comes over to me. He pins me against the sink and puts his hands on my breasts and kneads them. I can hardly breathe.

'I've been laid off. What do you think of that? he says. After nearly four years they just say, "Sorry you're no longer needed, off you go. We'll be working out your redundancy and will send it on. Bye." So, I'll be around for a bit, and you won't have to take my daughter to school, I can do it, till I find another job.' He gives me a leering grin. 'I'll be here with you alone and we can get up to whatever we like, that'll be one consolation.' I try to move aside saying I have things to do. But Guy says I don't need to bother so much now, as he'll be here to help. He says he wants me upstairs with him, straight away. Horror fills me. I don't know what to do. I follow him like an automaton up the stairs and into the bedroom. I stand while he undresses me and then I lie on the bed.

Twenty-Nine

Guy's been at home for three days now and the only time I'm alone is when he takes the child to school or picks her up. I've not left the house and I haven't dared reach for my typewriter. I've managed to write these few words in an exercise book in the middle of the night, when I was sure he was asleep. I've hidden it as well as I can. I long to see Stan or even smile at the Watcher and get water for her little dog.

At last, I have a reprieve. Guy is leaving to collect the child from school, then he's taking her into town to buy her some new shoes, and they'll have a meal out afterwards. So that gives me time to myself. My hands are trembling at the thought. Finally, he's going. He gives me one last squeeze on my bottom, then he leaves and I hear the front door close behind him. I take a deep breath and go to the bathroom to shower. Guy has wanted sex several times a day and I need to wash away his smell. I dry myself in front of the misty mirror and look at my naked body for the first time in ages. I've never given birth and therefore my stomach is flat and my breasts firm, which is what Guy likes about me. Suddenly, without any warning, Stan is standing behind me. I can see his reflection in the mirror. His face is above mine and he's smiling. I don't dare move. I can smell his aftershave, hear his soft breathing and feel warmth from his naked body. My legs turn to water. I hold onto the basin to steady myself. His breath is on my neck. I close my eyes. His lips touch my shoulder. His hands hold my arms. I can't tell where his flesh starts and mine ends. I'm aroused in a way I never thought possible. I'm wet, weak and breathless. I long to face him, to press my naked breasts against his chest. But I'm scared, so scared I'll break the spell. I can't know if this is real or imagined. I don't want these sensations to end. I knew he would feel good. I knew I'd want him. He puts a hand on my cheek and traces the curve of my lips with his fingers. I open my eyes and see his ice blue ones regarding me in the mirror with such sadness. A tear falls on my cheek, his image blurs. I turn to him.

But he's gone.

Stan straightens his tie in front of the mirror. He smiles at his reflection, and picks up his aftershave, pours a little in the palm of one hand, rubs his hands together and pats his cheeks with the stinging liquid. He regards himself critically. He's certainly smarter and the grey suit fits him well, but his stomach is still large. He sighs. *It's hard to lose weight when I'm frequently eating out in fancy restaurants.* There's a sadness, this morning, because he's meeting Eileen, probably for the last time. Her husband, Darius, is returning to help with the move into the farmhouse. Eileen's waiting for Stan when he arrives at her hotel. She's wearing a green jumper and her high heels show off her fine calves beneath a straight skirt. Her hair is swept up into a chignon and fastened with a green lacquered clasp, she looks marvellous and as he bends to kiss her cheek, he says so quietly, for her ears only.

She beams at him. 'Thank you darling you look very fetching too. I thought we'd go to Antonio's for lunch as it's quiet there and I've lots to tell you. I hear from Amy that you've lots to tell me too.' She takes his arm and squeezes it, 'It's so good to be with you, Stanley.'

They sit at a small table in the corner of the restaurant. Eileen has ordered a sparkling wine and the ice bucket stands to one side, the frosted bottle gleaming in the soft light. She twists the stem of her glass between her fingers and appears fascinated by the rising bubbles. Stan waits quietly for he senses that she is about to say something significant. It's unusual to see her so thoughtful and silent. He places a hand over hers and holds it. Eileen smiles, 'We've come a long way in a short time haven't we, Stanley. It's been a lovely journey from the very beginning and I wouldn't change anything. Although, I think I've messed your life up quite a bit.'

He presses her fingers to his lips, 'You haven't messed up anything, you've opened my eyes and it's been a wonderful experience.'

'I'm glad. You know Darius is coming tomorrow. We move in on Thursday and he has a two-week holiday so…' She looks at him again, her eyes searching for something in his gaze. 'I don't know what I mean to you, Stanley, but I must tell you how special you are to me. I'll miss our times together.' A tear brims onto her cheek and she dabs it with her napkin. 'I thought I'd be able to re-instate our outings, after Darius goes back to work. But it appears, he's off to the West Indies on a Trade Mission and he wants me to go with him. We'll be gone for a quite a while. We've decided to rent the farmhouse out for at least six months.'

Stan keeps hold of her hand and looks at the manicured nails and the heavy rings which she wears so boldly. He remembers the feel of those ringed fingers on his bare chest the first time she took him. He feels a tightening in his throat, 'I'll miss you, Eileen.'

'I'm so sorry, Stanley, I feel I'm leaving you at a disadvantage. I said I'd go on needing your services when you set up this business and I practically guaranteed you an income.'

'It's alright Eileen, things are already looking up. I have a wedding in a few weeks that's going to net me a fair whack. And I was going to tell you; Maureen has asked for me to escort her out on her birthday and beyond.'

'That awful woman!' Eileen is immediately back to her usual forceful self. 'Take my advice Stanley and steer clear of that woman, I knew she was trouble from the start.'

'Well, it's a one off and because she isn't fifty yet, I can refuse to put her on my books. However, she has introduced me to another contact, so that all helps the business, and I still have Amy.'

'Yes, that's true and she's a jewel.' Eileen studies Stan's face for a moment and seems to come to a decision, 'Will you come back to my hotel room this afternoon?'

'Is that really wise?' he asks cautiously, 'Won't your husband be staying there tomorrow?'

'Yes, but, on the first floor there is a Gents Toilet, if you go up there and wait for me, I'll take the lift. Once we're past reception no one will notice. I'll meet you and take you up to my apartment.'

Stan looks uncomfortable. 'I'm not sure Eileen, you can always come to my flat.'

'With respect Stanley dressed like this I'll be a tad noticeable. I was thinking, perhaps it would be a good idea for you to sell that place and buy something a little more select, where you can entertain ladies in style.' She puts her hand on his arm and leans towards him, 'I'm sorry, Stanley, it's not the interior that's the problem it's the location; the area. Have I hurt your feelings?'

'No,' Stan shakes his head. 'I know exactly what you mean, I want to escape the area too.'

'Well maybe this is something Maureen can help you with, she owes you a favour. She could value your place and send you details of other flats further in towards the city centre, there's a lot of new development going on I hear,' Eileen squeezes Stan's hand. 'Say you'll come to my room, please darling, just this once. You know how I love living dangerously.'

Stan laughs, 'I know only too well.' He looks at her pleading eyes, her enticing smile and knows he's lost. 'Yes, I'll come, you terrible woman.'

Eileen meets him outside the Gentlemen's toilets on the first floor of her hotel as arranged and they climb two flights of the back stairs giggling like naughty school children. When they finally reach her apartment, Stan gasps at the size of the sitting room and at the view over the city roof tops. The Cathedral tower rises into the grey sky, the sunlight shining through the delicate stone tracery of its four turrets. From this view point, Gloucester is a stunningly beautiful city, and Stan realises that he's never really appreciated how lovely it is. Turning to Eileen, he puts his arms around her, 'I can see why you have wanted to stay here this long, the view's breath-taking. It almost beats looking at you.'

She punches him playfully. 'Let me show you the bedroom.' She leads him into a large, airy room with more views across to the hills, a king-size bed stands in the centre of one long wall. 'This must cost you a fortune to stay here.'

'It's a bit pricey but I got a reduction for a long term let and Darius puts it all against Tax, so…'

Stan shuts her up with a lingering kiss, 'Come here you

mad, glorious woman,' he says. He pulls her to the bed, 'I don't want to talk money I want to lick you all over.' He pulls down the neck of her jumper, takes out one breast from inside her bra and kisses the firm nipple. He begins to suck and bite until Eileen whimpers out loud and presses against him, then he pulls her down onto the bed and starts to undress her. 'I'm going to give you a ravishing you won't forget. You'd better get used to being on your back for a long while.' Pulling off her jumper, he unhooks her bra and releases her generous breasts. Her perfume is heavy. *Opium?* She slips off her skirt, and her lace knickers so that she is completely naked. Eileen lies spread-eagled on the wide bed. Her hair has come loose and now falls over her face and shoulders and he stands looking down at her. *There's something very erotic about being fully dressed, while the woman you're with is naked.* He recalls the painting Eileen showed him by a French artist, *Manet, wasn't it? Le Déjeuner sur l'herbe*? Suddenly he understands some of its significance. Stan undresses slowly keeping his eyes on Eileen. She's breathing quickly, her eyes are dark with dilation. She licks her lips, begs him to hurry in a soft voice. But he keeps the advantage and takes his time. Sometimes he stops to stroke part of her body, then returns to removing his clothing. Finally naked, he climbs onto the large bed and lies half on top of her, kissing her from her neck to her mound of Venus. Pushing her legs apart he slides his fingers into her. She moans and he strokes till she cries out. Only then does he enter her.

Stan stays the night and they sleep lying close together. In the morning he's the first to awake. Tiptoeing to the bathroom, he dresses quietly. As he stands looking out at the new morning rising over the city, he wonders whether he should just leave. Goodbyes are painful and everything that can be said, has been said. He turns to look at her and sees that her eyes are open. 'I guess it's time for you to go.' She gives him a sad smile, 'Thanks Stanley, for last night, for everything. You are a lovely man.'

He walks over to the bed, sits next to her, and taking her hand kisses it. 'Yes, I'd better go before room service arrives and your husband with it. Take care Eileen, meeting you has been an education in every sense of the word. I'll never be able to forget you.' He kisses her just once on the mouth, and as she's about to speak, he puts a finger on her lips, 'Say nothing, you amazing woman, there's nothing to say.'

Stan closes the door of her apartment and walks very slowly to the stairs.

Thirty

It is 3.00am. The child and Guy are sleeping and I'm sitting at the kitchen table with my typewriter. I've thought of a plan. I searched and found an old typing manual of mine and I've typed out several exercises from it, these I've put in a file. If anyone finds me typing I can say I'm practicing so that I can look for work too. The pages I write can be slotted in behind these exercises until it's safe to put them with the others. This way I should be able to manage to write for a couple of hours each night. Of course, I probably won't see Stan or the Watcher at this time of the morning, but at least I can write about them.

Sitting in this dim, chilly kitchen with the night pressing against the window, seems to tinge my sentences with a sombre note. I empathise with my hero as he loses his close friend. I long to put my arms around him. I know how he feels about his run-down estate, and I want to help him escape.

In a mood of depression, Stan catches the bus home. The morning has lost its earlier promise and become grey, damp and cold. As he walks through his estate, the place looks seedier than ever, from the peeling paint and over flowing wheelie bins, to the fag ends and used condoms in the gutter. It's no better when he lets himself into his flat. The dull daylight intensifies the dinginess of the rooms. In comparison to Eileen's spacious, airy suite, his flat is claustrophobic. He goes into the bedroom, takes off his suit and hangs it up out of habit, then he strips off, stuffs his underclothes in the wash basket and goes into the bathroom. He's tempted to have a whisky but decides it's too early. He turns on the shower instead. Standing under the jet of warm water, he thinks of Eileen and his body responds telling him just how much he's going to miss her. He's lost two lovely women, Eileen and Linda. He recalls the words of that 'Lady Bracknell' character, from the play Maureen took him to; *'To lose one... may be regarded as a misfortune; to lose both looks like carelessness.'*

He steps out the shower, dries himself and dresses without looking in the mirror. He knows he'll become maudlin if he so much as catches a glimpse of his sad face. Going into the sitting room, he draws the curtains. A flashing light on his answerphone captures his attention, and he presses play. 'Hello Mr Baker,' says a low, husky voice he doesn't recognise. 'My name is Martina King. I am a friend of Maureen Carter. I am calling about your advert regarding The Over 50's Escort Agency. Please may I say I think this is a brilliant idea and I'd love to meet you to discuss several possible business opportunities I might be able to put your way. Do please call me, Mr Baker, I am available this evening, if you are free. Ciao.'

Stan's not sure why but there is something about her voice that makes him feel uneasy. He goes into the kitchen and makes himself a coffee then comes back, replays the message and listens while he sips his drink. Perhaps it's the stilted way she speaks that puts him off, her words are very precise and clipped showing that she is not an English speaker from birth. But it's more than that, the message isn't from someone wanting an escort for herself, it's more about business opportunities. What kind of business opportunities? He finishes his coffee and decides not to call back, he just isn't in the mood. Sitting down on the settee he turns on the TV and flicks through the channels till he finds a travel programme, and falls asleep in front of it.

He's awoken by the shrill ringing of the phone. Stan struggles into consciousness and grabs the receiver; 'Hello.'

'Hi, Mr Baker?' It's the husky-toned voice again. 'Is that Stanley Baker? Can you talk to me please?'

'Hi err… just give me a moment.' Stan struggles up from his prone position, *damn the woman she is certainly persistent.* 'Hi; sorry I was in the middle of something. How can I help?'

'Oh, I rang your number before and I left you a message. Did you get it? Only you have not called me.' She sounds almost peeved at that fact.

'No, I'm afraid I've been tied up. I did get your message though, it sounded intriguing.' Stan lies, hoping he is convincing.

'My name is Martina King and I would like to meet with you and discuss a few things. Can you meet me today?'

Is it his imagination or does she sound like she's issuing an order? 'Well, I am a bit busy right now. Can't you tell me more over the phone?'

'No, we need to meet. How about we say, eight o' clock at the Robert Raikes in town. Do you know it?'

'Yes but…' Stan is trying desperately to think of an excuse.

'Good I will see you there. Ciao.' And the phone goes dead before he can say anything else.

Stan gets up from the settee. *Blast the woman. I wish Maureen hadn't given her my details.* He starts to pace. Perhaps he should just ignore the whole thing. After all, does it matter if he stands her up? But then he remembers how lovely she looked at the Community Centre. He sighs, and goes and gets his suit out of the wardrobe again. *I'd better give it a press*, he groans.

At eight o'clock Stan is sitting at the small bar with a glass of single malt in his hand. Everything reminds him of his first meeting with Linda. The memory is painful. He recalls how nervous he'd been at the prospect of dating for the first time in years. It seems like a whole age has passed since that night, and here he is waiting for another beautiful, but imperious, woman to turn up. As Martina walks through the door of the hotel several heads turn to look at her. She's dressed in a dark red coat and wears high, black patent leather boots that shine as she walks. She's certainly stunning for her age. Her face is as firm and taught as a young woman's, the cheek bones are high under the wide, dark eyes, but she doesn't smile. Stan gains the impression that she regards the effect she has on men, as her due. She walks up to Stan and holds out her hand 'Have we met somewhere before?' She asks him, just twisting the edges of her mouth a touch, which he guesses constitutes a smile in her case.

'We haven't actually met, but I've seen you at the Community Centre a couple of times.'

'Oh yes, I hire a room there for seeing clients from time to time.' She takes off her coat and hands it to him. The wine-coloured dress she wears accentuates her figure. She's petite but has the presence of a taller woman.

Stan's not sure what to do with the coat so he hangs on to it lamely, asking, 'Shall we go and find a table? What would you like to drink?'

Martina walks into the next room and sits in a tall armchair, 'I would like a white wine, not too dry. You can put my coat on the back of that chair.' She points to the high carver opposite her.

'Oh yes,' says Stan, now totally discomforted, he quickly deposits the coat and goes to the bar. He gets himself a double measure of whisky for Dutch courage and carries the glasses back to the table. Sitting in the armchair opposite her, he raises his glass. 'Cheers,' he says.

'As you say, 'cheers.' But she doesn't attempt to raise her glass. 'Maureen has told me all about you. She rightly appreciates your ability to come up with a great idea after losing your position. I am a Life Coach. I teach people how to gain control of their lives and talents. You obviously do not need my input for that. However, if I may be blunt, you could do with some advice on your personal image. With my help your agency could grow into a very big business.'

Stan finds it hard not to let his mouth drop open at the cheek of the woman. *What on earth gives her the right to think he would want or need her help?* Still ,he attempts to be civil as he replies, 'I'm sorry, Martina, but I think you are mistaken about me and my business; I don't need anybody's help.

Martina picks up her wine and sips it genteelly. It appears as though she hasn't heard him, or if she has, she's decided to ignore what he's said. 'Mr Baker. Stanley, I don't think you realise what I am offering you. I can take your little agency and turn it into big business. I can make you a real success. For just a small percentage, I can create for you a client list of select ladies, who will appreciate you and your skills. What do you say to that idea, Stanley?'

Stanley can hardly believe it. This woman considers his agency to be a business opportunity which she can muscle in on. He's just about to reply angrily, when he thinks of Amy and her suggestion about pausing before he speaks. So, he puts the tips of his fingers together and takes his time to answer. Martina looks at him and a small frown forms between her brows, one exquisitely manicured finger taps impatiently on her wine glass as she waits for his reply. Finally, Stan takes a deep breath and says, 'Thank you, Martina, for the interest in my agency. However, I've not asked for, nor do I want, any input from you or anyone else.' He drinks the rest of his whisky and places the glass very carefully back on the table between them.

Martina glares at him. 'Very well, Stanley, but let me assure you that you make a big error in not taking my offer. You will be back and the terms will not be so generous then.' She gets up and puts her hand out for her coat. Stan stands and holds her coat for her, and as she puts it on, he smells her perfume. It's very light yet so subtle he can't place it. His senses tell him that she could be a very passionate woman if she allowed herself to be. For a moment, he almost feels sorry for her and for all the women of her kind, who think that equality means being better than men in the hard-nosed arena of big business. 'Good bye, Ms King,' he says holding out his hand. She ignores it, shrugs her shoulders as she picks up her bag and walks out of the room without saying anything.

Stan strolls home slowly, thinking of this bizarre woman and their recent conversation. When he lets himself into the flat the phone is ringing. He picks it up quite expecting it to be Martina, but it's Maureen on the other end of the line. 'Stanley, I've just had Martina phone me on her mobile. Whatever have you said to her? She's very angry.'

'She isn't the only one Maureen; the woman has the cheek of the devil.'

'Well, it doesn't do to make an enemy of her, Stanley, she has her fingers in so many people's pies around here that she can make or break you, and your business.'

'I can't help that, Maureen. I don't want her input in my agency, and I can't imagine why she's even interested in it. '

'Frankly neither can I, but she must see some potential in it or she wouldn't bother. If she does contact you again, just be nice to her and try not to anger her further. Alright? I'll leave you in peace, until the 14th that is. Ciao, Stanley.'

Thirty-One

For a couple of nights, now, I've been typing in the early hours. But it's making me so tense. I keep expecting Guy to wake up and find me. Today he has an allergy. He's been cutting the grass and strimming the edges of our garden and now his eyes are all red and itchy. He's got some antihistamine from the doctor but he's not supposed to drive while taking it, as they've told him it'll make him sleepy. This information has given me an idea. What if I manage to get hold of a few of these antihistamines and I give Guy a tablet each night in his evening meal? Will it make him too sleepy to wake up in the early hours, leaving me free to write as much as I can? An added bonus maybe, that he'll feel too tired for sex when he comes to bed. I know this is really wicked of me but I'm so tempted, just till I finish my story. I wish I could ask the Watcher what I should do.

When Guy and the child leave for school, I go to the kitchen and get a shock; the Watcher is there, sitting at the table. Her dog comes towards me wagging its tail and I stoop to fondle its ears. I sit opposite her and she smiles at me. Nervously, I ask inside my head, 'should I give Guy something that will make him sleep?' Her reply echoes in my mind as she looks into my eyes with concern. 'You need to do something to help yourself.' She gets up and puts the lead on her dog and they leave, but now that I've seen her, I feel comforted.

I run upstairs to the bedroom and go to Guy's drawer

and open it. The tablets are there. I pick them up with trembling fingers. I haven't much time. I open the carton and see that there are four strips of the tiny yellow pills. I take out one strip, close up the packet and put it back exactly where I found it. I'm just in time for I hear his key in the door. Quickly, I slip round to my side of the bed and hide the strip in my own drawer. Then I go down to meet him feeling unusually calm.

Amy sits opposite Stan and listens to his account of his meeting with Martina. She has a frown on her pretty face. They're at a table in her favourite restaurant, Chez Renard, waiting for their meal. 'You're right, it is a strange occurrence,' she says as she reaches for his hand across the table. 'But I think you handled it excellently darling and I'm sure you'll probably never hear from her again.'

Stan feels better now that he's shared it with her and resolves not to think about Martina any more. 'So, what would my lady like to do after her meal this evening?' he looks at her, thinking how lovely she is.

Amy smiles, the frown instantly gone as she puts her head on one side to consider. 'I think I would like to be escorted home this evening, Stanley,' She drops her voice to a whisper, 'and be taken to my large bed and...' she stops and giggles as the waiter arrives with their meals.

The waiter places the large white plates in front of them, each succulent meal presented to perfection. 'Bon Appetit, Madam et Monsieur,' he says as he backs away from their table before turning and leaving them in peace.

'Whatever the lady desires,' says Stan quietly pressing her knee under the table. 'Shall we play footsie out of sight of the waiters or shall I slide my hand up here?'

Amy pushes his hand away as it's reached half way up between her thighs. 'Stanley, behave,' she says, as she wriggles her skirt down to her knees.

'Beg pardon, my lady, but might I enquire if you have any knickers on?'

'Stanley, keep your voice down. You'll have us thrown out.' Amy picks up her fork. 'Eat, that is an order.'

'Yes, mi lady.' Stan looks down at the delicately carved slivers of roast duck placed on a bed of honey glazed winter vegetables and drizzled with an orange and saffron sauce. As he places the first forkful in his mouth, the flavours explode on his tongue. Stan no longer feels out of place in this restaurant, now that he pays the bills, the waiters treat him with deference. To Stan, eating at this gourmet establishment is like visiting an art gallery, where the exhibits are brought to you individually. The difference being, that here you consume the art.

After the meal Stan calls a Taxi and they're driven back to Amy's house. Sitting with his arm around Amy, he kisses her slowly from time to time. He's languidly relaxed as he looks out of the car window at the lit streets of suburbia. He wonders why in his mind the word 'suburbia' always conjures up pictures of these substantial semis owned by the middle classes but never offers the impression of the shabby estates, like the one he lives in.

In her large, luxurious living room Amy puts on some music. She pours two generous measures of single malt and they sit together on the rug in front of her 'coal effect' gas fire toasting their toes. For a while they sit in companionable silence watching the flames flicker and listening to the singer's soft voice. He turns to her and kisses her lightly on the lips; tiny, short kisses delicate and almost pure, just like he did the first time they met. She starts to respond and whispers, 'You are very dangerous with those tiny kisses.'

'I know,' he breathes. 'Someone once called them "butterfly kisses".' With a sudden pang in his heart, he momentarily thinks of Linda. He takes a large swig of his whiskey, and tries to forget her. He continues to kiss Amy till she puts down her glass and lies back onto the cushions. Stan does the same as he asks, 'and what is it the lady would like to do now?' he kisses her eyes, her nose, her cheeks, 'Does she wish to go to her large bed?' Stans hand moves along the hem of Amy's skirt which has ridden up her thighs showing the tops of stockings and suspenders. Running a finger along the smooth skin above the stocking he murmurs, 'I think it's time to find out if the lady wears knickers.' His hand travels upwards. 'Can this flimsy garment be termed a pair of knickers?' he laughs as he slips his fingers beneath it feeling for her wetness. Having removed the tiny garment he kisses her toes, her calves and turns her onto her back as he continues to kiss his way upwards.

'Shall we undress?' whispers Amy between short breaths.

'I shall,' he says, kissing her thighs above the stockings, 'but I want to take you fully clothed this time.' He leaves her lying on the rug, her skirt up around her waist, her hair spread across the cushions while he gets up and undresses. 'Because,' he says returning to her side and caressing her belly, 'if the lady has no objection?' he kisses her on the mouth and slips his tongue between her parted lips, 'I do find suspenders so very erotic,' he admits as he pushes her legs wide apart.

When Amy finally lies sleeping on the rug, Stan goes up

to her bedroom and gathers the quilt off the bed and takes it downstairs. He places it over her sleeping form as she is now quite naked, every item of her clothing having been removed before they finished. He lies down beside her and pushes back a strand of hair that has fallen across her face, she stirs but doesn't wake. Lying on his back he relaxes his muscles. His right knee is aching and he realises with regret that he's not as young as he was. *These gymnastics should really be done on a mattress from now on.*

The only light in the room comes from the fire as it flickers across the furniture and paintings. Once again, he pictures his dingy, little flat. He realises, with a touch of sadness, that renovating anything in that location would be a total waste of money. Stan's torn between the certainty and familiarity of his mother's flat, and the desire to have a new life with the kind of luxuries that surround him in this room. Paintings, for example; he'd love to be able to buy original paintings from struggling artists, or merely have a view from his window that would inspire rather than depress. He sighs deeply. *I'll speak to Maureen about selling the flat when I see her,* he decides, before slipping into a dreamless sleep.

Thirty-Two

It worked! Guy was so sleepy he could not get up this morning. I said it didn't matter and that I'd take the child to school. Then I made him a cup of tea and put in another tablet, adding lots of sugar, which he likes, and he drank it all down without complaint.

When I get back, I open the front door and stand in the quiet hall, listening. I creep upstairs to our bedroom but Guy is fast asleep and snoring steadily. I get out the typewriter and take it down to the kitchen table, I put the folder of typing exercises out just in case, but I can hear him snoring from here. I sit, fingers poised over the keys but nothing happens. I can't think of anything to write. I take out my typed sheets of what now constitutes a book, my book. I read the last few pages, but still no words rise into my mind. I begin to panic. I walk around the house in distress, what have I done? Drugged Guy for nothing? When I return to the kitchen it's a relief to see the Watcher there at the table, and I smile at her. She picks up her little dog, sits it on her lap and they both regard me for some time. Then I hear her voice say, 'Don't panic so much, you just have a bit of writer's block. Relax, it will return. The words will flow as soon as you stop chasing them.' I want to ask her. 'Do you write?' I do ask it in my head, just not out loud. But she must hear my words because she answers me. 'I have in the past. Now all I write is my diary every night.' 'Am I in your diary?' I ask silently. 'Of course, you are,' she smiles.

I like this kind of communication, this silent thinking to and fro and I start to imagine a world where this was the only kind of talking, how relaxing that would be? No white noise in the brain. Suddenly my fingers tingle and the words start coming in snatches, short phrases then whole sentences. Gradually they build into a flow and I type so quickly and easily that I don't see the Watcher go. But when I look up her chair is empty.

Stan parks the hired car in a side street just around the corner from Payntons. He doesn't want to turn up before the staff have had the chance to leave as he still feels escorting Maureen isn't a good idea and the fewer people who know the better. At ten past six he gets out and walks to the front door, Maureen is looking out of the window for him and opens the door immediately. 'Hi Stanley, thanks for coming.'

'Did you think I wouldn't come?' he asks taking a small envelope out of his pocket. 'Happy Birthday by the way, and he hands it to her and places a quick kiss on her cheek.

Maureen blushes. 'Why thank you Stanley.' But she doesn't open it, just slips it into her handbag. 'Shall we go?'

'Your carriage awaits,' Stan says, holding the door open.

'Have you bought a car?' she asks when she sees it.

'No, just hired it for the day, hop in.' He opens the passenger door for her.

At the restaurant they order pizzas and Stan pours two glasses of wine, then holding his up to hers he declares a toast, 'To your last year of the forties. What do you intend to do with it?'

Maureen clinks her glass against his. 'I intend to enjoy it,

Stanley!' she says giving him a beautiful smile.

'Have I ever told you that you should smile more often?'

'Frequently,' she laughs. 'And I mean to do it as often as I can.'

'I'm glad to hear that,' he says beginning to relax in her company. *Perhaps Amy's right about her, she isn't a bad woman.*

'Maureen,' Stan starts awkwardly. 'I need to apologise for my behaviour with Eileen. It put you into an impossible position, I realise that now.'

A frown darkens her face for a moment and then she smiles again. 'Thank you, Stanley. Shall we not to mention it again?'

'Agreed,' he says with relief. 'Now let's talk about you.'

'Oh gosh that's a facer.'

'Well tell me, are there any men in your life?'

'Ha, no and there hasn't been for a long time.' She stops talking as the waiter arrives with their meal and she starts cutting her pizza. 'I haven't had much time for personal relationships.'

'Has there never been anyone special in your life?' Stan asks with concern in his voice.

Maureen's face flushes, she picks up her glass and takes a large gulp of wine. 'Yes, Stanley, but it was a long time ago. I was in love with a young man, but he was stationed in Northern Ireland.'

'Sorry, that question was probably too personal,' Stan puts a hand on her arm, 'You don't have to tell me anything.'

'No, but actually it might be good to talk about it.' She stops eating and stares out of the window for a moment then takes a deep breath. 'His name was Colin, Colin Taylor. And he was twenty-five when he was killed in a bomb blast in County Down, trying to evacuate women and children. I remember the phone call. I'll never forget how chilled my blood felt in my veins. I seemed to lose heat. I sat there shivering for ages, though it was a hot afternoon in mid-summer.'

Stan feels awful, 'Oh, God, I'm so sorry. I shouldn't have opened up old wounds, not on your birthday.'

'It's okay, you weren't to know. Besides, Stanley, you don't know what a relief it is to speak of him. It makes him real again. Colin was a real person, flesh and blood, passionate and bloody minded but so lovely to me.' Maureen reaches for her bag and starts fumbling for a tissue, Stan hands her a clean handkerchief and she smiles at him through her tears. 'Thanks, Stanley, ever the gentleman, eh? Gosh a linen handkerchief, I haven't seen one of those in years.' She dabs carefully at her eyes trying to stop the mascara from running. 'Sorry I'll have to keep this,' she says looking at the black smudges, 'I'll wash it and return it to you.' She blows her nose and with a final dab at her eyes puts it into her bag.

'Don't worry, I'm just so sorry. Are you alright or do you want to leave?' Stan feels ashamed of himself. He'd been trying to strip away her hard shell to see for his own sake what was underneath, well now he knew.

'It's fine, Stanley, really. No one ever wants to know about me as a person they just relate to me at face value. She takes a sip of wine and holds the glass up to the light looking at its colour as she speaks. 'He was lovely you see. I thought us a perfect match…' She puts the glass down and cuts a slice of pizza. 'But it was all a long time ago and that young woman no longer exists.'

They eat in silence but Stan finds it difficult. His mouth is as dry as a desert and he has to take several sips of wine in order to swallow. He's relieved when it's time to leave for the theatre.

The play turns out to be very funny and Stan's stomach aches with laughter. The sadness of revelations made during the meal is forgotten. Stan drives her home and as he pulls up outside her house Maureen thanks him and leans over to kiss him on the cheek. 'I hardly dare ask you again, but would you like to come in for a coffee?'

Stan looks at her hopeful, lonely face and is unable to turn her down, 'I'd love to,' he says.

'Come in then.' She says getting out the car and she takes his arm as they walk up the path.

Her house is small but immaculate. The walls are white with several bright, abstract paintings strategically placed to add colour and warmth. She shows him into the sitting room. Stan has removed his shoes in the hall at her request and so becomes aware of the luxurious carpet under foot. The room is square, with a bay to the front, the sofas are of coffee leather and the fireplace is white with an art deco tile surround. Maureen pulls the heavy drapes across the bay window, puts on some soft music that Stan doesn't recognise, and bustles out of the room. 'Make yourself comfy and I'll get the kettle on,' she calls from the kitchen.

Stan sits on a comfortable sofa, and he looks around him with a feeling of surprise at the overall effect of the room. It's obviously been designed with skill. Above the fireplace a picture glows at him, the more he looks, the more it shimmers. It's a large, square canvas painted red but the red fades to a soft blue-grey towards its centre, and the gradation of colour fluctuates as he gazes. Four small squares equidistantly and centrally placed, focus the eye into the swirling colours. Maureen brings in a tray with the coffee and a plate of biscuits, she puts them on the large central coffee table and sees that Stan is gazing at her picture. 'Do you like it?'

'Yes, I think so, though I'm a bit bemused by it.'

'I love it. It's called 'Contemplation' and is by Penny Elfick, an artist friend from Somerset.' She pours him a small mug of coffee and hands it to him.

'Thanks,' says Stan tearing his eyes away from the picture, 'I didn't realise you were so into art. Are all these originals?'

'Pretty much. There are a couple of prints in the hall but otherwise I've collected originals from local artists as I've travelled around. I'm glad you like that one, it's my favourite.' Maureen comes and sits next to him and they drink their coffee in silence.

At last Stan puts down his mug and puts his arm around Maureen's shoulders. When she's finished her coffee, she puts her mug on the tray too, and settles back, leaning her head against him. They are quiet, listening to the strains of a violin and there seems nothing worth saying after all their talk over the meal. Stan has sudden empathy for this stoically brave woman whose fierce independence has isolated her from so many people and from personal happiness. He slowly strokes her arm with his thumb and he takes her hand and kisses the back of it. He feels her relax. He doesn't have to look at her to know she is succumbing to his warmth, his presence, his gentleness. He kisses her hair and whispers, 'Are you alright with this?'

'Oh yes, I'm happy,' her voice is soft and so unlike the Maureen he knew at work.

'Look at me then,' and as she turns her head to look into his eyes he bends and kisses her lips so lightly, so swiftly that her eyes widen and then he repeats the tiny kisses many times till her lips part and her breath quickens.

Gradually his kisses grow stronger, till he slips his tongue between her lips and she gasps, holding her hand against his face.

'Please Stanley,' she breathes in his ear, 'make love to me. It's been such a long time. I couldn't bear it if you left tonight.'

'Are you sure?' he pulls back and looks at her face that is flushed and softly beautiful.

'Yes,' she says, 'Yes if you are.'

'Then you'd better show me the way to your bed,' he smiles down at her. 'Actually, I could do with the bathroom first.'

When he comes out of the bathroom Maureen is already laying in her large white bed. As he stops to look at her, he thinks that everything about her and her house depicts virginity. He's never taken anyone's virginity and the thought of doing so does not appeal to him. He prefers experienced women who embrace their sexuality. But the fragile aspect of her face against the white pillow makes him realise that possibly for her, this will be the first sexual experience for many years. As he undresses, he watches her but she doesn't look at him. So, as he climbs in beside her, he asks again, 'Are you sure?'

Then she turns to him and smiles. 'Yes.'

He holds her against his warm body. For a long while he does nothing but stroke the hair back from her face. He's waiting for the tension to leave her eyes and her muscles. *Only then, will I begin.*

Thirty-Three

Once again, Guy is too sleepy to get up and after getting him a nice cup of tea, I take the child to school. On my return I set up my typewriter, the house is silent and it's almost as if he isn't there. I relax and as I do so the words start to form in my head. The typing goes well for about an hour, and I get up to make myself a drink. When I turn around the Watcher is there, I give her a smile and get a drink for her dog. It occurs to me, if I can give her dog a drink, why can't I get her one? So, I ask her in my head. 'Would you like a drink?' She looks at me for a moment as though making a decision and then nods her head and smiles. I make her a cup of coffee and place it on the table in front of her. I go back to my typing. The words are pouring from my fingers when I hear the bedroom door open. Then the bathroom door closes with a bang. I look up at the Watcher and our eyes meet. I know she sees the fear in mine for she frowns a little. She picks up her dog, and they're gone. I take up the metal bowl and empty it into the sink. I don't have time to put away my typewriter so I stuff the typed pages into the back of the exercise folder and put in a new piece of paper in the machine on which I type, 'The quick brown fox jumps over the lazy cat', several times down the page.

I manage this just in time as the door opens and Guy enters in his dressing gown. He looks dishevelled and unshaven and his eyes are puffy and red. 'What the hell are you doing?' he barks as he sits in the chair opposite, the very one vacated by the Watcher. 'I thought I'd practice a bit of typing,' I say attempting to keep fear out of my voice, 'Build up my speed.'

'Why for God's sake? It makes one hell of a racket when you've a headache.' He picks up the mug, the one I made for the Watcher. 'Whose is this coffee?' 'Oh, it's mine,' I say uncertainly. 'So, whose is that one?' he asks me, pointing to the mug next to me. 'Err... that's mine too. I forgot I'd made one and it went cold so I got another.' My heart's hammering in my head at these quick lies. 'Shall I get one for you and something for your headache?'

'Yes,' he growls. 'You're a mad woman. Get it quickly, I have one hell of a pounding in my ears and my throat's so sore I can hardly swallow. It must be those bloody pills the Doc gave me.' He crosses his arms on the table and lays his head on them.

I get him his coffee, two paracetamol tablets and a glass of water. He sits up and swallows the pills and sips his coffee watching me as I put the typewriter away. He puts his hand on my arm, stops me, pulls the paper out of the machine and reads it. 'Why have you decided to do this now?'

I reply, feeling my legs tremble, 'I thought I might be able to get some typing work?' I pray he doesn't feel it in my arm, he hates it if I 'shake and shiver' as he calls it. 'Come on, how are you going to do that when you're too scared to leave the house?' He pulls me to him and I stand next to him while he pulls down my jumper to gaze at my breasts. I can feel his hot breath on my skin. 'I don't know,' I answer, 'but I could get some work to do at home, there are several adverts...'

'Your job is to provide a nice home for me and my child, and to pleasure me whenever I need it, there's no need for you to work. I'll get another job soon enough, meanwhile you can provide me with some of that pleasure right now.' He kisses my breasts and starts to bite my nipples. I can barely stand it but my body begins to betray me for my nipples become hard and he laughs, 'Come on, you bitch, up those stairs.' 'I thought you were feeling ill?' I say in desperation. 'Well,' he says bending me backwards and kissing my mouth, 'I'm feeling better all of a sudden. Leave all this and get to that bed or I'll be having you on the hall carpet.'

Stan wakes in the morning and for a moment he's totally disoriented by the white walls. Then he remembers and looks at Maureen still sleeping beside him. His first reaction is one of dismay, but on reflection he realises it was probably an inevitable outcome, after Maureen's emotional revelation. He slips out of the bed and goes to the bathroom. Splashing cold water on his face he runs his fingers over his emerging beard. He badly needs a shave. He wonders how it is that all these women want him to make love to them. There must be something about him that he can't see. All he knows is, that once he's in bed with them, he makes every effort to give pleasure. To him there is nothing more erotic than a woman having an orgasm under his hands. He's never understood macho men that take women as a sport for their own enjoyment. *Making love is so much more than just having sex. It's an art form. Perhaps that's what they sense.* He dries his face on a white towel and opens the door. Maureen is just waking up and smiles sleepily at him. She throws off the covers and opens her arms wide. 'Come and give me a cuddle, Stanley.'

'You know what may happen if I do?' he sits on the edge of the bed. 'Don't you have to get to work?'

'I told them I'd be in late this morning so there's plenty of time.'

Stan climbs in beside her and she presses her trim body against him stroking his chest and his nipples till he hardens against her and she smiles as she feels him. 'That was beautiful last night, Mr Baker, but it's made me want more.'

Stan gives a mock sigh and raises his eyes to the ceiling. 'This is what happens,' he laughs. 'As soon as I lay my hands on a lady, she becomes insatiable. What can a mere man do?'

Maureen digs him in the ribs, 'Big head, turn on your back please.'

Stan obliges, throwing off all the covers as he turns over. He strokes her breasts, her belly her thighs and then puts his hands around her waist, 'Come and ride me,' he murmurs into her hair. She sits on top of him gasping as he enters. 'Now feel,' he whispers, 'move and feel. Think of nothing else. Isn't that amazing?'

'Yes,' she breathes. 'Oh my God, yes…' Maureen throws her head back as she sits tall and upright and he strokes her breasts, her legs and her knees. Her breathing becomes rapid. She moans and sighs as passion takes over, and as she comes, she calls out in a cracked voice, 'Colin!' Maureen collapses forward onto Stan's chest, tears running down her cheeks. Between sobs she says, 'I'm so sorry. I don't know why I thought of him at just that moment. Sorry, Stanley.'

He helps her climb off him and she lays down beside him curled into a foetal position. He turns towards her and holds her for a long time until the tears dry up and she wipes her smudged and blotchy face with the corner of the pillow case. She looks up at him through swollen lids and says again. 'I'm so sorry... That must have been horrible for you.'

'Stop apologising. It's fine. You needed that. That connection, that memory. You've buried it too deep and then when you abandoned yourself, it all came flooding out. I totally understand. Alright?'

'You're a lovely man and so suited to this occupation.'

Stan stops hugging her and sits up. 'What do you mean, occupation?'

'Why I mean your business; the escorting and providing a service for women.'

Stan is staggered. 'Do you mean that you think I was making love to you as part of the job?'

'Well, yes. Though you did it so sweetly it didn't feel like that. You were just what I needed. You said I needed to let those feelings out and I've done it with your expert help. She sits up, reaches for her dressing gown and wraps it around her.

Stan sits on the edge of the bed and puts his hands over his face. He's angry and hurt. And yet he can't blame her for thinking that way because he never explained that love making was not included in the package. 'Maureen, I made love to you because I felt a connection with you. Sensed a need in you, and I loved doing it. I wasn't thinking of charging you for it.'

Maureen sits down next to him, obviously thinking hard. 'Stanley, I'm very flattered,' she says, giving him a radiant smile. 'I'm honoured that you thought enough of me to give me that gift of love.' She moves closer to him and puts her arm around him, 'But you can't live on love and you need an income. If I pay you...'

'I can't talk about it this way.' Stan gets up. 'You don't

understand, I've never charged for making love to a woman. I've not even considered doing so. Even though Eileen said I should.'

'Amazingly for once, I'm in agreement with that woman. Stanley, sit down, please, and listen to me.'

Reluctantly Stan returns to her side and Maureen continues. 'The need of some women to be loved is as great as the need of others to be seen out with, and escorted by, a man. If you provide a full service, and the two don't necessarily go together, the one is a contract within your agency. But the other is a mutual consideration, and can only happen when the connection is made between you and the woman. However, it's still a service and you need to allow them to pay you. At the very least for the hours spent in their company.'

'No, no it cheapens it somehow.' Stan is desperate to explain how strongly he feels about it. 'I see the act of making love as something precious. Not something to be bought and sold.'

Maureen gives him a kiss on the lips. 'Nothing can cheapen what you've done for me. It was beautiful, it was what I needed, but I'm not in love with you and you aren't in love with me. So, when I pay you...'

'I won't accept it.'

'...when I pay you for the hours you've spent with me, it won't diminish the beauty of what happened between us. It'll just make me feel better because I'll be helping you to get back on your feet.'

Stan sits trying to think. His mind is in turmoil. He can see it makes sense to her. But to agree with her will break something sacred in his psyche.

'Stanley, trust me, this is the way of the world. Transactions are made between people but they don't need to be soulless. What you've done for me is priceless. I can't reimburse you for that. All I'll be doing is paying for your time.' Maureen gets off the bed and walks to the bathroom. 'I need to get ready for work. Please don't let this spoil things between us, Stanley. I'd love to do it all again, sometime, if you'll accept me as a regular client? Otherwise, I might stop smiling again.'

Stan looks at her standing in the doorway, her robe slipping open to reveal more than it covers, her face looking relaxed and pretty. He'd be a fool not to see how his attention has helped her. 'It would be a dreadful shame for you to stop smiling, your smile is beautiful,' he says as he gets off the bed and begins to dress. But Stan is still convinced that being paid for the privilege of making love to a woman, is a sin.

Thirty-Four

Guy is going for a job interview in Chippenham today. He's taken the child to school and he'll pick her up on his way back. That means I have the whole day to myself! I go to the bathroom and stand under the shower. The hot water relaxes me and I feel fresh and happy. I wrap a large towel around my body and stand in front of the mirror willing my hero to appear. 'It is safe,' I say out loud. 'Come to me now, we have time and I long to see you.' But nothing happens. So, I get out the typewriter, and pad down-stairs in my bare feet to the kitchen. I put in a fresh sheet of paper all ready to start. But as my fingers touch the keys, I experience an overwhelming desire to climb the stairs again. I give in to the impulse, and as I open the bathroom door, I see him. I catch my breath. He seems to hear me because he turns and for the first time I look straight into his eyes. They are so kind and full of love it scares me. I put out my hand and touch him on the chest and he puts his hand over mine and holds it. I step closer. He's half dressed in a shirt that's open to the waist, he's been shaving and there's a streak of blood on his cheek. I lick my finger and rub away the blood. His skin is smooth and soft. Lovely to touch. I lift up my face to him and as he bends to kiss me, I sway slightly. He puts his arms around me and holds me close. I can smell him, feel him, touch him. I hardly dare to breathe in case he vanishes. But he doesn't this time. Instead, he takes me by the hand and leads me into the bedroom.

We sit on the bed. That very same bed that I dread so often. Now I long to lay on it and to draw him down beside me. He sits and looks deep into my eyes and I know he knows all that's happened to me. He pushes my hair back from my face and strokes my cheek. In this way he tells me how special I am to him. I'm so happy. I lay back onto the bed and he takes the towel away so that I'm naked beneath his gaze. He smiles down at me. I feel dizzy and close my eyes, just for a moment.

When I open them, he's gone. But I'm not sad. I can't be sad, because I know I'm loved. Because I know he wants me to continue creating his story and to finish it. So, I get up, dress myself and go downstairs. I want to write while he's still in my head.

On the day of the wedding Stan is up early. He's already packed his overnight bag and he's looking as smart as he can. His best grey suit is back from the cleaners, he has on a new white shirt, and he's trying to choose a tie. Amy gave him a royal blue one and he picks that for good luck. He checks the time, picks up his bag and a set of car keys, then having double locked the door to his flat, he descends the stairs. The smart, blue Audi parked outside the flat has been hired for three days and Stan's looking forward to driving it. The street is still dark and deserted, he puts his bag in the boot of the car and climbs in behind the wheel. As he drives away from the estate he experiences a feeling of freedom, and wishes he was leaving for good.

Sasha's waiting for him at the bottom of her drive looking wonderful in a cerise dress and jacket. Her shoes, he notices, are high-heeled, blue suede. Stan can't help singing, *'Keep off, keep off, keep off of my blue suede shoes,'* as he draws up beside her. He gets out of the car, to open the door for her and she slides gracefully onto the passenger seat. Having put her case into the boot, he climbs back into the driver's seat, and smiles. 'You look stunning.'

'You look pretty good yourself, Stanley, and the car's a brilliant touch.' She gives him a peck on the cheek.

'You don't think it is too much of a statement for a writer?'

'Not at all, after all you have been a successful reporter remember.' Sasha's laugh is infectious.

'Let's go then, if you've got everything?'

'Yes, all I need.'

Stan drives off and they're both quiet as he heads the car towards the M4. He turns his head to check she isn't sleeping before asking, 'Do you mind if we go through all the things I need to remember.'

'No of course not. Ask whatever you need to.' Sasha puts her bag down on the floor and looks expectantly at Stan.' For the next few miles, he goes through everything he can think of. But he can't shift the feeling that he's forgotten something. 'Well, I hope I've got it all,' he says.

'You'll be fine, just take it slowly and I'll be there to cover any holes. Do you mind if I have a little sleep now?' She finds the release catch on her seat and drops the back down.

'Be my guest.' Stan drives onto the motorway and tries not to notice Sasha's legs, because as she sleeps the hem of her dress is riding up her thigh. She's certainly a lovely woman, if it wasn't for his nervousness over this role playing, he'd be enjoying himself immensely. Once again, he hums *'Keep off, keep off, keep off of my blue…* Stan smiles to himself, *perhaps it's a sign for me to behave myself.* But he wonders what's this woman's life is really like? Always waiting for her lover to be free; it isn't the life she deserves. *Still, it's her choice, I guess, and really none of my business.* An hour later he turns off the motorway at the services and gently wakes Sasha. 'Would you like some breakfast?'

She stretches and yawns then sits up pulling her dress down. 'Yes, that would be lovely. Where are we?'

'Somewhere east of Reading, I thought it best to stop before we hit the M25.' Stan gets out of the car and opens the door for Sasha. 'Come on, I'll stand you a coffee and a croissant.' In the café they sit feeling over-dressed amongst the throngs of blue jeans and T-shirts. Sasha's worried about marking her dress as she's eating a croissant, so Stan obliges by handing her a large clean linen handkerchief which she uses as a napkin.

Back on the road Stan drives faster, there isn't a lot of time left, and he doesn't want to get there late. They arrive at the hotel, however, before 1.00pm. The porter takes them up to their rooms, which turn out to be adjoining, with an interconnecting door. 'Did you particularly arrange this, Stanley?' Sasha asks raising her eyebrows. 'I shall have to remember to lock the door.'

Stan's a little embarrassed. 'I really didn't ask for connecting rooms. If you'd feel better, I can ask for another room.'

'Don't be silly, I'm only teasing,' she laughs. 'Let's say ten minutes to freshen up. Is that enough?'

'Yes, that's fine.' But while he's combing his hair, Stan hears Sasha turn the lock on her side of the door.

They walk to the church which is Victorian and gothic in design, quite pretty. Though for Stan it lacks the authority of a Norman Church with a sturdy square tower. There are many people milling around the entrance waiting for the right time to enter. Stan tries to swallow the insects that have started crawling out of his stomach. Sasha introduces him to her mother, who is a comely but distracted woman. Fortunately for Stan, the mother has no time to chat and he and Sasha follow her to a pew in the second row from the front. Sasha's father is absent with the bride, of course. Sasha looks around her, smiling at people she recognises and waving to one or two closer acquaintances, while Stan sits stiffly feeling very nervous and studying the order of service without seeing any of it. At last, the organ strikes up and the wedding march signals the presence of the bride. Stan hears the hushed rustle as all the women turn to catch a glimpse of the dress and make soft appreciative 'Ahh' sounds as the bride passes them. Stan watches the beautiful bride. She's a younger version of Sasha but with more poise and a regal touch to her walk; probably a direct result of her cream taffeta gown with a long train. Her hair is loose about her shoulders and softly curled under the veil. The bouquet she carries is of white roses and its simplicity emphasises her dark complexion. Stan glances sideways at Sasha and sees her eyes filling with tears. 'She's very lovely, my little sister, isn't she?' she whispers.

'Not as lovely as you,' he says without lying. The bride is beautiful, but somehow 'loveliness' isn't a word he would use to describe her. As the service begins Stan squeezes Sasha's hand, takes out his handkerchief, the one she used as a napkin earlier, and places it at her disposal on the seat next to her. This gentlemanly gesture makes her laugh and the tension leaves her face.

After the wedding is over and the photos are being taken, Sasha introduces Stan to her father. Stan feels his gut tighten; this moment will decide if the ruse works or not. However, he needn't have worried, her father seems genuinely pleased to meet him and says he's glad that Sasha has someone special at last. The irony of those words is not lost by either of them, and it's compounded when they're ushered next to the bride and groom to have their picture taken. Stan tries to look as though he belongs in that position, but he's poignantly aware of the bitter twist of fate; his face will be placed in this family's album for ever. With a relief, Stan sees the bride and groom climb into the shiny, black limousine, the white ribbons fluttering in the breeze as it's driven off to the reception. The rest of the party starts to disperse towards the large Inn, two streets away. Stan takes Sasha's arm as they cross the road. 'Phew, so far so good.'

'You're doing brilliantly, Stanley, don't worry,' she says squeezing his arm.

'Well, it's the next couple of hours that'll be the proof.' He's feeling distinctly queasy, but doesn't say so. 'I could do with a stiff drink.'

The happy couple are at the entrance of the restaurant to greet their guests, and when Sasha introduces Stan to her sister, he's aware of a pair of piercing eyes above the welcoming smile. 'So glad you could make it this time, I was wondering if we'd ever get the chance to meet you. We'll have to catch up, if I get any time that is.'

Stan and Sasha are directed to a large table to one side of the top table where most of her family will sit. This is an unexpected bonus for they'll be talking to long lost cousins and family friends most of the time. Stan takes two glasses of Champagne from a tray of filled glasses proffered by a waitress. He brings them over to Sasha. 'I think we need these. Let me suggest a quick toast, 'To subterfuge,' he says, the words are for her ears only and they drink, giggling.

'What's the joke?' a strong male voice says from the

other side of the table. They look round guiltily and Sasha smiles with relief. 'Oh, Tony, you made me jump. No joke we were just gasping for a drink. Stanley, this is my favourite cousin Tony; Tony this is Stanley my beau.'

'Pleased to meet you at last,' Tony says shaking Stan's hand. 'Sasha's mentioned you on several occasions, I hear you are a roving reporter.'

Stan smiles, 'I was but no longer. I've retired from that rat race now.'

'Sasha, I'm sure when you last mentioned this guy you said his name was 'Pip' or something.'

There are a few seconds silence and Stan's mouth goes dry while he desperately searches around for a reply. 'Oh yes, she used to call me that as a term of endearment for some reason. It came from 'Great Expectations', I believe. I wasn't too fond of it so she stopped, didn't you, my love?' Stan takes hold of Sasha's hand and kisses it.

Sasha blushes. 'Yes, that was ages ago, I'd forgotten I'd told anyone.'

Tony looks at them a little strangely. 'Oh well, "a rose by any other name..." I suppose,' he says laughing. 'I'm glad to see her happy, Stanley, she deserves to be. Keep it up.' And with that he disappears into the crowd.

'Oh my God,' Sasha says. 'I'm so sorry. I didn't think I'd mentioned his name to anyone. Well done you for quick thinking, I was at a loss for any excuse.' She kisses Stan on the cheek, 'You're a marvel.'

When the reception is finally over, they walk back to their hotel in silence. Stan is shattered. The strain of acting a part for so many hours has been exhausting. He slumps down in an armchair in the hotel lounge, leans his head back and closes his eyes. 'Sasha, would you mind ordering me a large, single malt. I didn't dare drink too much at the wedding in case I forgot who I was supposed to be.'

'Poor Stanley, of course. I've put you through it, haven't I?' I'll get us both one, I could do with unwinding too.' She returns with a tray containing two whiskies and two Irish coffees, 'I thought these would be an immediate pick-me-up. I hope you like Irish coffee.'

'I adore it, you brilliant woman.' Stan sits up, takes the tall glass and sips the hot, bitter-sweet liquid through the cool layer of cream. 'Oh, but that's good.'

'Well, you did it, Stanley. You created a believable persona and my family is delighted with you.' Sasha sits back with a sigh, 'Perhaps they'll stop cross-questioning me all the time. I do believe they thought I might still be a virgin.'

'I'm not a hundred per cent sure your sister was taken in. She gave me several very piercing looks with those beautiful eyes of hers.'

'Hm. Laura's very perceptive but she gave me a lovely hug before she left and she didn't mention anything.' Sasha slips off her high heels and stretches out her toes on the carpet.

'What? She didn't say, "That's a hunk of a man. I wish I'd met him before I was married?". You disappoint me. Stan attempts to look hurt.

Sasha laughs. 'No Stanley, she didn't, but my mother was impressed by you.'

'It's always the more mature women that go for me,' Stan sighs. They sit in silence for a while sipping their drinks and letting the whiskey do its work. Stan looks across at Sasha. *It's sad that she's forced into all this subterfuge. Wouldn't it be better if she told everyone the truth? Is being someone's mistress the last taboo?* he wonders. *Strange, you can be gay, bisexual, a masochist, tattoo yourself, pierce your body*

with metal, even change your gender, but you can't fall in love
with a married man, regardless of circumstances.

Sasha is sitting back in her chair; her legs are crossed and her bare feet look pretty in the smooth tights. She clasps the whisky glass in her hands and is lost in contemplation. Stan studies her profile. *If only I could paint her with that gleam of light on her dark hair, or describe her expression.* Sasha's face looks sad, and Stan can't imagine what today has cost her. 'A penny for them,' he says letting the words fall into the silence.

Sasha comes out of her trance and smiles tiredly at him. 'Sorry I was a long way away. Think I'll finish this and turn in if that's alright with you.'

'Of course, it's been a long day.' Stan drains his glass, smacks his lips in appreciation and stands up. He offers her his hand and steadies her while she puts on her shoes, then with a slight bow he gives her his arm and says, 'Will Madam permit me to escort her to her room.' Sasha laughs and accepts his arm. 'Oh Stanley, you make me laugh,' she says, giving him another kiss on the cheek.

Thirty-Five

I have the house to myself at last. I'm free to write. Guy has started his new job and will have to drive to Chippenham every weekday. So, after taking the child to school, the whole day is mine. He'll get home much later, and I can do my chores early evening. I'm relieved that I don't have to drug him anymore, it wasn't very fair. I'm sitting on the side of the bath, waiting for my hero to come. There'll be lots of days when he can come and go, just as he did before. I'll wait for the Watcher, too. I'm sure she'll arrive. I'll get her a coffee and we can sit and celebrate together. I know she'll be happy for me.

Guy's not a bad man, just narrow minded. He works hard, we have this nice house and he keeps me away from mental institutions. I don't want return to those places, they're full of truly sad people and the drugs they administer make you feel so unreal. I try to work out how they're supposed help? If you can't **feel** yourself, how can you get back to being yourself?

I leave the bathroom, fetch the typewriter and in the kitchen, I feed in a new sheet of paper. There are so many pages, now. I wonder if I should be making copies. Perhaps I could go to to the library to photocopy them? But it would cost a lot, and I don't feel up to it, right now. Sadly, neither Stan nor the Watcher have come but I don't mind too much, I know what I need to write. I know what's going to happen, and my fingers tap the keys as Stanley's story grows.

❖

Stan lies in bed staring up at the ceiling. Memories of the day's events move through his mind: Sasha walking through the crowd of people, acknowledging them but looking reserved. He wonders if it's always been that way, or whether her situation keeps her reigned in. *Oh, God, I'm getting quite the pocket psychologist. When did I start contemplating people so deeply? Before Mum died, I didn't contemplate much at all, I certainly didn't do deep-thinking. My circle of acquaintances was small, and I had no desire to find out what made people act the way they did. I thought it was the same with Mum, but as I've found out, she didn't really allow me to know her.*

His contemplation is broken by a small noise at the interconnecting door. He lifts his head from the pillow but it doesn't come again. However, as he relaxes back, he's sure he hears someone sobbing. *Is that Sasha crying?* He is surprised by how tight his chest feels at the thought. The sound at the door comes again, this time it's a definite turn of a key and the door opens a crack. 'Are you awake, Stanley?' Sasha's voice is plaintive.

Stan sits up and turns on the bedside lamp. 'Yes, are you alright?'

'Can I come in?' she says, 'I can't seem to sleep.' Sasha slides quietly through the opening and shuts the door behind her. She's wearing a cream silk nightie and dressing gown.

'Of course,' says Stan, reaching for his dressing gown as he never wears anything in bed. 'Just give me a second.' He slips into the en-suite to put it on properly. When he comes back into the room Sasha is pacing up and down. He can't help but be aware of how the shimmering material moves against her body as she walks. Stan tries his best not to find it alluring but fails, clears his throat and asks what's wrong.

'Oh, Stanley. I'm finding things so difficult. I'm sorry to disturb you but I kept tossing about.' She stands in front of him rubbing her hands together. 'I need… I'm sorry.' She looks small and lost.

He thinks of the old-fashioned term 'wringing' her hands and he's so overwhelmingly sorry for her that he moves towards her and takes her hands in his. 'You've already said sorry,' he says softly 'but what do you need?'

'I need you to hold me. I need someone to hold me and stay with me. Someone who won't leave before midnight in case the whole world turns into a pumpkin.' She looks up at him with such desperation in her eyes that he has to enfold her. His arms curve around her shivering body and he stands holding her and gently rocking, as though she's a child in need of protection. They stand for a long while like that till the shaking leaves her body. When she stops shivering, Stan whispers into her hair, 'Please can we sit down my left leg has gone to sleep.'

Sasha starts to laugh, 'I'm so sorry.'

'Will you stop apologising,' he says releasing her. As they sit on the edge of the bed, he adds, 'all this saying sorry must be a woman thing. Now, would you like a hot drink? I can see what there is next to the kettle but unfortunately there is no mini bar.'

'Is there a hot chocolate by any chance?' she asks, starting to shiver again.

Stan looks and finds one sachet. 'You're in luck.' He fills the kettle from the en-suite and turns it on then he comes back to her side. 'Come on, get into that bed,' he orders.

'Oooh Stanley,' she smiles sexily at him, 'you are so forceful.'

'Don't get any ideas I'm not getting in there with you,' he says. *Not that I wouldn't love to.* He carries on talking to hide his naughty thoughts, 'You're cold and need to get under the covers.' He plumps up the pillows behind her and pulls the duvet over her breasts that keep peeking at him from under the flimsy material of her nightie. By now the kettle is boiling, so, he goes to make her drink and gets a coffee for himself. When he brings them over to the bed, along with a small pack of biscuits he's found, she takes her mug and holds her hands round it to warm them. He sits on the side of the bed and opens the biscuits, 'Want one? They're ginger nuts.'

'Yes please.' Sasha takes one, dunks it into her chocolate and bites into its warm softness. 'Mm that's lovely. Thanks, Stanley you are wonderful. I feel cosseted.'

'Well just don't get any crumbs in the bed, if there is one thing, I can't stand it's a crumby…'

He gets no further for she plants a big kiss full on his lips; a kiss tasting of chocolate and spicy ginger. 'You are a sweet man,' she says in a husky voice.

Stan laughs, 'Not as sweet as you,' he licks his lips, 'that tasted very sweet.'

'Oh sorry,' she says wiping her mouth on the back of one hand.

'You're saying sorry again.' Stan drinks his coffee. 'And don't think of me as some kind of big teddy bear. I am a bear, but real bears can be dangerous.'

Sasha giggles, 'I just can't see you as dangerous.'

'Well, I am.' Stan wags a finger at her, 'You should be very careful for I'm a naughty man at times.'

She finishes her chocolate and hands him the empty mug. He takes the cups into the bathroom and washes them as best he can, when he returns, she's laid back on the pillows and he pulls the covers up to her chin. 'Now it's time you went to sleep, snuggle down.'

'Where are you going to sleep?'

'Next door in your bed. He goes towards the communicating door.

'Oh dear, I don't want to push you out of your bed,' Sasha says, throwing back the quilt and siting up.

'Well then you'll have to go back to your room but your bed will be cold.' He holds the door open for her but she doesn't move.

Instead, she pats the mattress next to her, 'If you get back in here with me it will be even warmer.'

Stan looks at her, his face showing real concern. 'Isn't your life complicated enough at the moment without muddying it any further?'

'Why should it muddy anything?' Sasha smiles, her eyes inviting. Stan sighs, he has so many conflicting thoughts running through his mind. He'd be mad not to make love to her when she is asking so sweetly but he feels responsible for her. It's her money that's paying him for being here, so, if he makes love to her then technically, she'd be paying for that, too. The notion puts him off somehow, and besides he told her mother he would look after her. He knows that was a false promise but… 'Are you going to stand deliberating all night?' she pats the bed again. 'Come on Stanley, I'm getting cold. You can just hold me if you like we don't have to do anything'

Oh, but we will. He climbs onto the bed next to her.

'Aren't you going to take off your dressing gown?' she says as she removes hers.

'For your information I don't wear anything in bed so I'm naked under this.'

'Well, I can be naked too if that helps,' she pulls the

flimsy nightdress up and over her head.'

Stan groans, 'I'd like to put it on record that I didn't think this was a good idea,' he says as he removes his dressing gown and climbs into the bed with her.

'Duly noted...' she giggles, 'Now hold me again just like before.' And he does. And she feels so good. Stan can't believe the thrill of her flesh against his chest. The touch of her hand on his back sends a shiver through him and when she kisses him it's electric. She responds to his every move; wherever he caresses her she flows under his fingers and when he finally enters her, the joy is indescribable. He moves, she moves, on and on like a dance, they turn and twist together sliding and slipping till finally she cries out and he allows his own crescendo. There's nothing to be said. They lie, like two stranded sea creatures clinging to each other as the tide ebbs. At last, she sleeps and Stan is able to slide himself onto his back and resume his contemplation of the ceiling. *What was that all about? I've never made love, or been made love to, with that intensity. Was it just the tension of the long day coupled with the whisky before bed? Was it my feelings of protection and concern that enhanced my longing for her?* Just before he slips into unconsciousness he realises, *and **she**'s paying **me** for a night like that!*

In the morning Sasha stirs and wakes Stan, 'Good morning, Mr Baker,' she says, kissing him slowly on the mouth. Stan wakes to this delightful sensation. 'How are we this morning?'

Stan rolls towards her. He's as hard as he's ever been. 'Can't you feel how I am?' he whispers as he reaches for her.

'Mr Baker, you are a naughty man,' she giggles. 'How much of the bear are you this morning?'

'If you don't want to find out you had better leave this

bed now, before it's too late.' He strokes her breasts and tweaks her nipples, snuffling her like an animal.'

'Oh, but I want to find out what you're really like when you're roused.'

'Well don't say you weren't warned.' He slips his hand between her thighs and strokes; his fingers slip inside her and she moans. When she begs him to, he climbs on top and the whole delightful dance begins again.

At the breakfast table they sit opposite each other. Stan eats hungrily, having ordered a full English, while Sasha nibbles at the continental buffet. 'You'll never put weight on eating that,' Stan laughs.

'That is the whole point, hopefully I won't.'

'You have a lovely body, if you don't mind me saying.' He leans forward and says quietly, 'I can give that opinion from personal experience.'

'Sasha sighs, 'Thank you Stanley, but I am afraid Phillip isn't of the same opinion. I need to watch my weight.'

'The man's an idiot.' Stan starts to feel very irritated by this overbearing dentist, and in a rash moment blurts out, 'He doesn't seem to value what he's got.'

'Stanley, please. This is none of your business.' Sasha pours herself another cup of coffee. 'You have to realise that I happen to love this man.'

'Does he love you?'

'Yes, he does.' She puts down her cup and looks at him sternly. 'What happened last night was very lovely and I enjoyed it immensely, but it doesn't alter what I feel for Pip.'

Stan has to admit he was hoping it might. He realises he's in danger of overstepping his remit. The thought sobers him very quickly, 'I apologise, Sasha, I was out of order.'

'That's OK. I do understand. But if I am to see you again, and I'd like to, then you have to accept that my situation is as it is.'

'Fair enough,' Stan's large plate of food no longer appeals. He pushes the plate away. 'I've had enough and if you're finished, shall we head back?'

'Yes, I think that would be best, I'll go and get my bags.' Sasha walks out of the restaurant looking cool and efficient and not at all like the lost child of the night before. *I'll never truly understand women.* Stan had been planning to take his time on the journey home and suggest stopping for lunch somewhere, but he realises that wouldn't be what the lady wants. *And **she** is paying the bill after all.*

Stan stands up straight and puts on a professional demeanour. From now on, this is what he'll have to do in many different circumstances, he realises.

Thirty-Six

The Watcher comes early today. I'm just taking my typewriter out of the airing cupboard when I hear small sharp sounds coming from downstairs. My heart begins to pound with a fear that Guy's returned unexpectedly. But when I hear it again, I realise it's the yapping of a small dog. I look over the bannisters into the animal's soft brown eyes, he seems so pleased to see me and his tail wags madly. I pick up the typewriter and run-down stairs, I'm excited to see him too. I stroke his soft fur, feel his little tongue lick my hand and think how lovely it would be to have a dog; a creature that would always be so eager for my company. The dog and I walk into the kitchen, where the Watcher sits in her usual chair. She smiles as I put the typewriter on the table, I get out his metal bowl and fill it with water. While he laps away, I fill the kettle. The Watcher and I sit opposite each other with mugs of tea and I look into her eyes. She has such kind eyes, but they look very tired. It's as though she's experienced too much; observed too often, and would welcome a break from watching the world.

She sips her tea and says, 'I'm not sure Stan is that happy.' I'm immediately concerned, 'Isn't he?' I think in my mind. 'No,' she shakes her head and wisps of grey hair escape from under her hat.' I look at her lined face. 'What can I do about it?' I silently ask. She shakes her head again. 'Just be aware and think kindly of him,' she says, her lips never moving. 'I always do,' I say.

❖

After dropping Sasha home, Stan returns to his flat. He's absolutely shattered and has just enough energy to fill the kettle before collapsing onto a kitchen chair. The hours of driving, the effort of pretence, the emotional rollercoaster of the previous night and this morning, have taken their toll. He makes coffee and takes it into the bedroom, strips off his clothes and can't even be bothered to hang up his suit. He sits on the edge of the bed, drinks his coffee and then lies back with a sigh. Pulling the duvet over his head, he shuts out the world and slips gratefully into unconsciousness.

He's awoken by the sharp ringing of the telephone. Cursing under his breath he climbs out of bed and staggers to the phone. 'Yes,' he barks down the receiver.

'Gosh Stan, are you in a foul mood?' Amy's voice enters his consciousness.

'Sorry Amy, I was asleep. How are you?' Stan perches stark naked on the arm of the settee.

'Better than you by the sound of it,' she laughs. 'I was going to ask how the wedding went.'

'Oh, good on the whole, though I have a couple of things I'd like to talk to you about.' He rubs his eyes with his free hand still feeling woozy.

'Shall I come over then? You can take me out to dinner, or we can get a take-away if you've removed your sore head by then.'

'Stan sighs, 'I'm not sure I'll be much company Amy, I'm a bit knackered.'

'Oh, but I have some news I have to discuss with you.' She is quiet for a bit then she says, 'Stanley, how about you go back to bed for a couple of hours and then have a shower and I'll be with you at eight with an Indian...or

Chinese if you prefer.'

'Alright, but can it be Chinese? Chicken something or other, not too spicy. I'll leave it to you. See you later then.' He stumbles back to bed, remembers to put his alarm on for two hours, and rolls back under the duvet.

Amy arrives on the dot of eight with the food and fortunately, Stan's managed to get himself up in time to tidy up and put a clean tablecloth over the faded Formica table. She puts the packs of food out on the table and then stands next to Stan waiting to be kissed. When he makes no move, she reaches up and pecks him on the cheek. 'Gosh you are in a way, aren't you? Here sit down and eat, I'll open a bottle of wine.' She bustles about his kitchen finding glasses, cork screw and a bottle of white Chablis. 'I'm guessing that playing a persona was more exhausting than you thought. Come on, tuck in,' she says as she puts more rice on his plate.

Stan takes a mouthful of sweet and sour chicken and realises how hungry he is. After a few more mouthfuls he begins to feel almost human, and grins across at Amy, 'This is the best thing you could have done for me. Thank you again.'

'Thanks for what?'

'Thanks for being there for me and getting me just what I required. You seem to have a knack for turning up just when I need you.' He picks up his glass of wine and takes a long drink, its sharp sweetness cuts through the remaining fog in his brain.

Amy smiles, 'You're welcome. Now tell me how the wedding was and did you bed Sasha?'

Stan nearly chokes on a piece of chicken. 'Err... there's nothing like being forthright!

'Well?' Amy says, looking him straight in the eye.

Stan can feel himself turning red, 'I may have done.'

'Stanley, you old goat, you really did, didn't you? How do you do it?'

'Well, I didn't do anything much, she sort of wanted it. That's one of the things I wanted to talk to you about. It seems I am giving those extra services I didn't intend to, while being paid for the time I'm spending with them, and it makes me feel weird. With Sasha and Maureen, I...'

'You've slept with Maureen?' Amy's fork hits her plate with a crash.

'Well... yes. You were right about her she's had a rather sad life and it was her birthday and...' Stan stops eating and doesn't quite know what else to say.

'OK, Stanley,' Amy puts her hand on his and squeezes it, 'There's nothing wrong in providing extras. It's like Eileen said, it's bound to happen sometimes. So, are you going to see these two ladies regularly?'

'I'm not sure. Sasha said she would definitely be in touch and Maureen wants me to make it a regular thing but she isn't fifty till next year. And I'm not convinced a regular basis is wise.'

'Hmm...is there anyone else?' Amy asks, she seems rather pensive.

'Well, there is something else I wanted to run past you.' Stan describes his meeting with Martina.

When he's finished Amy says nothing and they finish their food in silence. Stan's worried that she's thinking he's gone too far and he longs to hear her opinion on everything, but he respects her need for silence. They put the dishes in the sink and take the rest of the wine into the lounge, Stan puts on a 'Dire Straits' album but low volume, so it's not intrusive. Amy's so quiet he begins to get concerned. He sits next to her, puts an arm around her shoulders, and asks, 'What's the matter Amy? Is it something I've said?'

Amy smiles and squeezes his hand. 'No, Stanley, I've something to tell you and I don't know how to put it. I think I'm about to disappoint you.'

'How on earth can you do that? You're not pregnant, are you? You know when we did it au naturel. I thought it was unwise but…'

Amy laughs, 'No darling it's not that.'

'Phew!' Stan says with relief.

'Would you have minded very much if I was?'

Stan is stumped. He has to think for a moment. 'I'm not sure. I'm relieved you're not because I think we're too old to have a family. But on the other hand, I'd feel awfully proud of you and…' And suddenly Stan has to stop talking because there's a constriction in his throat. *Why am I being so emotional? I've never wanted children,. But if it happened, it seems I'd be pleased about it.*

Amy kisses him. 'It's alright Stan, it hasn't happened. What I have to say, is about these dancing classes I've started, twice a week. I've been asked to join an amateur dance troupe and that means going on stage at various local venues, like the Guildhall. But it means I'll have lots of rehearsals.' Amy takes a deep breath. 'It means I won't need you to escort me as often. I won't have the time and so, I won't be able to pay you as much. Not as much as I promised anyway.'

'Oh, is that all!' Stan hugs her. 'I thought you were about to give me the elbow. I thought I'd offended you by sleeping with all these women.'

'Oh Stanley, no. I'm pleased for you, though I expect you to be safe, of course. You're only allowed 'au naturel' with me, understood.'

'Understood Madam.' Putting his hands on her face, he turns her towards him, kissing her lips with his little kisses till her lips part. Stan asks urgently, 'Would Madam allow me that privilege now?' Amy stands up guiding his hands to her breasts as they go into the bedroom. 'I'm afraid the bed isn't made,' he says between kisses. 'It doesn't matter we'll mess it anyway,' she breathes, pulling off her skirt. She stops kissing him long enough to take her top off over her head, her breasts rise delightfully as she holds up her arms and Stan lifts them out of the flimsy lace bra and kisses her nipples. She puts her arms around his neck and presses her body against him, 'I need you to make my body sing,' she pleads, moving from him to the bed. She lies naked except for a silk thong. Stan struggles out of his trousers and kneeling by her places a kiss on that silk garment before slowly drawing it from between her legs. Every inch along the way he kisses the space it leaves uncovered.

Much later, as they lie side by side Amy becomes serious once more, 'Stan, I'm really sorry to drop you in it, financially speaking that is. I want to be sure you're going to manage. So, I'll pay half the usual amount for two months, and then drop it to one evening's escort a week after that.'

'Amy, you don't owe me anything. Both you and Eileen have done your best for me and now it is up to me to make a living. The thing that makes me really sad is that I shall only see you once a week, how shall I manage?'

Amy laughs. 'You'll have your work cut out to satisfy all these women who are lining up for your services.' Amy gets out of bed and reaches for Stan's dressing gown, 'I need to go to the bathroom be back in a bit.'

Stan lies on his back, *I mustn't let Amy feel bad that her life's moving on.* He tries to work out just how much he is going to have. *Eileen's still sending me £100 per month, mad woman. Amy'll pay me £400 per month, of which half may go in expenses. As long as I go on getting clients, I'll manage. I won't be able to afford a car, though. But the money from the wedding will help with living expenses and I'll have to hire vehicles when needed.* Stan's mind runs on, wondering what would have happened if Amy was pregnant. He imagines holding the small, warm bundle of his own child. He knows now, he wouldn't be a bitter parent. He couldn't be like the man who raised him. His biological father was totally unlike Reginald, and this makes all the difference to Stan. *I might have made an alright Dad;* he thinks with sadness. Amy comes bouncing back into the bed cuddling up to him for warmth, 'Stan I've been thinking, you should take Maureen on as a client. It'll add some regular income and then you should go and see this Martina again and see what she has in mind, at least for the short term.'

Stan struggles to extricate himself from his fantasy of fatherhood, and tries to focus on what Amy's saying. 'Alright, I'll think about it. But for now, can you give me a hug because you'll be going soon and I want as much of you as I can get.'

'It's alright Stan, I've drunk too much to drive so, I'll be here till the morning. You can have as much of me as you want till then.'

'What a bonus. Where shall I start? Toes first I reckon,' he teases, bending down and taking her big toe between his lips. Amy shrieks and nearly kicks him, but he doesn't give up.

Thirty-Seven

It's early in the morning, Guy's still in the shower, and suddenly Stan appears. I'm horrified to see him sitting on the edge of my bed, 'You can't be here yet,' I say to him in panic. 'Please disappear.' He turns to me and smiles sadly, places his head against my belly and tries to put his arms around me, but I back away as though I've been burnt. I can hear Guy turning off the shower, he'll be coming into the bedroom any second. 'You must go,' I hiss. 'Please go now.' I stop talking as the bathroom door opens. 'But come back later,' I say my mind as he walks away.

'Who are you talking to?' asks Guy as he enters towelling his hair. 'No-one,' I say as calmly as I can, but I feel myself shaking. 'You're not talking to yourself again, are you? We don't want any more of that madness do we,' he says as he comes up behind me and puts his hands on my breasts. 'I like having my little woman around all the time. I don't want you having to go away, even for a short time.' I try to laugh it off but his words fill me with fear; the fear that always lurks at the edge of my mind. If I see the hero of my story while Guy is in the room, then surely that will be madness.

Guy turns me round and lifts up my nightie, stroking the backs of my legs. 'You're going to be late.' I say urgently, trying to walk away, but he pulls me back. 'It won't take long.' I know I'm trapped. 'But what about the child?' He sits on the edge of the bed in the same place as Stanley sat. 'Come here and sit on me,' he says. 'Hold your nightie down at the front, and if she comes in, we'll say we're playing at bouncing you up and down. Which we are,' he says leering at me. 'There we are.' He holds me around the waist and lifts me up and down. I can feel his hardness thrusting deep inside and it hurts. I try to do it for him but he stops me and holds my hips pushing me down onto him. 'I've always fancied doing this in public,' he says. 'You could get a wide skirt in the summer and I could sit you on top of me like this and no one would know but us.' I try to relax and just let it happen but it's taking so long. I'm so scared the child will come in to see why her father is making all that noise.

After they've gone, I shower and when I feel clean again, I walk through the rooms calling out, but he doesn't return and I'm so sad. I get out my typewriter. But I sit in front of it for a long time before I begin to write.

Amy leaves first thing the next morning and Stan feels bereft. All his beautiful women seem to be abandoning him. The three lovely ladies who helped him feel alive, who helped create his new life, are moving on. He paces up and down his flat. The grey autumn day darkens the windows and he turns on the lights, but it doesn't help his mood. He stares out of his kitchen window and sees the Watcher walking to the backdoor of the block of flats opposite. She disappears inside but there's no sign of her little dog, *which is strange because I've never seen the one without the other.* He's distracted from his gloomy reverie, and when the Watcher doesn't reappear, he decides to put on his shoes and a jacket and go to see what's happening.

It's cold outside, and a sharp wind blows around the

corner of the flats. Stan turns up his collar and walks the narrow passage that winds between the tall, brick walls to the concrete back yard. There's no-one about, not even kids on bikes, which is odd. He turns into the yard and sees that the old pair of trousers have at last fallen from the line and are spread out on the damp pavement. *They're ruined now.* He picks them up to throw them away. As he approaches the bins at the rear of the flats, he hears a soft whimper. Stan stuffs the ruined garment into one of the bins, walks around the back of the others and sees the Watcher's little dog tied to one of them. The dog stops whimpering when he sees Stan and starts yelping. 'Hello boy,' he says softly, stooping to stroke the animal's head. 'What are you doing here?' The animal's lead is tied so high up on the bin that the poor dog can't sit. Stan releases the lead and the dog starts leaping about overjoyed to be freed. There's still no sign of the Watcher and Stan wonders what he should do. He decides to take the dog back to his flat and give it some water. From there he can keep an eye on the yard through his kitchen window.

Back in his kitchen he makes himself a sandwich and throws the crusts to the little animal, who swallows them as though he hasn't eaten for a week. Stan is just wondering whether to take the dog round to the Watcher's flat, when he sees her nosing around the bin area. He opens his window and calls but she doesn't hear so he whistles piercingly through the palms of his hands, something he hasn't done since he was a kid. The Watcher looks up, her face is drawn and worried, but she sees him, and he beckons her to come up. She leaves the yard at a shuffling run.

The Watcher is finding it hard to breathe and when Stan gets to her, she seems on the point of collapse. He helps her up the stairs and sits her down on the settee. 'Thanks,' she says between puffs.

'What's happened?' Stan asks her.

'I can't find Mutty… I've been over the whole estate.'

'It's alright, he's here,' says Stan patting the Watcher's frail hand. 'He's in the kitchen wolfing down half a tin of corned beef.' Stan goes to kitchen door, opens it and Mutty rushes out and jumps onto the settee next to the Watcher.

'Oh Mutty!' The Watcher is laughing and crying with relief, 'Where have you been? You naughty boy.'

'It's not his fault,' says Stan stroking the dog's head. 'I found him tied up behind the bins and his lead was pulled so tight he couldn't sit, poor animal.'

The Watcher looks really pale and Stan's worried about her. 'I'm going to get you some sweet tea and something stronger too, then when you've drunk it all, you can tell me what happened.' Stan brings in two small glasses of whisky and hands her one. 'Get that down you, the tea's nearly ready.'

'Oh, thank you, Stanley, I'm glad you found him. I was so worried.'

'Don't talk for the moment, just sip that and calm down, I'll get the tea.' When he returns the Watcher's looking better and her little dog is curled up beside her, his head in her lap, and his eyes close as she strokes him.

'I dropped the lead when we were out on our walk and he ran off before I could pick it up again,' she says. 'I called and called but he never came back which is very strange. Now I know why not. I went back home in case he'd gone there but nothing and then this note was stuffed through the letter box.' The Watcher shows Stan a screwed-up piece of paper:

'You'd better search the estate for your dog,
he's tied up somewhere.
Get to him before he needs to sleep.'

'I ran outside but couldn't see anyone. I went everywhere I could think of.' She ruffles the dog's coat with the back of her hand.

'Has anything like this happened before? asks Stan.

'Not to Mutty, no, but I've had a few notes stuffed through the letterbox. I don't usually take much notice.'

'What do they say?'

'Oh, I don't know, things like, "Keep your nose out you meddlesome old biddy" and "Stop poking your nose in or we'll cut it off."'

'Have you told the police?'

'The Police would probably agree with them. I've been told off for taking photos of parked vehicles before now.' says the Watcher, with a rueful smile.

'Why were you taking photos?' Stan is intrigued.

'Well, last summer things were going missing around the estate: hanging baskets, garden ornaments, tubs of flowers, that sort of thing. Also, I heard that drugs were being sold to school kids. The police couldn't catch them. On my evening walks I'd see vans waiting with engines running; several of them in different places, so I thought I'd take a few photos. A couple of people complained and a policeman came round to warn me off. I told him what I'd seen but he took no notice. I even saw people talking to the drivers, and passing packages and money. I managed to take a couple of shots of that. But then my camera was stolen.'

Stan was unsure what to say. He'd heard about drugs on the estate but nothing had ever come his way. 'I think you should be careful.' He stroked the dog's soft fur, 'We wouldn't want you or this little chap getting hurt. Obviously today, someone was intent on diverting your attention elsewhere in case you noticed something they didn't want you to.'

'I guess so,' says the Watcher. I'll try and stop. Trouble is I can't help noticing things.'

'The trouble is you've got a reputation for watching everything, so even if you stop looking you won't lose that.' says Stan with concern. 'Anyway, no harm done, this time, thankfully. You rest as long as you want and I'll walk you home when you're ready.'

After the Watcher has had another whisky and a little snooze, Stan escorts them back to their flat. In her kitchen Stan stays for another, 'wee dram' as the Watcher calls it, and she asks him, 'How's your business doing?'

Stan hesitates, not sure how much to tell her. 'It's doing alright, but I've lost a couple of friends. Eileen has gone travelling with her husband and now Amy is involved with a dance group and only needs escorting once a week, so…'

'So, earnings are down,' she finishes for him.

Stan nods gazing gloomily into his empty glass. 'I've had two new clients: Sasha, who wanted me to escort her to a wedding, which went well I think, and Maureen, who had me escort her out on her birthday.'

'Maureen. Do you mean your old boss?'

'Yeah, though she's not over 50 yet but I don't think I can afford to turn her down.'

'Stop staring at that empty glass Stanley, here let me top you up.' The Watcher pours him another generous measure.

'Thanks,' Stan takes a large sip letting the taste of peat and honey slide over his tongue. The warmth of it spreads through his body and he gives the Watcher a rueful smile, 'That's better,' he says. Then he decides asks to her about Martina. 'Have you heard of a Martina King around these parts?'

The Watcher frowns as she searches her memory. 'The name doesn't ring a bell,' she says. 'Have you got a photo? I can recognise any face I've seen, but I'm not so good with their names.'

'No, I don't. She's looks Eurasian. She's probably in her late forties; she's petite and attractive with black hair cut into a bob and she wears very smart clothes. If you saw her you wouldn't forget her.'

'Does she go to the Community Centre by any chance?'

'Yes, she rents a room there from time to time, to see clients, she says.'

'I've seen a woman around here that fits that description, she's often talking to young, good-looking guys, but I don't know who she is. What about her?'

Stan explains about their meeting. 'She seems to be interested in my Escort Agency, but I don't know why. She's a business acquaintance of Maureen's.'

'I'll try to find out a bit more if you like?' says the Watcher. 'Perhaps you should have another conversation and find out exactly what she's got in mind. You can't really afford to miss a good opportunity.'

'True,' Stan takes another sip of his drink, 'but there's something about her I don't like. I suppose I'll ring her sometime. Maureen says I should stay on the right side of her.'

'Well, you don't always have to like your business associates. I'll check her out, if I can.'

'Thanks, but don't get yourself into any more trouble over it.'

The Watcher gets up and moves stiffly around her kitchen. 'Sorry Stanley, but I need a rest, chasing after Mutty has wacked me out.'

'Of course,' Stan stands up and drains his glass. 'Sorry I kept you talking.' He pats the little dog's head, 'Glad I found you, little fellow. I'll be around tomorrow to see how you are and to replace that bottle. Take care.'

Stan walks slowly back through the blocks of shabby flats and wonders what on earth a woman like Martina would want with guys from an area like this. *Perhaps she's looking for individuals trying to escape this estate. Desperate people are more likely to take desperate measures. Am I desperate enough to take her up on her offer?'* As he reaches the stairs, he hears the telephone ringing. He runs up the last few steps, rushes into his flat, and picks up the phone, 'Over 50s Escort Agency can I help you.'

'Hi Stanley, its Maureen.'

'Hi, how are you?' Stan sits on the settee and tries to get his breath back.

'I'm fine, are you all right, you sound out of breath.'

'I just ran up the stairs; not that fit I'm afraid. How can I help?

'Oh, I was wondering. Are you free to escort me to the theatre next Thursday? Have you decided whether you can take me on your books under fifty?' Her voice sounds hopeful, as though she's crossing metaphorical fingers.

Oh, what the hell. 'When do you want me to pick you up?'

'Oh, that's such good news. Um… could you come to work like last time?'

'Certainly can. Do you want to eat first? Same place?'

'Oh, Stanley that would be lovely, thanks,' she sounds really happy. 'See you then.' She pauses and then says, 'Oh Stanley?'

'Yes?'

'Have you called Martina yet? She was asking after you. She says she apologises if she came over as rather forthright.'

'No, I haven't, though I was thinking about it.'

'You should, give her another chance. Anyway, look forward to seeing you Thursday, Ciao!'

Stan shakes his head as he replaces the receiver. Maureen's a strange lady but he seems to be what she wants and after all it is more money in the bank. He sits next to the phone and picks up Martina's card. He stares at it for some time trying to make up his mind. Then, he takes a deep breath and dials the number, a mobile number he realises.

Thirty-Eight

I try not to expect Stan to appear every day, because I get so disappointed if I don't see him. But this morning, as soon as I get home, I know he's here. I rush upstairs and go into the bedroom. He's sitting on my side of the bed; he turns and gives me a sad smile. I smile back and sit next to him. Gently I put my hand on his knee and he covers it with his large, warm hand. He strokes my wrist with his thumb. I move closer and lay my head on his shoulder. It's very quiet in the house. There's only the faint ticking of the clock and the sound of our breathing. He pushes my hair back from my forehead, gently cups my face in his hands and kisses me. Fire races through my blood. I'm weak at his touch. We lay back on the bed, he puts his arms around me and we cuddle. He strokes my body slowly: my breasts, my belly, and each place melts under his hands. I've never felt like this before, I desperately want him to make love to me. But he goes no further, just holds me and it's enough.

Now he's gone and I've put the typewriter on the table. I'm trying to capture what happened, but words are inadequate. I can't find a vocabulary sufficiently eloquent to describe what I felt.

He's done it. Stan's spoken to Martina and he's going to the Community Centre tomorrow morning to meet her and talk business. He paces the sitting room in agitation. He's just made a momentous change in his life and not necessarily for the better. But as yet, there's no commitment, he's only going for a discussion. Stan knows he'll probably capitulate out of necessity. He'll agree to whatever plan she puts forward because he's no other choice. There've been no calls, no enquiries about his Agency since Sasha booked her wedding, and she hasn't got back to him again. He can't live on escorting Amy once a week and Maureen's occasional theatre trips. So, what else can he do? He considers advertising on-line but he needs to assess the cost of setting up a website and that means paying someone to design it. To run this business properly he needs a car and a mobile phone, not to mention a decent place to live and entertain in. Stan sighs and pads into the kitchen to put on the kettle. He eyes the whisky bottle and is tempted, but he hears his mother's voice, 'Alcohol won't help you in the end.' So, he replaces it in the cupboard and goes to the biscuit tin instead.

After a sleepless night, Stan is up early, nerves are kicking in. He shaves, trimming his moustache and goatee to a neat length then gets into the shower and lets the hot water relax his muscles. He cleans his teeth, polishes his shoes, and considers what to wear. *Not the suit. A linen shirt and black jeans, perhaps,* Stan regards himself in the mirror. *I wish I could understand Martina's interest in me and my agency.* Stan checks the clock, *I need to be at the Community Centre before nine fifteen, it's still too early.* He puts on his leather jacket, transfers his keys and wallet into the pockets and sits on the edge of the settee waiting for the time to pass. *I bloody know I should cancel this appointment, but I can't afford to.* At exactly nine o'clock Stan opens the door and goes down stairs. The morning is cold but bright and the sunlight on the Autumn trees makes them glow against the blue sky. Stan takes a deep breath and watches steam waft as he breathes out. Zipping up his jacket against the cold he walks like a condemned man towards his appointment. At the Community Centre, the café isn't open yet but the lady's bustling about in the kitchen and steam's rising from several pans. She gives him a big cheery smile. 'Bit cold ducks. You should wear a scarf these mornings. You got an appointment?'

'Yes, with Martina.' Stan says.

'Oh her.' She makes a little shrug of her shoulders, 'Well she'll be down in a minute I expect. I'd take a seat if I were you.' And she returns to her bubbling pans and the chopping of vegetables.

Stan sits at one of the tables covered with blue and white checked tablecloths He'd forgotten how pleasant this place was. Getting his lunches here could really save him money. He tries to take deep breaths to calm his nerves; he's always hated waiting for appointments of any kind. He taps his fingers on the top of the table and is about to get up, when the door to the stairs opens and Martina walks up to him. 'Hello, Stanley,' she says, holding out her hand. He stands up and shakes it. 'Nice to see you again,' she says with the slightest of smiles. 'Please follow me.' Stan follows her up the stairs to the first floor. Despite his nervousness, he can't help noticing her shapely legs as she leads him into a large office. A big desk fills the space, there's an executive's chair behind it and two chairs in front. Stan takes one of these. Martina sits opposite him and for a moment nothing's said while study each other.

'Thanks for coming, Stanley. I'm aware how important this could be for you so I want to get straight to the point.' She puts her arms on the desk in front of her with her hands open, palms up and she leans towards him. 'I think you have a really brilliant business idea. I know the last time we met we got off on a wrong footing. I'd had a bad day and was too pushy, for that I apologise.' She gives Stan a smile, her scarlet lips curve upwards revealing a flash of perfect white teeth.

Stan's shaken by the sudden change; *did he get the wrong impression of her?* 'Well, yes,' he says, 'I felt you were rather invasive.'

Martina sits back in the black swivel chair and crosses her legs showing an enticing glimpse of thigh. She regards Stan for a moment. 'That's understandable, Stanley, and as I said I am reappraising how we might work together. I can certainly introduce several ladies to your Escort Agency for a modest one-off fee per client. How does that sound?'

Stan begins to relax slightly, 'How much of a modest fee?' he asks, wondering how much he should trust the eminently reasonable version of this woman.

'Well let's say fifty percent of your first night's takings, after that whatever you make through escorting them in the future is all yours. How does that sound?'

Stan uses Amy's silent treatment and slows the speed of his replies; he puts his fingers together and frowns a bit. 'Could we say forty percent, since I enclose expenses in my fees?'

Martina's lips twitch but she doesn't smile again, 'Very well I'll consider that.' She uncrosses her legs and leans forward. 'Can I be frank with you, Stanley?'

'Yes, of course.' Stan says wondering what's coming.

'You seem an unlikely candidate for an Escort Agency although I am reliably informed that you are a brilliant escort. My friend Maureen speaks very highly of you and that is praise indeed.' She pauses for a moment as though forming the next few sentences in her mind.

Why do I feel as though I'm at a job interview for my own business?

'If I am to help you, I will need you to smarten yourself up. I can get you cut price offers at a gym, a spa and a good class hairdresser, not to mention several men's clothing establishments that cater for the larger gentleman.' Martina looks dispassionately at him, 'Is that acceptable?'

'Yes, I want to lose weight, if it doesn't cost too much…'

'I'll make sure that it doesn't, Stanley. Now the other thing I need to mention is this age restriction on your Agency. Can that be altered to include say forty-year-old ladies?'

'No. I can only escort more mature ladies as these are the ones I can relate to, and I do seem to offer them what they're looking for.'

'But Stanley there are so many beautiful ladies out there, think of what you are missing.'

'Look Ms. King, if this is the drift of your ideas about my business then you're wasting your time. I only want to escort mature women. No young thing is going to want me to accompany them to the kind of venues they are likely to frequent.' Stan moves to the edge of his seat preparatory to getting up.

Martina regards him dispassionately and her lips tighten. She mutters something under her breath, but out loud she says, 'OK, Stanley, if that is the way you want it. It is your business after all.'

'Thank you for accepting that,' Stan says, feeling peeved and making a move to get up.

Martina holds up a hand. 'Come on, Stanley, don't think of going. I have to push to see where your boundaries lie. Alright?'

'OK.' Stan sits back in his chair somewhat mollified.

'Now, it's a pity because I was going to ask you if you would consider employing other gentlemen escorts, perhaps for the younger clients? No, don't get up, I've taken your opinions on board. It is just that I have a couple of lovely young men who are looking for just this kind of work, but I guess they can work with your older women.'

Stan is becoming increasingly irritated with this woman who just doesn't listen, however lovely she may look. 'Let me spell it out for the last time,' he says as firmly as he can. 'My agency is for the 'over 50s' and it's an 'Escort only' business. I don't wish to employ gigolos however lovely they may be.'

'Alright, Stanley, I understand. I think we should start with my referrals and then as you get acquainted with my methods perhaps, we can take things further. Shall we shake on that?'

Martina gets up gracefully and walks around the desk to stand in front of Stan, who stands up and mechanically takes her hand. He notices that she holds onto his hand for just a little longer than is necessary, and he becomes aware of her animal magnetism. There's a tingle of it under his fingertips. In spite of himself, he regards her in a new light. She flashes him another of her glorious smiles. 'Well done, Stanley, I'll get my associate to draw up a contract.'

Stan is shocked. 'What contract?'

'Oh, it is nothing to worry about. It will just mention the fee for the first date etc. It will only be a page or so for us to sign for our mutual benefit. You can read it all through before you sign.' Martina squeezes his arm reassuringly and he catches a whiff of her perfume, light and yet subtle, so unforgettable. She opens the door for him. 'Lovely to do business with you, Stanley. Come and see me next week, same time, and I will have a few referrals all ready for you.'

Outside, Stan's sensibilities return. He feels as if he's been asleep or mesmerized. He tries to remember what they've agreed. Surely there's nothing to worry about, if she's just going to provide him with a few ladies to escort. He goes to the supermarket and buys two bottles of whiskey and returns home past the Watcher's flat. He knocks on her door but she isn't in, so he leaves the carrier bag, with one of the bottles in it, on the doorstep behind a large flower pot. He scribbles a note and pushes it through her letterbox. Hopefully she won't be out for long.

As soon as Stan gets home the phone rings. 'Hello, The Over 50s…'

'Stanley, it's me, Maureen.'

'Oh. Hi.'

'I've just had a call from Martina, she's very excited. I wanted to congratulate you. I know your business will do well with her backing. See you. Ciao' Stan puts the phone down and wonders why the call has given him a bad feeling. Maureen and Martina are too close for his comfort, and he questions just how much Maureen tells Martina about their time together.

Thirty-Nine

My feelings for this man I've created are causing me a problem. Every time Guy reaches for me I find myself recoiling from his touch. I mustn't do this. If he senses my reluctance, he'll get cross. Fortunately, he's very busy with his new job but some evenings, before he goes to sleep, he still wants me to pleasure him. So far, I've been able to comply without shaking or showing signs of dismay. But he's noticed something. If I say I'm tired, he says, 'You're always tired these days, perhaps you should see the doctor.' I say, 'There's no need.' And I force myself to let him do what he wants with me.

When I return home this morning, Stan's sitting on my bed. I'm so pleased to see him. But he reaches for me in a different way as though he needs comfort. So, I hug him as I might a child and we sit in each other's arms for a long time. I rock him gently, as I used to rock myself when the emptiness closed in. When at last he seems better, I stop. He gets up to go and smiles at me; a sad smile, with love for me in his eyes.

After he's gone, I type all morning, creating his story. The feeling of being loved lingers and fills me with joy. At the end of the morning, I type a little note:

'I love you so.'

Should I leave it for him on the side of my bed tomorrow morning, after Guy's left for work? If he comes, he'll read it before I return and then at least he'll know.

When Stan wakes, he lies on his back looking at the light falling from the edge of his curtains; it's a grey light that comes with the shortening days at the start of winter. The thought of winter depresses him. *Nearly a week's passed and I haven't earned a thing, the phone's remained silent and except for my outing with Maureen, there's nothing in the diary. Amy doesn't want escorting for nearly a month,* he sighs, and rolls out of bed. In the bathroom he pours water into the basin and continues thinking. *I'm due to meet Martina, today, to sign a contract, and that's worrying. I'm seriously concerned that Martina, and the women she refers to me, will expect me to sell sex as well as escort services. But what can I do?*

Stan gets to the Community Centre early. The cold, raw November morning makes him turn up his jacket collar and twine his scarf around his neck, so, the contrasting warmth of the building is welcome. Unfortunately, his friendly cook has been replaced by a surly, older man, who merely nods at him. He sits on the edge of a chair and waits for Martina. When she finally arrives, she holds the door open for him to follow her. Up in her office, Stan sits once again opposite her but this time in front of him on the large desk are several sheets of paper.

'Right, Stanley, there is your gym membership,' she says as she pushes a slim folder towards him. 'It has your membership card and all the info about the place but also, I've included a session with a personal trainer, free of charge. What do you think?'

Stan takes the folder and looks quickly through it. 'Thanks, yes, I'll look into that.' He tries to smile and look enthusiastic.

'Good. The next thing is a list of half a dozen ladies who require your services. Their telephone numbers are next to their names. They've been told about your Agency and will be expecting a call from you. Do you have a mobile phone, Stanley?'

'No, sorry I...' Stan stammers.

'I thought not. Not a problem.' She opens the top draw of the desk, takes out a brand-new Nokia and hands it to him. 'I will lend you this one, it has a pay as you go Sim with ten pounds of credit on it, which you will have to top up when it runs out.' She gives him another slip of paper. 'This is your number. I suggest you add it to your advert and give it to all your ladies.'

'Thanks,' mutters Stan as he puts the strip of paper into his wallet.

'Right, now for the contract.' Martina picks up the last two sheets of paper and brings them around to Stan's chair and bends over to show him the document. Stan can smell her perfume, the light yet unforgettable fragrance of her. He looks up to see her black glossy hair fall across her face. She's dressed in skinny jeans and those high, black patent leather boots and her legs look shapely. He tries hard to not let her close proximity distract his concentration. 'You will see it mentions a forty percent one off charge for the first introductory appointment.' Martina continues in an efficient tone pointing at the relevant paragraph on the document, 'And then no further charges for future arrangements between you and that lady. However, I have stipulated that there should be a minimum uptake by you of four referrals a month, which of course I will guarantee to provide. I think that is reasonable, don't you? After that you can choose who you wish to retain on your books.'

'Err…' Stan tries to say something.

'Please do not interrupt, Stanley. You can mention any concerns you may have when I have finished. This agreement is to continue for one year, when the said contract can be reviewed, altered and renewed by mutual consent. But because it is all so new to you, Stanley, I have agreed a break clause in the first year after four months. The clause can only be invoked on that date and should either of the parties forget or be unavailable on that date, then the full year contract will remain in place. Should you refuse to pay the said percentage of the initial fee, then the contract will cease but you will be liable to compensate me to an equivalent sum of forty percent of your fee, four times per month, for the remainder of that year. I think that is only fair. In return I guarantee to provide you, for the first four months, with a mobile phone, gym membership and any help or advice you may need.' Martina beams one of her gracious smiles at him and says in a husky voice, 'Relax, Stanley. I assure you it is all quite straight forward.'

She takes the document back to her side of the desk, sits and signs her name at the bottom of the last page. Then she pushes the papers and the pen across to him for his decision and signature. 'Over to you, Stanley.'

Stan picks up the pen and looks through the typewritten pages. He can't see any problems but he still feels it's all a bad idea. Martina is tapping one exquisitely manicured nail on the table as he tries to consider his options, but he doesn't really have any. So, with his heart beating hard in his chest, he signs his name next to Martina's neat signature.

'Well done, Stanley, you will not regret it. Now any questions?' she asks as she gets up and moves towards the door.

Stan shakes his head. 'None that I can think of at the moment,' he says, being totally unable to recall what he was about to ask her when she stopped him. He smiles tentatively, 'just…'

'Yes Stanley?' her voice has a slight edge of impatience in it.

'What if these ladies don't want my services when I call them?'

'In that highly unlikely scenario, I will send you further introductions. OK?' Martina opens the door for Stanley to leave. 'Just one last thing Stanley, your address.'

'Yes,' Stan asks, 'what about it?'

'It is rather unfortunate. With the guarantee of a regular income, I would suggest that you talk to Maureen about putting your flat on the market and buying something in a more salubrious location? Failing that I have several high-class apartments for rent in Gloucester Docks; you could become a tenant of mine. Think about it, Stanley. Goodbye.' She shakes his hand and flashes her teeth once more as she dismisses him.

Outside, Stan tries to remember what he's signed and realises she hasn't offered him a copy of the contract. He considers going back but feels such an idiot. He should have asked for one. *What was the date of the break clause? I think it was it in March?* He decides he'll request a copy of the document when he pays her his first percentage fee at the end of the month. He walks slowly wondering when he should ring this list of names. It feels a bit awkward; a bit like cold calling, even though they'll know about him. He's walking with his head down and doesn't see the Watcher coming towards him on the other side of the road.

She calls across to him. 'Morning, Stanley, are you OK?'

He looks up, sees her and crosses over to pat her dog.

'Sorry I was miles away.'

'I could see that,' she says smiling. 'Time for a quick glass? I got your bottle by the way, many thanks, much appreciated and it's my favourite brand.'

'Well, that was lucky. It's a bit early for me, but I could do with a coffee. If that's alright?' On the way back to her flat he tells her about the contract with Martina.

In the Watcher's warm kitchen with a hot mug of coffee in his hand he begins to feel a bit better about everything. 'Did you find out anything about Martina?' He asks her, while she cuts generous slices of cake that she made yesterday.

'A little. She seems to be getting involved with several things around here: property management for example; she has invested in a new development of 2 and 3 bed houses on Berkley fields.'

'What that scrubby bit of ground near the by-pass?'

'Yep, and also, I hear she's the one to contact if you need a short-term loan. Evidently, she'll even lend to youngsters who are unemployed.'

'Why would she want to do that?' Stan thinks out loud.

'Exactly!' The Watcher brings over the sliced cake and two plates. 'They say she gets them to pay her back by getting them to do stuff for her, but when I ask "such as?" they all clam up on me.' She hands Stan a slice.

'Thanks,' says Stan. 'This looks delicious.' He takes a great bite and eats hungrily, talking with his mouth full. 'But you haven't heard she's done anything illegal?'

'No Stanley, I haven't.'

'Well, that's a relief anyway.' Stan finishes his cake,

'Want some more?' The Watcher asks him smiling.

'No thanks, I'd better not, I'm supposed to be losing weight and getting trim. I'll ring these ladies tonight, and hopefully I'll get some clients. If I haven't enough clients on my books by March, I'll use the break clause and get out.'

'Good idea.' The Watcher clears away the plates and gives her dog a small piece of cake, making him beg for it.

Stan laughs at the trick then asks seriously, 'Have there been any other attempts to steal him?'

'No thankfully. I don't know what that was all about but you might be right, it stopped me noticing anything else.' The Watcher gives Stan a piercing look. 'Are you going to put the flat up for sale then, Stanley?'

'I'll certainly think about it. I suppose it depends on what I can get for it and what I can buy with that money.'

The Watcher picks up her little dog and it regards him with bright excited eyes. 'We'll miss you, when you do go,' she says. Stan reluctantly leaves her cosy flat and walks out into the freezing foggy day.

That evening Stan sits by his phone, places Martina's list in front of him and taking a deep breath, dials the first number. The phone rings several times and then an answer machine cuts in: 'Sorry Laurie and Vanessa are otherwise engaged and can't come to the phone please leave a message and we'll get back to you.' Stan decides not to leave a message for Vanessa, not knowing what her relationship with Laurie is. He writes Ans. Ph. on the list by the side of her name. Try again. He punches in the next number and crosses his fingers while it rings and rings. He's just about to replace the receiver when it's answered by a breathless female voice. 'Hi Brenda here, who's calling?' Stan stutters a bit, 'Hello, err... It's Stanley Baker, from the Over 50s Escort Agency, I think Martina King will have mentioned me to you?'

'Oh hello. Yes, she did mention you, but I'm suited for this week. Could you call again next week and I'll see how I am?' The voice is less breathless but still rather hoarse for a woman. Stan attempts to sound professional and not disappointed. 'Of course, I can, Brenda, or I can give you my mobile number and you can call me if you prefer.' There's a rustling sound on the line, 'No, I'm a bit tied up at the moment,' she says, as someone giggles, Stan doesn't think its Brenda. 'OK, I'll call next week,' he says, but she hangs up before he can finish. Stan sighs, puts the phone down and goes into the kitchen to make coffee. This is turning out to be more difficult than he'd imagined. Carrying a large whiskey back to the phone as well as the coffee, he tries number three. This time the phone is answered immediately and before Stan can say anything a woman's voice says, in an urgent whisper, 'Is that you, Jack?' 'No, my name is Stanley, Stanley Baker.' Stan starts to explain but she interrupts. 'Sorry, thought you were someone else. Who did you say you were?' The woman's voice is still low not much more than a whisper. Stan tries again, '...from the Over 50s Escort Agency. Martina King said she'd told you about me.' 'Oh yeah, she did, but look I'm waiting for a call. Rather urgent, so if you don't mind. Call me again sometime? Bye.'

Stan looks at the list, three names left. *This doesn't bode well,* He takes a large slurp of whiskey as panic starts to build. *How on Earth am I to pay Martina if I can't actually find anyone to escort? Oh well, she'll just have to get me some more names, I suppose.* He tries the fourth name. *Annabelle, a pretty name,* The phone rings twice, and is then answered by a soft cultured voice, 'Hello.'

'Oh hello, my name is Stanley,' once again Stan is interrupted but this time successfully. 'Oh, hello Stanley, you must be the guy from the Escort Agency, yes?' 'That's right,' says Stan with relief. 'I guess Martina has mentioned me?' 'Too right she has and with such glowing credentials I can't wait to make your acquaintance.' The last few words are uttered with a definite sexual drawl. Stan swallows hard. 'So, when and where would you like me to escort you?'

'Oh, darling you are so quaint! Well, you can find me here at my flat and we'll decide from there shall we?' Stan can hear her flicking the pages of what he guesses is a diary. 'Let's see,' she drawls, 'how about Thursday?'

Sod it, that's when I'm seeing Maureen. 'I'm sorry,' he says. 'I'm already booked that day.'

'Ooh, in demand are we. Oh well, how about Friday, say eight o'clock?'

'That's fine and your address?' Annabelle gives him her address and coos her goodbye. Stan takes another mouthful of whisky but this time as a toast to success. Before he can make another, call the phone rings, he answers and at first can hear nothing but breathing, 'Hello? Who is it?'

'Stanley, sorry, I was about to hang up,' says a small soft voice he could barely recognise.

'Sasha? Is that you?' Stan is sure it is, but he hasn't heard from her since the day after the wedding.

Sasha sighs. 'Oh, Stanley, I could do with your help.'

'Sasha, what's the matter?' Stan's now very concerned.

'Heard any good fireworks lately?' she asks.

'Well, yes a few. Oh, of course, it's November 5th, your Birthday. Happy Birthday.' He's pleased with himself for remembering.

'Yes, it is, only, it's not a very happy one.' There's the sound of her blowing her nose and snuffling.

'Sasha, are you crying?'

'Have been. Oh Stan, never become a mistress.' She gives a small laugh.

'I'll try and remember that,' says Stan feeling sudden sympathy for her. 'Do you need to talk?'

'Yes, I do. Are you busy this evening?'

'No, I have nothing on.'

'Really!' she laughs louder.

Stan laughs with her, 'I am glad you can still crack the jokes. But how can I help?'

'Can I book you to escort me out for my Birthday treat?'

'I'd be honoured to escort such a lovely lady,' Stan's spirits start to rise. 'Where are we going and where shall I pick you up?'

After replacing the phone, Stan is left with conflicting emotions. He's sorry for her situation and cross with the lover who keeps letting her down. But he's also happy to hear from her again. Then he immediately feels a heel. *Sasha's distraught, and I'm just pleased she's picked my shoulder to cry on. I mustn't criticize her man, and I mustn't expect to be more than a friend for this evening.* Even so he leaves his flat happier than he has been all week, and he completely forgets to phone the last two names on Martina's list.

Forty

I feel so silly. When I get home this morning, Stan hasn't appeared and my note is exactly where I put it. I just hope he didn't come early, sit there, read it and then go. Tearing the note into tiny pieces, I throw it in the bin. What a stupid fool. To do something like that's a frightful risk. Guy might have come home unexpectedly?

I bring the typewriter down to the kitchen, switch on the kettle and sit waiting for it to boil. Once again, it's hard to find words. I make coffee and drink it while staring at the blank white sheet of paper in the machine. I type, 'Chapter 40' and then nothing. I know where the story's going. Well, more or less, and that's why I can't write it. There's a resistance. Part of me has no desire to cross this next threshold, and neither, I think, does Stanley. I pace around the kitchen. Outside the day is grey and gloomy, in keeping with my mood. I'm deeply sad for my hero. Whatever I write will inevitably change things for him and for me. I sit with my hands resting on the keys, waiting, but it's useless. When I look up the Watcher is sitting opposite me with her dog on her lap. I smile at her and she says words that sound in my mind, 'Don't give up!'

I say, 'I won't, but I'm stuck.'

'You'll manage.' I hear her say and then she's gone. A long time later, I begin to type, sporadically, painfully. It's like pulling tiny pieces of skin from my fingers, but I struggle on.

❖

Sasha's waiting when Stan pulls up in his hired car. She's wearing a fitted, black coat and high heels and as he opens the passenger door for her to climb in, he sees that the dress under the coat is red, short, and shows her legs to perfection. He feels a sharp sting of desire; she looks fabulous and he tells her so. She smiles, giving him a kiss on the cheek.

Stan's bought her a white orchid plant which delights her. 'Oh, that is so sweet of you, how did you know I love them?'

'I guessed.' he says as he drives off.

They go to an early showing of 'The Sixth Sense' and afterwards to a small Italian restaurant where Stan has booked a table. Sasha is impressed with the venue. A pianist is playing a baby grand in one corner of the large room and every table is lit by flickering candles. 'This is lovely, Stanley. You have a knack of knowing how to please me.'

'I'm glad I get it right,' Stan says and looks into her eyes but he sees with concern that they are filling with tears. He hands her a freshly laundered handkerchief.

'Oh,' she sniffs, 'you are such a gallant man. I do love you.'

Stan tries not to take her meaning literally but it thrills him to hear her say those words. He reaches out and puts a hand on hers. Outside the window there are intermittent flashes of light and several explosions. The deep throated detonations sound more like a military attack, only the blue and green stars show that the blasts are fireworks. Sasha dabs at her eyes then puts the handkerchief in her lap and squeezes his hand. 'Phillip couldn't be with me tonight. He intended to take me out, but when he came at lunch time to bring my present, his wife phoned him on his mobile and said his daughter was ill, and would he get back early. I heard her voice, Stanley, she was very correct, almost clipped. I wonder if she knows about us.' Sasha stops talking as the waiter arrives. They give their order, and she continues, 'I also wonder if their daughter is really that ill, or whether his wife uses this as an excuse to call him back. I rarely get to see him in the evenings now. Usually, he comes in the afternoon. He's even cancelled patients on occasions, just to make sure we get some time together. I try to be understanding and our love making is as wonderful as ever, but when it comes to special occasions like this, it's hard not to complain.'

'I can't imagine how you cope with the situation. It must be very difficult for everyone,' Stan says the words as gently as he can. Sasha bends her head. 'Yes, it is. I have to accept that,' she sniffs and looks up at him. 'But I've decided, I don't have to remain at home like some overgrown wallflower if he can't be with me. So, if you are in agreement, I'd like to book your services once a month and we can do this kind of thing again. In the summer, perhaps we can go to the coast for the day. What do you say?'

'I'd be delighted to take you wherever you wish to go, Sasha,' Stan says. He stands up, and asks, 'By the way, what's your favourite song?'

'I don't know. Um... 'Smoke Gets in Your Eyes' is a lovely one.' Stan walks over to the piano and whispers something to the pianist and when he returns to the table Sasha asks, 'What are you up to Mr Baker?'

'Wait and see. Would you like a desert?' Stan hands her the menu.

'No, just a coffee and perhaps a Baileys?'

Stan calls the waiter. As their drinks arrive, the pianist starts to play Sasha's song. She's delighted and gives him a chaste kiss on his lips.

Much later, when they reach her house, Sasha gives him a long and lingering kiss on the mouth. Stan puts his arms around her and starts to draw her to him but she stops him. 'I've had the most wonderful evening but I'm tired now and need to go to bed,' she says. 'On my own.'

Stan tries to cover his disappointment. 'Of course, Sasha, I understand,' he says as he watches her open her front door. She stands for a moment, a silhouette against the hall light, before the door closes.

Stan's about to drive away when he feels a vibration against his leg. It makes him jump. He fishes in his pocket and brings out the mobile phone that he'd completely forgotten about. He presses the button and hesitantly speaks. 'Yes. The Over 50s Escort Agency how can I help?'

'I thought you were supposed to ring me,' the voice sounds peevish. 'Martina said you were desperate for work but it doesn't seem that way or you'd have rung wouldn't you.' 'I'm sorry, says Stan. Who is this?' 'Tina, Tina Carson, you were supposed to call me, I'm on your list.' The woman sounds querulous.

'Oh, I'm so sorry. I'm out working at the moment; can I call you back?' Stan tries to remember the last two names on the list.

'On the job are we,' the woman gives a raucous laugh. 'Nice to know you're in demand,' she snorts. 'Look it's urgent, I need you to come here Saturday afternoon, my hubby will be out at the races so we won't be disturbed.'

Stan's stomach churns. 'Wouldn't you rather go out somewhere?' he suggests hopefully.

'No way. Quite out of the question. I can't be **seen** with you. Will three o'clock, do you?' Stan hesitates, but without waiting for his reply she says, 'I'll expect you then.' and hangs up.

Stan drives home feeling totally deflated. *It's begun, work any day of the week, and what work!* he shudders at the thought of what it might be. *There's nothing I can do; my lovely women have deserted me and I need to make money to live.* The first steps have been taken and now he has to follow through, if he doesn't, he'll owe Martina a whole load of money he can't afford to pay.

He parks the car outside his block and slowly walks up to his shabby flat, which looks cold and unwelcoming. He picks up the post from the hall carpet and goes into the kitchen, turning on the light. The sink is full of washing up. The water is brown and globules of fat have congealed on its surface. As he tips the water away, there's a smell of rancid oil. He fills the kettle, opens the cupboard and restores the whisky to its normal place on the work top. He pours himself a generous measure. Taking it into the sitting room, he sits on the sagging sofa, remembering how he felt after his mother's funeral. *Perhaps it isn't that easy to get over depression,* he stares out of the window at the sulphur glow of the street lamps and listens to the roar of motorbikes as they race around the estate. *What I need more than anything else, is to get out of here. That's why I'm doing this after all. I'll talk to Maureen tomorrow,* he decides. *I'll go into the office before it closes and put the flat on the market. Then maybe I'll ask Martina about renting one of her apartments in the Docks.* 'Yes, that's what I'll do.' he says out loud to himself, as he gets up and pulls the curtains, checking on the hire car that he hopes won't be vandalised before the morning. He finishes his whisky and lets its warmth run through him. Kicking off his shoes, he turns on the TV and falls asleep to the sound of canned laughter on a comedy show.

Next morning, he uncurls himself painfully from the settee, turns off the TV, and gropes his way into the bathroom. After a very hot shower, he feels almost human. He dresses and attacks the filthy kitchen. Then he rings Maureen's work number.

'Stanley!' Maureen's voice is full of her joy at hearing from him.

He takes a deep breath and plunges in, 'Hi, Maureen. This is a business call, actually. I need your professional services. I want to sell my flat.'

'Oh right,' her voice immediately turns business-like. 'I'm glad you've chosen us to sell it for you. 'We'll have to do a valuation but I'm sure it won't be difficult to sell.' He can hear her turning the pages of the diary, 'I'm afraid we're rather busy at present. Just a minute, Stanley.' He can hear her getting up to close her office door, when she returns, she asks in a quiet voice, 'Do you intend buying anything?'

'I thought I might rent for a while.'

'Oh, a good idea, that way there'll be no chain, which is always a help. 'Right, Stanley, how about I come and measure up this afternoon before we go out?' Her voice comes over the phone softly, 'I could get there around five thirty and go through everything with you and then we can go out afterwards. What do you say? Otherwise, I can't manage anything for at least a couple of weeks and that's getting a little near Christmas.'

Stan agrees. 'We could eat here if you like before the theatre.'

'Good idea!' Maureen sounds really enthusiastic. 'I'll see you then. Ciao darling.'

Forty-One

I've very little time to write this morning as Guy's only working half a day. He's coming home early and we're going Christmas shopping after we collect the child from school. This is a problem for me on three fronts: firstly, I won't be able to write, secondly, he'll probably want sex before we leave, and thirdly, I'll have to go out into the crowds of shoppers. I find it hard to explain my panic when surrounded by so many people. I guess it's a kind of claustrophobia but with the added anxiety that I'm semi-naked while everyone else is fully clothed. I know it's silly to imagine that everyone is looking at me; why would a mouse of a woman draw that kind of attention? One of my counsellors called it 'paranoia' but that doesn't describe the terror that hits me as I am dragged into the swirl of a crowd. All those eyes swivelling towards me and focusing on me, seeking out my deepest secrets.

If I could stay here in the arms of my love, I'd be safe. He could lead me out by the hand because he wouldn't push or stress me. I might manage all sorts of things with him. I need to continue his story. I catch hold of the words as they start to flood through me.

Stan becomes aware of a heavy perfume as he struggles out of sleep. He opens his eyes and for a moment can't remember where on earth he is. Looking at the pillow next to him he sees Maureen's face, and memory returns. His head aches, his mouth feels like a sewer and he has a desperate need to pee. Rolling himself out of the soft bed, he gropes his way to Maureen's en-suite and fumbles for the light switch. Light ricochets from the white tiles, from glass, and from the chrome fittings. He keeps his eyes closed as he pees but when he's finished, he glances into the mirror and groans. There are deep bags under his eyes. *Too much whisky.* He regards his reflection while waiting for the water to run really cold, then he cups his hands and sluices his face several times. Gradually, his brain breaks through the fog; he returns to the bedroom where Maureen is waking up. She searches for her watch, while swearing softly, 'Hell, what time is it?' She finds it under the pillow, 'Shit, its seven o'clock. Sorry Stanley I have to rush.' Climbing out of bed, she gives him a quick peck on the cheek, 'Turn the kettle on for me, please,' she says as she heads for the bathroom.

Stan dresses and goes down to her kitchen. All the walls in Maureen's house are white and Stan finds himself longing for a soft pastel shade that's easier on the eyes first thing in the morning. He makes coffee, takes his black and strong and sips the scalding liquid gratefully. Then he returns to her bedroom and puts Maureen's coffee on her dressing table. She comes from the shower wrapped in an enormous towel, her hair dark with water, and Stan thinks how young she looks like that. Going up to her he kisses her damp mouth. She kisses him back then breaks away. 'Sorry darling, I just have no time left. I'll be round sometime soon to take those photos of your flat and then we'll put it straight on the market. OK?'

'OK. Thanks, Maureen, see you soon then.'

But Maureen has disappeared into the bathroom again

and shut the door. Stan picks up his keys and goes out to the car.

Back in his flat he takes a shower, changes into jeans and a sweatshirt and gets himself some breakfast. He runs through Martina's list of ladies and ticks off Tina Carson, so the only one left is Amina Patel. Checking his watch, he sees it's nine thirty, should he try and call now or leave it for a bit? Getting out his diary, he writes 4 hours, next to Sasha's name on Wednesday, puts in 10 hours, next to Maureen's name yesterday, and writes Annabelle's name at eight o'clock in today's page, and Tina's name in on Saturday at three.

At least that's a bit of an improvement, and I still have one more to call to make. He dials the number. It rings several times and he's just about to give up when a woman answers, Stan introduces himself.

'Yes, I did get your name from Martina. I have to admit I've never hired an escort before.' Her voice is soft, melodious and hesitant.

'Well, what would you like me to do for you Amina?' Stan prompts. 'Do you wish to go out for a meal for instance?'

'Yes... Yes, that would be nice,' she sounds relieved. 'Shall we say Monday at seven?'

'Perfect, I look forward to it,' he says, also relieved. 'Just give me your address and I'll pick you up.'

Stan writes her name and address in his diary. *Hopefully, with this lady, I might be in control of the situation again.*

At six o'clock he starts to get ready. He shaves and trims his beard and moustache then moisturises his face. *Who'd have thought, a year ago, I'd be doing all this beautifying.* After a light meal of salad and ham, he polishes his shoes, cleans his teeth and puts on a fresh shirt and his suit. He stands in front of the mirror, pulling in his stomach and studying himself, *I really must start that gym, I don't I look too bad though,* and picking up his keys, he turns out the lights and shuts the door. With a queasy sensation in his gut, Stan walks to the car.

Annabelle's ground floor flat is in a large square near the centre of Gloucester. One of the few squares of Georgian town houses left in the area. He climbs the worn stone steps to the wide door and finds three intercom buttons. He presses the lowest one and Annabelle's voice answers. Stan introduces himself and the door buzzes and releases the catch. The hallway is wide and imposing with a curved staircase, but before Stan has a chance to look at the architecture, the door on his right is flung open by a tall, graceful woman in her early fifties. She's dressed in a long coffee coloured dressing gown. 'Come in, please,' she says and she turns and walks ahead of him into a beautiful sitting room. Stan's taken by its generous dimensions: the high ceiling retains its original plaster coving and the wide bay has heavy taffeta drapes in a pale green. The room is carpeted in a rich cream and the large leather sofas are the same colour. On the walls are several Art Deco prints. A Cotswold stone fireplace takes a large part of one wall, with a gilt Georgian clock on the mantelpiece, set between two bronze candle sticks. Stan's glad he decided to wear the suit, anything else would feel out of place in this grandeur. Annabelle comes towards him, the silk of her gown moves across her body seductively, 'Please sit down, Stanley, what would you like to drink?'

'Err... it depends if you want me to drive you anywhere?' he says hopefully.

Annabelle smiles at him, 'I'm not really dressed for going places. Besides we have everything we could want right here.' She gives him a mincing twirl showing her cleavage.

Stan's last vain hope dies, 'I'll have a whisky then, please?'

'Blend or single malt?'

'Oh, single malt, please,' he replies, thankful for the choice.

'Man, after my own heart,' she says going over to a tray of drinks on a sideboard and pouring two generous measures. She sits on the sofa and hands him his drink. She lifts her glass, clinks it against his and takes a generous gulp.

Stan watches her. She's a handsome woman, not beautiful in the conventional sense, but graceful and her thick brown hair is shiny with only a fine sprinkling of grey, and when she looks at him her eyes are large and a warm brown. 'Your flat is very beautiful,' he says, then looking at the painting before him he asks, 'Is that an original?'

'Yes, done by a friend of mine, lovely isn't it. I'm not a purist, I choose paintings because they enhance the décor and not just for themselves. I've been told that is a heinous crime but I don't care.' She takes a long look at Stan as she finishes her drink. 'If you don't mind me saying, you are a trifle more rotund than I was expecting.'

Stan nearly chokes on his drink, 'I guess you're into plain speaking then.'

She laughs throwing back her head. 'Glad you're not offended. Yes, I always call a spade a shit shovel. You'll do fine.'

'I'm glad about that.' Stan finishes his drink in one and lets the heat of the whisky relax him. 'And what will I do for?'

Annabelle puts her face next to his, 'Seduction,' she breathes into his ear, leaning forward and taking the glass out of his hand.

Stan feels the blood rush into his face. He tries not to be embarrassed, but he's not used to being seduced by a woman straight off, with no preamble and no chance of getting to know one another. Stan freezes as he feels her hands on his body under his jacket. It's all he can do to stop himself pushing her away. 'I need to take off my jacket first,' he mutters.

'Good idea, it's hot in here. Take off whatever you need to.' She gets up, and lights the candles on the mantelpiece then turns off the lights. 'Would you like some music?'

'Yes. OK. Good idea. What have you got?' Stan says, trying to buy time, as he takes off his jacket, loosens his tie a little and undoes the top button of his shirt. *God, I feel so hot!*

'I like jazz,' Annabelle speaks in a husky voice, 'but for now I think something a bit softer. I have an album of "in the mood music" that always turns me on.' She puts the music on low volume, returns to the sofa and unties her gown to reveal a low-cut Basque which pushes up her breasts to perfection. She leans over Stan's lap and traces a finger across his goatee. 'That will feel delicious on my skin when you kiss me all over.'

Stan gulps. His mouth is totally dry as he tries to kiss her with a reasonable approximation of passion. But he's forced to extricate himself from her arms, *it's like wrestling with a giant octopus,* he thinks desperately. 'I'm sorry Annabelle,' he says with sweat running down his face, 'but I do need the bathroom.'

'Of course, Stanley. I'm sorry for not suggesting that before we got started. It's through there and so is the bedroom. I'll be on the bed when you're ready, we might as well be comfortable.' She gives him a kiss, and he stumbles to the door on shaky knees, goes into the bathroom and locks the door behind him.

The bathroom is large and luxurious with a shower and a bath and large mirrors everywhere. Stan uses the loo and then washes his hands and splashes cool water on his face. He leaves the water running into the basin as he stares at himself in one of the mirrors, *Christ, what am I going to do? Can I say I'm suddenly ill? But then I won't get paid and I need to pay Martina. No, I'll just have to go through with it.* He swallows hard trying to quell the rising revulsion for the woman and the situation. *She's not unattractive, and she deserves a good time for her money, poor woman. But can I give her what she thinks she's paying for?* Stan knows enough about seduction to make it as pleasurable as he can. *Hopefully, I'll be able to finish inside her, but if I can't at least she should be somewhat satisfied by then.* He takes a deep breath, turns off the taps and opens the door.

'In here, Stanley,' she calls, her voice low and sexy.

Suppressing a shudder, he follows the sound of her voice and finds her lying on a wide bed in a room festooned with fairy lights. They're draped over mirrors and picture frames, twined round twigs in vases and wound round the brass rails of her bedstead. The overall effect is more like a fairground than a boudoir, but that's the least of Stan's concerns. He sits on the bed by her side. She's taken off the dressing gown and is just in the Basque, and a pair of thin panties. He leans over and kisses her face with his little quick kisses but she grabs him around the neck and pulls him on to her, kissing him full on the mouth. She starts to undo his shirt and then his trousers, and he has to push her away because he doesn't want her to know he's not yet erect. Desperately he thrusts her back on the bed and tells her, 'Lie still.' while he's wondering what to do next. Sensing that she likes this, he decides to direct her. He instructs her to close her eyes, while he struggles out of his trousers, pants and socks. When he's naked, he lies down but orders her to keep her arms by her side; because he can't stand the thought of her hands all over his naked body. He starts to kiss her breasts more forcefully than he usually would, he releases them from the Basque and bites the nipples. She starts to moan and writhe and begs him to let her use her arms. He answers, 'No.' She complies. Then he pulls down the flimsy knickers, over her legs and finally her feet. This makes her beg again to move her arms, and once again he refuses to let her.

Stan's beginning to see how he might get through this situation. This is not the play of the sensuous that he loves to have with his women. However, it does have an erotic element and she's obviously enjoying it. He leans his heavy body on top of her and she sighs, he bites her neck and her breasts and she moans. He hesitates for a moment, then taking a deep breath, he slides his hand between her thighs and upwards till he feels how very aroused she is. For the first time in his life this wetness disgusts him. He has to force himself on, moving his fingers rhythmically till her body tenses, he continues till she starts to breathe fast, until her hips begin to grind beneath him. Still, he holds her down with his weight till she's crying out for him to do something, to come into her. He stops for a moment, which seems to drive her wild. Telling her not to move, he feels himself and is relieved to find that he's erect. Putting on a condom as quickly as his shaking hands will let him, he returns to her side. Raising her hips, he drives into her, hard. She shrieks and moans as he thrusts. Stan does not come. When he's sure she is satisfied, he stops.

He covers her up with the bedspread and goes to the bathroom. He throws away the condom. Washing the frightful moisture off his hands, he soaps his fingers several times. When he returns to the bedroom, he's relieved to find Annabelle is lying there asleep. Stan has no wish to disturb her. Dressing as quickly and as quietly as possible, he grabs his jacket from the sitting room and leaves.

In the car he breathes deeply. He looks at the clock. Nine thirty! He was only there for one and a half hours. It seemed like forever. He'll charge for two hours but it won't pay well. Stan drives home and when he gets into his flat, he starts to shake uncontrollably. Going straight into the kitchen, he reaches for the whisky. *Am I beginning to rely on this stuff?*. *Oh, to hell with it,* and he pours himself a very generous measure before stripping off and climbing into the shower.

Sleep comes to Stan in brief snatches. He drifts through dreams of naked bodies and feelings of loss and disappointment. When he finally wakes, he relives the night before over and over again. He tries to come to terms with the horror of it. Tries to dupe himself into thinking of it as offering a service, fulfilling a need. But, however he wraps it up, he knows the naked truth; he's now a male prostitute and Martina is, for all intents and purposes, his pimp. He gets out of bed, showers again and makes himself a sandwich. Then gets ready to do it all over again with another, unknown female.

Forty-Two

It's been a very long weekend and I've been desperate to get back to Stanley's story. The shopping trip was hell. Gus was so impatient with me. I don't know why we have to shop so many weeks before Christmas anyway. The child got over excited and we nearly lost her in the crowds, which of course was my fault. When we got home, he was shouting and banging about the house. This went on all weekend except when he wanted sex on Sunday morning. Unfortunately, by that time I really couldn't face it with him and that started him off again. In the end I gave in and stayed in bed with him for another hour, till he was satisfied.

I'm sitting in front of my typewriter waiting for the echoes of that horrible time to die away. I so need to see my love this morning, just to have his arms around me and know he understands. Guy calls me cold and frigid. But now, I know I'm not. It can be so different with a man that gives me time to respond; a man I love. Guy wants instant gratification and gets so cross if I don't deliver.

The Watcher hasn't appeared. I recall her words the last time I saw her, *'Don't give up.'* I won't give up because writing is all that's keeping me sane. Well, I think it is. Either that or it's sending me totally mad. I find it hard to tell the difference.

Tina Carson's house is on a new estate just outside the City of Gloucester. It's small but neat and detached. Stan decides to park his car in a side street in case of nosey neighbours and at exactly three o'clock he rings her door bell. The woman who opens the door to him is short and plump with red hair, that he is sure is out of a bottle. She gives him a quick smile, 'Stanley?' she checks. When he nods, she pulls him inside and furtively looks out of the door to check no one's watching. He stands in the tiny hallway waiting to be directed. 'Oh, come through,' she says leading him into a tiny sitting room where there's only room for two small settees, a coffee table and TV. She sits on one of the settees and her short black skirt rides half way up her chunky thighs. *Thank goodness she's wearing thick black tights.* Tina pats the cushion beside her, 'Have a seat, don't be shy.' Stan sits. 'Would you like something to drink?' she adds.

'Yes, that would be nice. Coffee, please?' Stan says. *At least, coffee should take longer to make, and drink.*

'Right you are. Won't be a tick, make yourself comfy. There're some magazines in the rack that you might be interested in; might help you, if you know what I mean. They always help my Hubby when I'm being demanding.' Tina laughs and leaves the room.

God, can I really go through this again?

He riffles through the magazines and realises they're soft porn. In fact, two or three are not all that soft. One in particular has photos of a very lovely woman with big breasts and 'come to bed' eyes. He's intrigued in spite of himself, though he's more attracted by her face than her ample bosom. Hearing Tina rattling cups, he hastily replaces the magazine. Stan doesn't have time to turn the pages back to the beginning. Tina comes in with a small tray. 'Coffee and biscuits,' she laughs, 'We've got to keep your strength up.' She puts the tray on the coffee table and sees the disturbed magazine rack. 'Been having a butcher's, have you? That girl with the big boobs turns my hubby on something rotten. Thank goodness.'

'Err... I'm guessing you don't want me to escort you out anywhere?' Stan asks, all hope dying.

'Ooh no, Stanley, it would never do to be seen out. There are so many nosey parkers around here you wouldn't believe. We'll just have a cosy chat here. There's no rush. John, my hubby, won't be back before seven o'clock at the earliest.' Tina chatters on, just as she might at a church jumble sale. Her ample bust is squashed into a tight black jumper with a V neck that shows off her cleavage. Her hair is pulled back in a high pony tail and her face wears a slightly surprised expression; eyes wide open, almost innocent. 'See that picture next to the telly? That's me and John about four years ago on our fiftieth birthdays. We had a big party. Our birthdays are both on the same day. Isn't that strange? That's how we met actually. We were both in the same pub celebrating with our friends. Didn't know each other from Adam. But when John heard them singing "Happy Birthday", he came over and asked who was the birthday girl? Then he bought me a drink. I thought him cute. And the rest is history.' Tina giggles like a school girl.

Stan tries to get a word in. 'How do you know Martina?'

'Oh, she helped my boy get a mortgage after he got married.' *So, mortgages are another business strategy for Martina.* Tina drinks her coffee and continues between gulps, 'I was talking to her one day and mentioned that I occasionally liked a bit of spice in my sex life. She told me about you and your agency. I said that sounds just up my street.' She puts her cup down on the tray, 'And here we are.' She smiles at him. 'Now, you finish your coffee and the magazine if you like, while I'll go and slip into something more alluring.'

Stan drains his cup and paces around the little square of carpet between the settees. *This is going to be more difficult than last night. She's about as sexy as a camel, poor woman. Even her husband has to read porn before he can get interested.* But when Tina comes back into the room, she looks quite different. Her red hair is down round her face and shoulders and she's wearing a green, silk wrap which shows her skin to perfection. Her eyes are large and her face flushed. Stan finds that as long as Tina doesn't say anything, he can appreciate her need to be sexy. He thinks he can deal with that. She comes up to him and lifts her head to kiss him. 'What should we do now?' she asks giggling a bit.

Stan sits her down and takes her hands. 'You look lovely,' he says. 'Now, will you do just what I ask you?'

Tina's eyes widen. She opens her mouth to speak, but Stan puts his finger on her lips. 'No. That is the first request. Don't talk. OK? Just nod your head.' Tina, nods her head several times. All the while keeping her eyes on his face. She looks slightly scared. 'Good.' says Stan. 'Now, I'm not meaning anything kinky or dangerous, but will you leave everything to me?' She nods again but her breath comes quickly and her pupils grow large and dark. 'Right, show me your bedroom.'

She turns and leads him back into the tiny hall and up the stairs. 'Our...' she starts to say.

'Shh! Quiet.' Stan puts a finger on his lips. 'Whichever room you want us to use?'

She smiles and looks relieved. They go into the spare bedroom. There he tells her to lay down on the bed and not to move till he comes back. She nods and he goes into the family bathroom to wash his hands. Stan begins to shake at the memory of the previous night. *However, this time, I know how to control the situation. Dominance appears to work.* He looks at his reflection in the mirror, *'You managed it last night, so, you can bloody do it again for this poor soul.* Stan walks back to the bedroom. He slowly undresses himself and then undoes her wrap. He presses his warm body against hers, kissing her face. When her hands come up to hold him, he tells her to keep them by her side, which she does. Then he proceeds to stroke her. Tina starts to moan in her throat as he pinches her nipples. He strokes her stomach and moves his hand down. Tina begins to pant and roll her head from side to side. 'Please,' she murmurs. 'Shh! Quiet, remember?' he says holding his hand over her mouth. 'I'm in control.'

Once again when he needs to, Stan's relieved to have an erection of sorts. He manages to put on a condom. Then he pushes into her. Gritting his teeth, he continues till he feels she's satisfied. He doesn't climax.

In the bathroom he removes the condom and washes his hands over and over. But they don't feel clean. This time, he's brought his clothes into the bathroom and so he dresses quickly. Tina is downstairs, her wrap tightly closed around her body. She looks flushed and almost pretty. She gives him a hug and a kiss, before handing him an envelope.

'I usually invoice clients,' he says, reluctant to take the cold cash.

'But you can't invoice me with John around. I'd rather do it this way.' She pushes the envelope towards him insistently, 'I think it's the right amount.'

'I'm sure it is,' he says taking it and stuffing it straight into the inside pocket of his jacket. Stan finds the whole transaction so distasteful. Tina stands in front of him in the tiny hallway, her big eyes look into his. 'Thank you,' she says in a small voice. After opening the front door just wide enough for him to squeeze through, Tina shuts it quickly behind him. Stan walks down the road towards his car. He's convinced he sees several curtains twitch as he drives away.

Back in his flat Stan takes out the envelope and puts it on the kitchen table. He makes coffee, pours a glass of single malt, and then sits looking at the envelope. This taking money for sex is abhorrent. This isn't what he wants his business to turn into. Bloody Martina. She was supposed to be introducing him to women who wanted escorting. Not sending him to service frustrated old cows. *It isn't even cost effective, all I get is around eighty pounds and I have to hire a car to do it. Then I have to give Martina forty percent of it, so I'm selling myself for around twenty pounds an hour. Just like any street whore. How sordid is that?* Stan downs the whiskey in one and momentarily feels better. *On top of everything else, it will probably drive me to drink.*

At last, he has the nerve to take out the cash from the envelope and count it. Tina has given him a hundred pounds and he was only there just over an hour. Stan suddenly feels mean. Mean in every sense of the word. After all, none of this is the fault of these women. In different circumstances he'd probably find some kind of connection with them. If he did, he might make love to them, not just have sex with them. This is a concept he's always hated. *I'll have to confront Martina, and tell her she's nothing but a female pimp...* But he knows he won't.

Stan takes the bottle of whisky and his glass into the sitting room. He turns on the lights and as it is dark already, he pulls the curtains. He sits on the settee, turns on the TV with the remote and starts some serious drinking. He wakes several hours later feeling cold and stiff. The empty whisky bottle is on the floor beside him. His head is pounding and he can't remember why he's drunk so much. Stan struggles off the sofa and into the kitchen for a glass of water. Drinking it, he suddenly feels worse and rushes to the loo to be sick. He collapses onto his bed and pulls the duvet over himself trying to get warm. That's when his memory returns. The events of the last two days replay in lurid detail. Coiling himself into a foetal position, he starts to rock. Just like he used to as boy, when Reg beat him. Stan continues rocking till, sleep takes over.

The constant ringing of the phone pulls Stan out of his deep sleep. He rolls off the bed and stumbles into the sitting room to answer it. 'Hi Stanley. It's Maureen. Are you there?'

Stan tries to lick his lips but his mouth is so dry he can hardly speak. 'Hi… err… Hang on a moment.' He goes to the kitchen, pours a glass of water and drinks thirstily, then goes back and picks up the phone.

'Stanley are you alright? Maureen says sounding concerned.

'Yes, just a bit hung over.'

'Oh right, a goodnight, was it?' she laughs.

'No. It was a bloody awful one.' Stan sits down on the sofa.

'Oh dear. Do you want to talk about it?'

'Not really.'

'I was calling to see if I could come over and take the photos of your flat, it'd save time but are you up to doing that?'

Stan sighs. 'Yeah, why not. Can you give me a couple of hours to get the place tidy?'

'OK, I'll be over about mid-day. Ciao darling.'

Over the next hour Stan makes himself several cups of black coffee which he drinks, sitting at the kitchen table staring at the painted gloss walls. *Why would anyone want to buy this God forsaken place?* He decides not to say anything to Maureen about his predicament, not yet anyway.

Maureen arrives with camera and lunch. Sitting on the settee, Stan frowns at the carrier bag she offers him. But she says, 'I know what it's like Stanley and I know food is the last thing you'll think of, but it's what you need. Trust me.' She gives him a kiss on the lips and slips into the kitchen. She makes fresh coffee and they sit at the kitchen table and eat. Surprisingly Stan is hungry, and he wolfs down his sandwich. Maureen laughs as she watches him. 'I guess you're not going to tell me what this binge was all about?' Stan shakes his head and so she carries on, 'Well, I'll talk about your flat then. I'll need an outside photo and perhaps two interior ones.' She looks around the kitchen and frowns, 'Can I look around?'

'Go ahead,' says Stan, 'But I'll be surprised if you can find two areas you can use.'

She pops her head round the kitchen door, 'I don't suppose you intend to upgrade the kitchen or bathroom, do you?'

'Definitely not.' Stan is honest. 'There's no money to do that.'

'Shame, that always adds value to a property.' Maureen disappears again then comes back for her camera which she's left on the table. 'I've found two shots; one in the sitting room showing the wide window and the other your office which looks more modern than the rest.' When she's finished, she comes back into the kitchen. Stan is sitting with his head in his hands. Putting her arm around his shoulders, she gives him a hug. 'How about I make us another coffee and you tell Auntie Maureen all about it?'

Stan sighs and rubs his face with his hands, 'I'm not sure I can tell you.'

Maureen brings the hot steaming mugs over to the table and fetches a packet of biscuits which she puts in front of him. 'Just start at the beginning,' she says sitting down. When Stan's managed to tell her as much as his disgust and embarrassment will allow, Maureen sits quietly for a while. 'So, these introductions that Martina has given you are not women who want escorting at all?'

Stan shakes his head. 'No. Apart from anything else, Maureen, it doesn't pay me enough. I'd have to do two or three visits a day… God forbid.' He lifts his head and looks at her, 'I just can't do it, Maureen!'

She puts her hand on his. 'I can see that Stanley and you shouldn't have to. I'll go and talk to Martina.'

'But what can you say? I signed a contract with her!'

'You signed a contract as an Escort Agency not as a gigolo. I'll talk business to her; she's bound to see how much more money she can make by introducing a more select clientele.' Maureen gets up and picks up her camera. 'Leave it with me and I'll see what I can do.' She bends down and gives him a kiss. 'Don't see me out, but cheer up a bit, eh? Ciao.'

Forty-Three

When I return from the school, I instantly know Stan is in the house. I can't find him upstairs, so, I collect my typewriter and take it to the kitchen. As I open the door. I see him sitting in my seat, opposite the Watcher as though they're having a conversation. This scenario shocks me. The realisation that they might communicate when I'm not around, freaks me out. I set the machine down between them. Time seems to stop, though I still hear the clock ticking. I breathe. But I don't know what to say. They're silent too. Only the little dog snuffles as he licks toast crumbs from my kitchen floor. I get him a bowl of water and while he's drinking, I sit down between these two characters of mine. Plucking up courage I say, 'Would you like me to leave you alone so you can go on talking?' They smile and shake their heads. Then the Watcher says, 'Stan was just explaining his predicament.'

I suppose, his predicament is down to me. However, not many writers have to explain themselves to their characters. I feel weird. The world of my imagination is colliding with reality. 'I'm sorry,' I say, but I...' words fail me. 'I think I need to go and lie down.' I get up in a hurry, ignore the little dog who is trying to get me to notice him, and rush upstairs to my room. I lie on the bed, head spinning.

The peace in the room slowly relaxes me. I drift into a light sleep. Someone is stroking my face. I open my eyes to see Stanley smiling down at me. 'Sorry,' he says as he bends to kiss me. I put my arms around his neck and he lies beside me. We kiss and the world shifts as he makes love to me. He's so gentle and I am tender, my flesh molten under his touch. When he enters me, a small part of my mind tells me this is impossible. But reality is extinguished as he moves, and I am impelled to move with him. Afterwards, we lie side by side. I drift in and out of sleep. When he finally turns away, the feeling of separation is sharp. He sits up and kisses me.

Then he's gone.

Monday dawns cold and grey. Stan crawls out from under his duvet. *Today,* he decides, *I won't drink any whisky as it's becoming a habit.* He can't be bothered to shower, so he dresses and goes for a walk around the estate. There's a powdering of frost on the grass, the icy air chills his lungs and makes him cough. He stops, winds his scarf across his mouth and walks on, head down, gazing at the pavement. When he finally raises his head, he realises he's walked into an unfamiliar part of the estate, an area behind the Community Centre. He looks around him at the rows of tiny terraced houses, and then he sees her, right at the end of the road near some traffic lights. There's no doubt about it, it's Martina. Stan moves behind a couple of scrubby bushes and watches. She's wearing a faux fur coat with the collar turned up and those same high shiny boots. A large, black saloon is parked half on the pavement and she's talking to the driver. The man is gesticulating, possibly shouting. Martina holds up her hand and he stops. She says something then stamps her foot on the pavement. The man throws something away on to the grass verge, gets back in the car and drives off revving the engine in anger. Martina shrugs her shoulders and turns towards the Community Centre. Stan watches her go into the building. Without thinking, he walks up to the kerb where the black car was parked and there, in the frosted grass, is a small piece of screwed up paper. It isn't covered with frost so Stan's sure it must be what the young man threw away. He looks around to see if anyone's watching and then picks it up and puts it into his pocket. *What kind of shady deals is Martina involved in? More to the point, what the hell have I done signing any kind of contract with the woman?* Stan heads for home feeling trapped and scared at the turn of events in his life. *All I want is to be with my three fabulous women; Linda, Eileen and Amy.* He avoids thinking too much about Linda but wonders, *What's Amy been doing recently? Every time I try to call, I get her answerphone.* When he reaches the corner of his street, he sees a white van pulling away from his block of flats. As he gets closer, he sees that a Payntons 'For Sale' board has just been erected outside the entrance of his block. His flat is now officially on the market. Soon, people will be trouping through his living room looking critically at his home. He stands and looks at the sign, torn between the desire to escape this estate and a need to keep contact with his past and the memories of his mother.

'Hello, Stanley.' The voice pulls him out of his reverie and he turns to see the Watcher walking up to him. She stands with him to gaze at the sign as well. 'So, you're really moving.'

'So, it seems,' Stan replies.

'Where will you go?' she asks, bending to pick up her little dog, 'Out of Gloucester?'

Stan turns to her, 'I'm not sure, I might be renting to begin with anyway.'

'We'll miss you, won't we Mutty?' The little animal looks at Stan with its brown liquid eyes.

'I've not gone yet,' Stan laughs, 'I'll walk you both home. I'll come and visit when I can.'

'I hope you do,' smiles the Watcher, and then she looks serious. 'Are you thinking of renting from Martina by any chance?'

'I was thinking of it. Why?'

'Hmm,' the Watcher frowns, 'I haven't been able to find any direct evidence of illegal activity with Martina's businesses. But people round here don't like her or trust her. She seems to sniff out people's weaknesses. Then plays on them in order to get people to do what she wants. Just be careful and don't rely on her too much.' The Watcher puts her hand on Stan's arm and gives it a squeeze. 'Have you time for a drink?'

'A coffee would be good,' he says, 'But nothing stronger, I've been imbibing a bit too much lately.'

Stan sits at the Watcher's kitchen table, while she makes coffee for them both. *For all its shabbiness, there's something homely about this flat.* He studies the photos on the wall. He can see pictures of parked vans, some of them parked in the streets behind the Community Centre. He's just about to turn back to the table and his coffee when he sees a picture of a car that looks familiar; a large black saloon.

'When did you take this photo?' he asks the Watcher, unpinning it from the wall and handing it to her.

'That's one of the last pictures I took last summer before my camera was stolen.' The Watcher thinks for a moment, 'I'm pretty sure I had a few more shots of that vehicle but they must have been taken on the new roll of film that was in the camera at the time. Why?'

'I'm pretty sure I saw this car pulled up behind the

Community centre. Martina was having a tiff with the driver.' Stan suddenly remembers the piece of paper. He fishes into his pocket and pulls it out. 'The driver threw this out of the window in anger,' says Stan. 'After he'd gone I picked it up.'

'What is it?' asks the Watcher.

'Not sure.' Stan uncrumples it, 'It looks like some kind of a ticket.'

'The Watcher looks over his shoulder, 'Looks like a pawn ticket. Don't expect you've ever seen one of those?'

'No, I haven't. Are there any pawn shops left?'

'There's one in the City Centre, you'd think it was a second-hand jeweller, but it pawns watches and things,' says the Watcher, taking the ticket to look closer at it. 'But why would you pawn something and then throw the ticket away?'

Stan thinks for a moment then says, 'I just wonder if… What's the date on the ticket?'

'I can hardly read it but it looks like July 1998.'

'Might they pawn things like cameras?' asks Stan.

'You mean it might be…'

'It might be your camera,' Stan finishes her sentence.

The Watcher looks at Stan for a few moments her eyes wide with shock. 'Surely that's not possible, is it?'

'Only one way to find out,' laughs Stan. 'Of course, if it is you'll have to pay whatever they gave for it. Do you want me to go and see what it is?'

'No, Stanley. Thanks all the same, you've got more than enough to get on with. If I can keep the ticket, I'll go when I'm next in town.'

'Of course, says Stan, 'but let me know how you get on. Now, I better get going. I'll come and see you before I finally leave.'

As soon as he enters his flat, the phone rings and when he answers it, he hears Amy's cheerful voice. His mood lifts immediately, 'Amy it's so good to hear you. How are you? I've missed you.'

'I've missed you too Stanley. Are you free tonight?'

Stan groans, 'I'm sorry Amy I've a job on tonight,'

'Business looking up then?' she sounds a little disappointed.

'You could say that,' Stan says feeling desperate. 'Can you see me tomorrow? Please say you can, I'm longing to see you.'

'Yes Stanley, we can make it tomorrow. Come and pick me up early, say around six?'

'I'll be there,' Stan grins, 'and I can't wait, I've so much to tell you.'

'Me too. See you then darling.'

Amy's husky voice makes his skin tingle and as he puts the phone down, he realises he has a massive erection. He walks with some difficulty into the kitchen and smiles to himself as he makes breakfast. The aromas of coffee and toast make him realise how hungry he is. So, he has four slices of toast, and breaks open a new pot of marmalade to celebrate. *Sod the diet, the truth is that this girth doesn't seem to be causing me too much trouble with the ladies.* Stan spreads the butter thick, watching it melt into the hot toasted bread. Then feeling better about things, Stan has a shower and rings Maureen.

'Stanley, how's things?' she asks. 'Just to let you know, I spoke to Martina and she is going to look into finding you a more up market clientele. She says if you rent one of her apartments, she'll certainly be able to do that for you, as you'll be able to entertain there.'

'Oh, that is a relief, so as soon as we manage to sell this

flat, I'll certainly consider it.' Stan really feels that things might be looking up.

'Oh, darling, I don't think you should wait for that. Martina suggests you move as soon as possible.'

'Oh, really?' Stan hesitates, feeling rushed. 'But why the hurry?'

'Well, she has one apartment available at the moment but she can't just keep it for you, at least, not for long or she'll be losing money on it. If you take it as soon as possible then she'll let it to you at a discount until you've sold the flat. Besides it means you can give your property a good old make over which will help to sell it for the best price.' Maureen pauses, 'Stanley?'

Stan feels very unsure. 'It's just a bit quick,' he says, the Watcher's words about Martina are still in his mind.

'Well, I'll be covering your sale and Martina's rental so we can keep things simple. I tell you what why don't I take you over to see it; say tomorrow afternoon?'

'I can't make tomorrow, sorry.' Stan is now feeling very rushed.

'OK, let's say Wednesday morning, then we can go on somewhere for lunch, what do you say to that?' Her voice is soft but persuasive. 'I've Wednesday afternoon off this week so we could make a day of it if you like.'

'Stan shrugs. 'Alright. Yes, let's do that. But Maureen, I'm worried I can't afford to rent it, until I sell this flat.'

'We'll discuss it all on Wednesday,' she laughs. 'Now I really must dash. Ciao darling!'

Forty-Four

Now I have two men: one who wants my body for his own desire, and one who wants to give me pleasure. I've never known anything so wonderful as my lover inside me; both of us dissolved into one.

But this knowledge of how love should be, has made my life much more difficult. When Guy takes my body with his rough hands, pummelling my flesh and owning my body, I want to strike him down. In those moments I could plunge a knife into his heart for the way he treats me, even though I understand he knows no better. I lay there and tell myself that it'll only last a short time. I think of the days to come, when Guy leaves the house to me and my typewriter. To when the Watcher sits at my table with her dog, or my lover appears in my bedroom and makes love to me. Those are the moments I keep to myself. They are the magic that keeps me sane. I've a life Guy knows nothing about. I've tricked him. I'm not the simpleton he thinks I am.

But, living this secret life makes me tired. I have to remember not to say anything that might reveal it. This makes me tense and when I'm stressed, I get clumsy and Guy gets impatient. I'm also scared that my two lives are blending into each other. I mustn't see Stanley while Guy is here. It's too disorientating.

I record these words like a kind of diary every day before I continue the story. They clear my mind. Today no one comes and I'm glad. It freaked me out to see my two characters talking together. It's as though they exist without me.

Stan spends the rest of the day watching mind-numbing daytime TV. This is so he doesn't have to think about the evening to come. When the six o'clock news starts, he suddenly remembers he's got to meet the new client, Amina, at seven. He turns off the TV and rushes to get ready. He hopes this evening will be one where he can get to know the lady, make connections, laugh with her and relax. Stan has kept the hire car over the weekend, despite being worried about the cost.

As he climbs into the driver's seat, he thinks, *my first purchase after I sell the flat, will be a good reliable car.* He drives to the address that Amina has given him and for some reason, he is reassured to see she lives in a street of 1930's semi-detached houses. Pulling up outside her house, he sees the lace curtain in the bay move. A few seconds later the front door opens and a diminutive figure steps out dressed in a dark shapeless coat that shows nothing of her figure. She waves her hand uncertainly and turns to lock the door before walking towards the car. Stan holds the door open for her. 'Hello,' she says as she climbs in. 'I'm Amina.' Her voice is light, trembles a bit and her smile is nervous.

'I guessed,' Stan laughs, 'Unless you've ordered a taxi and I'm at the wrong address. I'm Stanley, but feel free to call me Stan.'

Amina gives a little giggle but sits stiffly in the seat, her bag on her lap, her coat wrapped tight around her. She stares straight ahead as Stan drives towards the centre of

Gloucester. Stan's not sure how to behave. He tries light conversation but she merely nods her head or gives a yes or no answer.

'Are you happy with Italian food, or would you prefer Indian cuisine?' he asks. 'I've booked a table at a little Italian Restaurant I know.'

'Italian is fine,' breathes Amina

'Are you sure?' Stan asks anxiously. 'We can always choose somewhere else. It's early and a Monday evening, so we should get in anywhere you like'

'No, it's fine.' Amina grasps her bag tighter, the knuckles of her fingers showing pale in the dim light.

Stan is stumped. When they pull up at some traffic lights, he places one warm hand on top of her cold, tightly clasped fingers and says softly, 'Relax Amina, I'm not going to eat you.' She gives a nervous laugh but she doesn't pull away from his touch and when he moves his hand back to the gear stick, she puts her bag on the floor of the car and strokes her coat with her hands.

At the restaurant the waiter shows them to their table and waits to take her coat. Amina stands awkwardly, obviously unsure what to do. 'I should give him your coat,' Stan prompts gently. 'You'll be rather warm otherwise.'

She gives him a weak smile and takes off her coat. Underneath she is wearing a straight grey skirt and a grey jumper; her long black hair is streaked with grey and is pulled back from her face, clasped by a gold slide at the back of her head. Her deep olive skin is dusky around her eyes. As far as he can tell she wears no make-up, except perhaps a touch of mascara. Her eyes, when she finally looks at him, are a warm, dark brown and their expression appears kind but confused by life. Stan calls for the wine list straight away and chooses a Pinot Grigio, thinking that perhaps with a little wine Amina may relax enough to talk to him. He carries on an inane conversation till the wine arrives and then he pours her a large glass which she drinks quite quickly. They order their meal and while they wait Stan tries again. 'Tell me about yourself, Amina.'

She sits holding her wine glass and shrugs her thin shoulders, 'I'm not sure there's much to tell.' She looks up at him, 'I'm not good at making polite conversation, I'm afraid.'

Stan smiles, 'Well let's make impolite conversation then.'

Amina laughs, her first real laugh and her cheeks darken, the wine is doing its job. 'You are funny,' she says looking at him over the rim of her glass as she sips more wine. She giggles again.

Stan takes the glass from her fingers and places it back on the table, 'I should go careful on that till our food arrives. Do you drink much?'

'No, I do have wine on special occasions, you know birthdays and christenings.'

'Do you go to many christenings?'

She giggles again, 'More than you might imagine. I have two brothers and two sisters and they all have families.'

'So, Auntie Amina, what else do you do with your time?' Stan asks kindly.

Amina looks at Stan, and seems to consider him for the first time. 'Thank you,' she says simply. Stan raises an eyebrow and she smiles, 'For putting me at my ease. She picks up the wine glass again and sips at the cool wine. 'This helps too,' she grins. 'Well, what can I tell you?' she sits back in her chair. 'There's nothing very interesting. I've looked after my aged parents for many years. My father died five years ago and my mother survived for another four years. She died last summer.'

'I'm sorry,' he says. 'My mother died earlier this year and I looked after her for many years, so I can empathise with what you're feeling.'

Amina looks at him in surprise. 'It never occurred to me that someone who runs your kind of business would have any idea of my kind of life.'

'Well, that's the fascinating thing about people,' Stan says. 'You can never tell what their lives are like from the face they show to the world.' Stan leans over and puts his hand on Amina's arm, 'But you do have a family to turn to.'

'Yes, you would think so but they find their little sister rather dull, I think. They're happy for me to keep my parent's house in exchange for not having to concern themselves about my welfare.' She stops talking as their food arrives. For a few minutes they eat in silence before Amina says, 'I can feel the question you are dying to ask me.'

'Really?' Stan raises his eyebrows, 'And what is that?'

'Why did I decide to contact the Over 50's Escort Agency?

'OK.' Stan laughs, 'Why did you?'

'I know Martina, through my brother, who sometimes does business with her. She suggested I get out and about now, and in case I couldn't find any men to escort me, she gave me your details.'

Stan can't help asking, 'What line of business is your brother in?' This curiosity about Martina is becoming obsessive.

'Ahmed is a self-made man. He deals in anything that might land him a healthy financial return, often regardless of moral or legal issues. I don't ask too many questions.' Amina holds out her glass and Stan refills it. She twists the stem between her fingers and looks at him over the rim,

'Can I be honest with you?'

'I hope so.'

Amina glances around the restaurant. Very few of the tables are occupied and no one is sitting near to them but she leans forward and says in a low voice, 'I'm a virgin.'

Stan stops eating and swallows hard. This wasn't what he was expecting. Putting down his fork, he wipes his mouth on his napkin and wonders how on earth he is to respond to that revelation. But he doesn't have to as Amina continues, 'Sorry that's a bit of a shock isn't it, at my age and in today's society.' She pushes her plate to one side and places her wine glass in front of her, 'Shall we say a virtual virgin, in as much as there have been a couple of clumsy attempts at sex in my life, with two different men, but at neither time did complete coitus happen.'

Stan is shocked at the change in this woman. She's gone from a silent, uptight ball of nerves, and in less than an hour with half a bottle of wine in her, she's become someone who can declare the most intimate details of her life. He gives her what he hopes is a reassuring smile, 'That must have been awful for you.'

'Not really, I wasn't in love or anything. I was due to be married at eighteen to a boy my parents had chosen for me. He was the first attempt. I know what you're thinking, how, as good Indian children, did we get to that stage before marriage? Well, my family are not totally traditional and they allowed us time together. But I don't think I'm a very passionate person, and it was an embarrassing moment for both of us. Besides I wanted to go to train as a teacher. So, the boy ran as fast as he could back to his mother, I became a teacher, and life just passed by. When my father got ill, the most sensible thing was for me to look after him.' She takes another large gulp of wine. 'You see I was still living at home so it was no problem. I was very fond of my Father. Anyway, the reason I'm going on about all this is to tell you why I contacted you. I'd like to experience a bit of life now. A bit of wining and dining, and perhaps to finally lose that virginity.'

Stan is flabbergasted. He could never have imagined being asked to deflower a virgin, not when dating women over fifty. He takes a long drink of his wine and then puts his glass down quickly as he remembers he's driving. 'Amina, I'm more than happy to escort you wherever you would like to go. And to see where that takes us. But I think maybe you should look for a man you can have a relationship with. Someone special.'

Amina smiles at him and her eyes are wide and dark, 'I think I may have found him.'

Stan feels panic and attempts to stop any romantic ideas she might be building around him. 'Amina this is my job, my living. This is what I do. I put ladies at their ease. I found I had a talent for it and then friends suggested I could turn that talent into a business. You pay me to take you out and that is no basis for a close relationship.'

'I know Stan, but that's all I want. Someone who is attentive, who can help me relax and who I find attractive. I don't want a full-time partner or husband, I'm happy the way things are. I have my house and I may return to teaching or tutoring kids for their GCSE's. I just want to know what it is like to be made love to and to feel good about myself.'

Oh Lord, the thought of it, makes me uneasy. That's not my thing. I prefer an equal level of experience in the women I make love to. He decides to slow things down. 'Alright, Amina. This is what I suggest. I'll escort you whenever you want me to. And, as I've already said, we'll see where that leads us. But at the same time, I want you to look at some dating sites and read the profiles of the men you see there. If anyone appeals to you, email them a message and start a conversation.'

Amina frowns, 'I'm not sure. I'll think about that but I'd like to see you again before Christmas, say next week?' She asks him and her big brown eyes sparkle.

Gosh, she looks almost beautiful. 'Fine,' he says. 'When would you like to meet?'

Forty-Five

I'm worried about Stanley and I want to talk to the Watcher but she hasn't appeared for a couple of days now. It seems I'm unable to call these apparitions when I need them. They are the ones who decide to visit. It seems it's got little to do with my conscious mind. I can't alter the way the story is unravelling. It creates itself. The characters determine their own lives, despite walking around in my mind, even when I am not typing.

Guy is becoming irritated with my distracted manner, 'away with the fairies' he calls it. I manage to do most of the routine tasks but if he asks me to do something extra, I forget and this infuriates him.

I fear the return of my old madness. I can't let that happen. I can't go back into that unit where everyone smokes and the air is stale with the smell of sweat. Where you're woken at night by the screams of some poor demented soul. I can't go back to the sickly-sweet staff, who think they know how to help you, while prescribing pills that cloud your brain. My typing is what I cling to. When the words are pouring out from my fingers, then I feel calm. Then, I become totally myself. I keep thinking of the Watcher's words to me, 'You are a writer...' and I realise that's what I've always been. I wrote in my head long before I found the typewriter.

Amy is in his bed. That's all Stan can think of as he caresses her breasts. Her smooth legs are half under his body, her hair is tousled and swept across the pillow, her eyes are closed and there's a slight smile on her lips. He kisses her and she stirs and sighs, 'Oh, I have missed you, Mr Baker.' Her hands trace the hairs on his chest, stroke over his nipples that are still tender from her bite. He feels so alive. This is what he loves. The sensations of mutual pleasure and sensual sex. 'I don't suppose we could do it, again could we?' she says reaching between his legs and stroking him.

He laughs, 'Not quite yet, you little minx. I'm an old man remember.' He turns her over onto her belly and strokes the backs of her legs. His hand moves up into the moistness of her, 'I could satisfy you another way,' Stan says. He strokes with his fingers till she starts to moan.

Amy rolls away from his hands. 'No,' she says sulkily. 'I want to wait for you, I want you inside me. She climbs off the bed. 'I have to go to the bathroom anyway,' she says smiling down at him. 'Let's have a drink.'

Stan stands up slowly, his back aches and his knees take a moment to move. He stumbles to the kitchen to pour two glasses of wine. *God, I need to get fitter if I'm to do this every day.* Back in his bed they sit side by side sipping the cool Chablis. 'So, tell me,' Amy says, 'When are you moving?'

'Very soon, it seems.' Stan sounds sad. 'I'm going to see the apartment tomorrow, and if I like it, Martina wants me to take it immediately.'

'Wow, so this is the last time in this flat. I shall miss 'coming' here,' she giggles.

'You'll miss slumming it with your bit of rough you mean,' he says finishing his drink and turning to her. 'Living in superior surroundings won't change me you know.'

Amy looks at him, suddenly serious. 'It might, Stanley. Can you trust this Martina?'

'I don't know. She does worry me but I can see no other way of getting out of this estate. The flat might take months to sell and I need to move this agency on. Anyway, Maureen seems to have my welfare at heart.'

'As well as her own,' Amy says with a slight frown. 'Remember, she gets commission on the sale and the rental.' She finishes her drink and lays down beside him. 'Don't let them rush you, Stanley. You're too trusting sometimes. Listen would you like me to meet Martina? Suss her out? I could come and see the flat with you tomorrow, if you like?'

'I would like that but you probably won't see Martina, just Maureen. It would be good to move in before Christmas. I could have a party and invite my friends and clients. You could meet Amina.'

'Who is Amina?'

'This Indian lady I escorted yesterday. Would you believe she says she's a virgin?' Stan looks worried.

'Wow, that's amazing, how old is she?'

'Fifty.' Stan frowns.

Amy attempts to smooth the lines between his brows with her fingers. 'Is that a problem for you?'

'Well... Yes, it is really. I've not 'deflowered' anyone. It's not my scene.'

Amy puts her arms around his wide girth. 'Well, Stanley, I can't think of anyone better to lose one's virginity to. You're so concerned and gentle it would make that first time very beautiful.'

'But I prefer experienced women who know what they want and what they like,' he says, leaning over Amy and sliding his hands between her legs once more.

'Like me, you mean?' she laughs.

The next morning Stan arrives early at Gloucester Docks. He walks around the whole area. Most of the old warehouses are destined to be converted into blocks of flats. Many are under refurbishment and their windows overlook the cobbled Quayside. But on the far side of the main dock basin, are two newly built blocks of apartments, they have balconies and larger windows. However, they're designed to blend in with the surroundings. It's a fresh, sunny morning and light from the surface of the canal is reflected onto the old brick walls. Several, newly painted narrow boats are moored alongside the paved concourse. *Certainly, these flats are close to the centre of the city, yet the area seems quiet enough, except for builder's hammers and the cries of sea gulls.* Stan sees Maureen walking towards him with a folder under her arm. She's dressed in a grey suit and high heels and looks very professional. 'Stanley!' she calls. 'Isn't this a lovely day?' She gives him a kiss on the cheek. 'Are you ready to see this? I think you'll be impressed. Follow me.'

Stan follows. Tense as he is, he can't help noticing how attractive her bottom looks in the pencil skirt. Maureen leads the way to the new block of flats. 'I think these are the best blocks in this development, or will be when they're completed. Martina owns several of these flats over-looking the basin. Very desirable properties. The one we're looking at is only a one bed, but it has generous room sizes and a balcony.' Maureen presses the button for the lift which falls silently and opens with a sigh. 'Number 17 is on the third floor.'

When Maureen unlocks the door, there's a strong smell

of paint. It's been carpeted throughout in a light beige, the walls are off white, and everything is glossy and new. The kitchen is compact with white goods provided. The white tiled bathroom has a bath with shower over and a folding glass shower screen. The bedroom is large with built in wardrobes. But it's the sitting room which captivates Stan. Sunlight floods in to the large, square room. One wall consists almost entirely of a glass patio door that open onto the balcony.

'So, what do you think Stanley? Will it do?' Maureen is looking keenly at him.

'Do! It's bloody fantastic! I love it. It's so big. But can I afford it?'

'Darling Stanley,' Maureen coos at him. 'You can't afford **not** to take it. Think about it. It's so central, you can entertain here and you don't have to be ashamed of your address. Sorry, but your flat isn't in the best area, is it?'

Stan nods. Maureen's right, but somehow, he feels an element of betrayal in admitting it. All the same he's very tempted. 'How much does Martina want for it?'

'Until your flat sells she is willing to take £350 per month, then it will go up to £450 for the first year with a review after that. It really is a bargain. You'll never have an opportunity like this again.' Maureen takes some papers out of her folder and puts them on the worktop in the kitchen. 'I have the agreement ready for you to sign, if you want to have a look.'

Stan picks up the papers but there's so much small print to read, he just skims over it. *Basically, it seems alright. Martina won't take the full rent until my flat sells and considering that might be months it's a marvellous opportunity.*

'Also,' Maureen adds, 'she's waving the deposit. You could be in before Christmas. You'd be comfortable and warm and free of that depressing estate. Well?' Maureen asks a little impatiently.

'I don't know it seems great…'

'Oh Stanley, no buts. This is the best deal you'll ever get, trust me.' She puts an arm around his shoulders and squeezes. 'Come on sign. It's quite painless.'

'How much time have I got to consider things?' he asks, still feeling pressured.

'Well, you haven't really. I've got another viewing this afternoon, you can't expect Martina to wait, Stanley.' Maureen holds out the pen to him.

Stan takes it and crossing his fingers behind his back, he sighs. 'Where do I sign?'

Maureen shows him and he scribbles his signature and drops the pen onto the draining board. 'Well done! I know you won't regret it and I want to be the first to stay here, please. We'll drink Champagne and have a wild time.' She kisses him full on the lips and he tastes lipstick and a faint tang of peppermint. She goes back into the sitting room, shuts all the doors, and they make their way to the lift. 'Let's go and celebrate with lunch.' Maureen says, taking hold of his arm as they walk into town.

During lunch Stan is very quiet and Maureen asks, 'Are you regretting your decision?'

'No, I don't think so.' Stan picks at his food. 'What do you know about Martina?'

'Well, she's widowed. She married a man much older than herself when she was in her twenties. It was a good financial move, he died a few years later and left her very well provided for. She has a keen business sense and has invested well. Fingers in many pies, especially around Gloucester.' Maureen finishes her steak and salad and pushes her plate aside. 'There are big development plans for the old dock area. All those derelict buildings and wharfs will become a vibrant new shopping complex. When that happens, Martina is set to make a mint as she's bought several of the old buildings.' Maureen lights a cigarette. 'Do you mind?' she asks Stan.

'No carry on,' he pushes his plate away half finished. 'So, why is she interested in me?'

'She must see you as a good business opportunity. I think she's investing in dating agencies as well.' Maureen smiles at Stan. 'Relax, Stanley, everything is working out for you. If you want to move on you have to grab every chance that comes. What shall we do this afternoon?' She looks at her watch, 'I'm now officially on leave, so escort me where you will.'

Stan laughs in spite of his concerns. Maybe Maureen's right. Time to relax and have some fun and when he thinks about it, he's getting paid for the pleasure of her company for however long she wants him. That can't be bad. 'How about going to see a film?' he asks.

The next morning, he wakes with a headache. *Much too much wine last night.* Maureen's gone but there's a note in his kitchen which he reads while waiting for the kettle to boil. 'Lovely time last night, thank you Stanley darling. Will be in touch regards getting you the keys. Suggest you find a removal firm a.s.a.p. Ciao.'

He scrunches it up and throws it in the bin and gets out the yellow pages to look up removals. *No time like the present I suppose.* He dials two numbers and on the second call manages to get someone who is prepared to come out this afternoon to give an estimate of costs. He takes his tea and toast into the sitting room and eats his breakfast standing in front of the window. *I'll miss this view; despite its depressing aspect, it's my view and has been for many years. It's familiar and comfortable and I belong to it somehow. Will I feel so at home in my new surroundings?*

Later that afternoon the man comes to estimate the amount of stuff Stan wants moving. 'When do you want to move, gov?'

'As soon as possible, I suppose. Any chance before Christmas?'

'Yeah, I can do you the end of next week if you want. Say Friday morning? Where are you going?' Stan tells him. 'Nice part of town that. Wouldn't mind living there, myself but the wife likes her garden too much.' He writes on his paperwork and hands copies to Stan. 'Me and the boys'll be here Friday morning, eight o'clock sharp. Let's hope it's not raining. Cheers.'

Forty-Six

I think I'm cracking up! I type these words sitting in the kitchen in my torn nightie and dressing gown. Guy has left and taken the child to his mother's. I'll try to write what happened, but I'm very frightened about what he's going to do. My fingers tremble, so I have to type slowly or I miss the keys.

The truth is, I can't stand Guy touching me. It's so different to the way Stanley loves me. Each time Guy takes me, I screw up courage and let him do what he wants. But last night was too much. He made me watch a porn film and when he'd drunk enough, he wanted us to re-enact it. It was horrible. He entered me like an animal. He told me to suck him while he pulled at my nipples then he took me in so many positions. He tied me up, licked me, bit me. It went on for so long.

But horror of horrors, while this is happening, I see Stanley enter the room. In a panic I try to cover myself and push Guy away. But he's into the enjoyment of his game and he rips the sheet from my grasp, turns me over roughly and enters me while I'm on my back. I'm lying across the bed with my head hanging. Guy pounds away within me as my eyes meet Stanley's. I see the look of agony on his face, and I know he feels my pain, my degradation. I can't bear it.

I see him turn away as Guy stops pounding and towers over me. His mouth is wet with drool, his eyes shine. 'Right my little bitch, you've had your fun, now it's my turn,' he says. He pulls me onto the bed so that my head is supported but my legs dangle. Then he kneels across my breasts and stuffs his erection into my mouth. He lets his head fall back with a moan as I move my tongue. He thrusts into my throat. I gag. I can hardly breathe. My eyes search for Stanley as he moves towards the door. He looks back at me with such sorrow. I can't imagine what I look like under Guy, stuffed full of him. My shame and anger rise together as he shuts the door behind him.

Suddenly, I fear I'll never see him again. That he'll despise me. That I'll never feel gentleness. All I'll ever know is this rough usage by this bastard, who doesn't understand the meaning of love. My panic rises. I know I can't take this treatment day and night. I can't be at the mercy of Guy's every whim. He thrusts deeper into my throat as he nears his climax. I choke but he doesn't notice. My hands fly to his chest. I try to push him away. He just thrusts harder. My jaws ache, and my tongue is sore. I bite down hard.

Guy shrieks and pulls back. My mouth is free, though filled with the taste of blood. He hits me across the face, before jumping off the bed and running to the bathroom. I hear him running water, moaning and swearing to himself. All those foul words spew out of his mouth in a torrent of abuse. Those words that come from his pornographic films. Words that I hate so much. Words I will not write. Words that degrade women.

I get up. I put on my torn night dress and my dressing gown. I feel sore and dirty but I can't get into the bathroom. I go downstairs and sit in the kitchen waiting. I hear him swearing and moving about. He goes into the child's room and speaks to her and after a long while I hear them both come downstairs. I stand in the kitchen doorway and see them in the hall with suitcases. Guy turns and spits at me. 'You're a mad woman. I'll make sure they put you back where you belong.' Then he leaves with his daughter and the door slams. The house is so quiet.

After a long while I go upstairs. I climb into the shower, and much later I dress myself before getting out my typewriter.

Stan stands on the balcony of his new flat, it's a cold crisp morning with a pale sun shining through thin cloud. He watches the people on the narrow boats going about their business. *What must it be like to live in such a small space? It's a kind of freedom, I guess, to move on whenever you want.* He returns into the lounge. It looks sumptuous. *It should do with the cost of the new furniture, The old stuff looked shabby so, of course I'm in debt, till the flat sells anyway, but I've paid this month's rent and dues to Martina.*

Maureen's lent Stan two pictures; abstracts on a watery theme. He's placed them on the wall opposite the balcony. Tonight, he's throwing a party. The remaining unpacked boxes have been moved into his bedroom and he's covered them with a curtain so they look like a table. In the end Stan didn't bring much from the flat. *Throwing away the past is harder than I realised. I still have so much of Mum's stuff to go through.*

Stan looks at the clock, it's ten thirty and he needs to shop for wine and some Christmas decorations. He puts on his leather jacket over his zipped-up hoodie and jeans. *To hell with looking smart.* He goes over the road to his designated parking place and climbs into his car; a second-hand VW Golf in a mid-blue.

At the supermarket he trundles his trolley around the aisles, picking items he needs. *I must go and see the Watcher before Christmas. I'll get a bottle of her favourite whisky. I'll go to the flat too, I'd like to say 'Happy Christmas' to Mum's corner of the sitting room. It hardly seems possible that we spent such a happy day less than a year ago. I cooked a Christmas dinner and she managed to eat a little of it. Then we played cards till she got tired. So much has happened since that day, I don't think you'd recognise me now, Mum.*

With these thoughts in his head Stan gets to the checkouts. He's waiting patiently in a queue, when he notices the couple that are paying for their Christmas shop. The man is smart, *'dapper'* his mother would have called him, and next to him is a pretty blonde, or silver haired, woman. It's hard to determine the exact colour of her hair. *She's younger than the man and she reminds me of someone.* He looks again, *Linda!* His heart is suddenly pounding in his chest. *It is her.* They've paid and are pushing their loaded trolley away. Linda is hanging onto the man's arm, looking up at his face and laughing. She looks happy and it brings a lump to Stan's throat. He wants to run after them. Wants to call out her name and tell her how he's missed her. But he's trapped in a sea of shoppers with their trolleys and besides what would be the point?

It's a sadder Stan that returns with his purchases to the fine flat he now lives in. After unpacking the groceries, he has to have a couple of single malts before he feels like putting up the decorations he's bought. Maureen will join him soon to help with preparations and he wonders if his time with her tonight will constitute an 'escort' situation for which he'll invoice her, or whether she is staying as a friend. The whole thing is complex. He considers whether he should invoice Amy, as well. Come to that, what about any of the other women he escorts, who may turn up this evening? Perhaps it's a way to make his fortune: escort multiple women to parties. *Would I service them all in an orgy*, he thinks bitterly, *or give them drinks and ask them to queue?* Stan shakes his head at the stupidity of his situation.

Maureen arrives looking lovely in a red dress and shoes, in her hair is a sprig of artificial holly. 'You look beautiful,' Stan says as he kisses her and she giggles like a girl. He forgets about Linda and throws himself into the party preparations. He changes into a suit and tie, chosen by Maureen, and at seven thirty Amy arrives with two bottles of Champagne.

'I've brought one to toast Christmas, and one to toast your New Home,' she laughs and kisses him full on the mouth for a long time. Stan's arms go around her and he holds her close, until Maureen clears her throat and they break away from each other.

'Oh, I'm sorry Maureen,' says Stan feeling slightly embarrassed. 'This is Amy. Amy this is Maureen, I forgot you two haven't actually met before.'

Stan watches as the two women take stock of each other. Amy walks over to Maureen holding out her hand, 'Hi, so pleased to meet you. I've heard a lot about you.' Then turning to Stan, she says, 'I've a piece of news for you, Stanley.' Amy's eyes sparkle in the lights that Stan has hung over the patio doors.

'Good or bad?' Stan asks cautiously. 'Because if it's bad I don't want to know till tomorrow.'

'I think it's good. Eileen's coming back to Newlands Farm, what do you think of that?'

'That's brilliant but I thought she was away for six months or more? '

'She was but she and her husband have split up and she hopes to be here in the New Year. She wants to throw a party to which we are all invited.' Amy gives a little dance around Stan hugging his arm.

Maureen, doesn't look happy. 'That woman again, I thought I'd seen the last of her. Well, I won't be asked to her party that's for sure.'

'Oh, but you are,' Amy laughs. 'I told her about how you've been helping Stanley since you had to sack him and she's thrilled. She's looking forward to meeting you again and thanking you. Eileen felt so bad about the whole thing.'

'Hmm. Well, I suppose...' but Maureen doesn't finish as the buzzer sounds and several guests are arriving all at once.

The party is going well, the drink is flowing and all his friends, his women, seem to be getting on. Amina hasn't come and neither has Martina, although Maureen assures him that Martina will be there. The noise is getting too much for Stan, so he slides open the patio doors just wide enough to get his stomach through and then closes them behind him.

The chill night air is welcome on his face, the silhouettes of the warehouses loom dark against the saffron coloured sky that covers the City of Gloucester. Below him the water gleams like oil, with the lights from the boats reflected in its calm surface. It is beautiful, and yet all Stan feels is it's strangeness. He misses that rough piece of grass outside the window of his old flat. He misses the dark road lit in patches by the street lamps. He misses seeing the Watcher pass by with her little dog in tow. He wonders how long it will take for him to settle here. Everyone is happy for him it seems and they've toasted his good luck. But something inside him is sounding an alarm. Stan's scared of the future.

Scared of what Martina might ask him to do for her, and scared of being beholden to her. The Patio door opens and a woman's figure steps onto the balcony. 'Hello Stanley, are you surveying your new surroundings? Beautiful, isn't it?' The woman is Martina. *The very devil.*

She comes up close to him and he can smell that allusive perfume again, only today it seems heavier, stronger. 'Yes, it's lovely,' he says, and feeling he owes her more than that, he adds, 'I need to thank you for making all this possible.'

'You're welcome, Stanley. It's up to you to make a success of things. That way we all get paid.'

'Now,' she says coming closer to him. 'Let's see what all these ladies are attracted to.' Martina puts her hands on his shoulders and raises her face to kiss him. The kiss is long and passionate. Stan's surprised she should want to kiss him, but what surprises him more, is how his body responds to her. He has a sudden surge of desire and goes to put his arms around her but as soon as he does, she stops him.

'No, Stanley, no touching,' she says as she moves to lean over the balcony and looks down into the water. 'Sorry, Stanley, you aren't my type. I prefer men younger and…' she pats his stomach, 'fitter. But you kiss well.' Martina's hand grabs at his crotch.

Stan is immediately horrified because he knows she'll feel his erection but he can't escape. Laughing at his predicament, she says, 'Perhaps one day in one of my kinkier moods I could use you.'

Stan bridles at the effrontery of this woman. It's like he's an animal in a cattle market. He almost expects her to lift his lip to check his teeth. He's angry and humiliated but what can he say? He daren't offend her. But it seems Martina has had her fun. Seeing she's managed to thoroughly discomfort him; she's no longer interested. She laughs again, a short snort of a laugh. 'Well, Stanley, I would suggest we go back to the party and mingle. You're neglecting your guests.' She turns and opens the patio door.

Stan waits for a few moments struggling with the ambivalent feelings he has about her. Her physical presence excites his body, but her disdain for him infuriates and he's trapped by the sum total of what he owes her. He's never met a more masculine woman in approach, but he's never been so close to a woman who's as alluring as she is.

When everyone has gone Amy, Maureen and Stan clear up. Amy snuggles up to Stan over the washing up. 'What's going to happen now Stanley, do you want me to stay?'

Stan feels sad, and awkwardly explains that he's promised Maureen she can be the first to stay. 'I'm sorry Amy,' he hugs her and whispers in her ear, 'I would rather it was you but...'

Amy pats him on the shoulder. 'Don't worry, I can wait my turn,' she whispers back and then as Maureen comes into the kitchen she moves away and says, 'Can you ring me a taxi, Stanley?'

'Of course,' he says and goes into the sitting room to fetch his mobile.

Later in bed he makes love to Maureen slowly and carefully making sure she is satisfied, but he doesn't come. As she drifts off to sleep beside him, he thinks of Amy and how sweet she is. Stan decides that when he is earning enough, he won't take money for being with her anymore. He hopes she wasn't offended that Maureen was staying tonight. He lies on his back and thinks of all his women with tenderness, and wonders idly, what it will be like to see Eileen again. But just before he falls asleep, he thinks of

Linda, and there's a pain in his heart. In his mind's eye he sees her surrounded by family; hers and perhaps the offspring of the man she is with, maybe even step grandchildren, which she would love.

He sighs as he turns over and feels Maureen's warmth in his bed. *I'll never have a family but I guess life's given me compensations.*

Forty-Seven

It's morning, and I've been alone in the house for a whole day and a night. I've heard nothing from Guy. I'm sitting at the kitchen table, typing, with many sheets of paper in a pile in front of me. I look up and smile at the Watcher, who has just entered with her little dog. His claws make a clicking sound on the floor, his tail is wagging as he looks up at me. I get up and pour some water for him and he drinks. But as I go to turn on the kettle the phone rings in the hall. I go to answer it.

I recognise the voice immediately, and my skin crawls. The sweet, female voice coos softly at me, 'We've been informed of a situation by your partner... The mental health team will be around for a chat in about an hour, then we'll see where we go from there,' she says. I say nothing, just put the phone down and return to the kitchen. The Watcher looks up at me with sympathy. 'Are you alright?' she asks. I look at her in surprise. 'You spoke to me?'

'Desperate times require desperate measures.' she says. 'Is there anything I can do to help?'

I'm tempted to say, 'Stop freaking me out.' But then I think, the Watcher is my only friend, so I say, 'Thank you. But there's nothing to be done.'

'Well, perhaps we'll see about that,' she says, picking up her little dog. They both look at me; two pairs of sad eyes. 'This book's finished.' I say, pointing to the files and sheets of paper. 'Will there be a sequel? she asks.

'I don't know,' I say. 'I hope so. I can't leave Stan in his predicament. But I may have to say goodbye for a while.' The Watcher frowns but nods her head. She stands up, puts her hand on my arm and they leave.

I'm sitting at the kitchen table, thinking of the day when the fat, white man first appeared in the bathroom. The day before I began to create Stanley. I've no regrets, a world without Stanley would be a dark world indeed. I type these last few words with trembling fingers, and plan what to do when I've finished.

I'll pull out the paper from the machine, put it in the file with the rest and pack up my typing. I'll stuff this machine back into the airing cupboard, hide the files under my clothes in the bottom of my suitcase and then if they take me away, I'll have it with me. I must keep this book a secret. I must protect it. It's all I have. Then I'll screw up my courage and sit on the stairs, waiting for them.

I hear the sound of a vehicle drawing up. Car doors slam and footsteps sound on the path. I tense up, I'm not quite ready for them, yet. But nothing happens.

I hear voices outside. I go to the sink, move the net curtain aside and look out. Immediately I'm bemused. The two nurses are standing at the top of the path talking to the Watcher. She's standing with her back to me, as though she's just left the house. Her little dog sits by her side. It's certainly her. I couldn't mistake the shabby raincoat belted at the waist, nor the grey hair sticking out from under her old battered hat. But how can they be talking to her? Why can they even see her?

I open the window a little. I can hear the Watcher's voice saying, '…definitely an abusive relationship.' and 'I don't know how she stood it for so long.' They shake their heads and thank her. The Watcher looks back at the house, sees me at the window and raises her hand. Then she walks away, her little dog at her heels. The doorbell rings. I take a deep breath and go and open it.

It would have broken my heart to leave this house without saying goodbye to Stanley. But it seems I won't have to. I have a reprieve.

The mental health team have left and I'm sitting in my kitchen. It is **my** kitchen now, well, for the time being anyway. They were very kind. They made me tea and sat me down in the sitting room. They talked for ages, but they didn't tell me off for what I did to Guy. In fact, they seemed very cross with him. They said the rent is paid till the end of January and so I can stay on here till then, if I want to. I said I did. They said they'll do a visit each week and they gave me an emergency number I can call. Then one of them added; 'Your neighbour will keep an eye on you, too.' I was totally confused. 'Who?' I asked. 'You know,' she said, 'Mrs Grey. The nice old lady with the little dog.'

The house is beautifully silent. I haven't put the typewriter away. I won't have to move it now. It can stay on the table. I sit down in front of it, put in a new piece of white paper and place my fingers on the keys, waiting for the words.

The author of **'Creating Stanley'**

J.J.R. Lay

Other works by this author.
(Written under the name, Josephine Lay)

Short Stories

Saffron Tones
Revised edition 2019

Poetry

A Quietus
2021

Unravelling
2019

Inside Reality
Revised second edition 2018

J.J.R. Lay is a writer and poet living on the edge of the City of Gloucester.

She has a BA (hons) in Creative Studies in English & English Literature & an MA in Creative Writing for Young People (both from Bath Spa University).

In 2015, she wrote her first adult novel. That novel has been adapted, re-written, and is now entitled, *Creating Stanley* (2022).

She has also published a volume of short stories, entitled *Saffron Tones (2017)* and three collections of poetry: *Inside Reality (2018)*, *Unravelling* (2019) and *A Quietus* (2021) all written under the name of Josephine Lay.

Lightning Source UK Ltd.
Milton Keynes UK
UKHW010922100622
404171UK00003B/95